Praise 1

MW00364124

"Quality fiction and real h
Angleton's *Gentleman of Mis*......... offers the best of both. This is an
engaging story with surprises on every page".

—Jeff Guinn, *New York Times* bestselling author of
The Last Gunfight and *Manson*

"Against a thorough and expertly researched historical setting,
charismatic miscreant Lyman Moreau cloaks his tooth-and-claw
survival instinct in the appearance and manner of a gentleman. As
he moves constantly to stay ahead of the law, he leads the reader
into encounters with mischief, mummies, murder, and Mormons.
An intriguing and entertaining reading adventure."

—J. J. Zerr, author of *Sundown Town Duty Station*
and *The Happy Life of Preston Katt*

"Adventures abound in this compelling tale of a flawed man on an
unforgettable journey. With a meticulous eye for detail, Angleton
spins a dark tale of intrigue, mystery, and forbidden love against the
vivid backdrop of a fascinating era. Don't miss it!"

—Pat Wahler, award winning author of *I am Mrs.
Jesse James*

"*Gentleman of Misfortune* by Sarah Angleton is a fascinating story built
around tantalizing facts . . . well-researched and delightful to read."

—M. M. Holaday, author of *The Open Road*

Also by Sarah Angleton:
Launching Sheep & Other Stories from the Intersection of History and Nonsense

Gentleman

Of

Misfortune

A Novel

Published by Bright Button Press

Cover Design by Steven Varble
Author Photo by Karen Anderson Designs, Inc.

For more information contact:

Bright Button Press, LLC
P.O. Box 203
Foristell, MO 63348

Publisher's Cataloging- in-Publication Data
provided by Five Rainbows Cataloging Services
Names: Angleton, Sarah, author.
Title: Gentleman of misfortune / Sarah Angleton.
Description: Wentzville, MO: Bright Button Press, 2018.
Identifiers: LCCN 2018906407 | ISBN 978-0-9987853-3-2 (pbk.) |
978-0-9987853-4-9 (ebook)
Subjects: LCSH: Mummies--Fiction. | Swindlers and swindling--Fiction. |
    Entertainers--Fiction. | Voyages and travels--Fiction. | Historical
    fiction. | BISAC: FICTION / Historical / General. | GSAFD:
    Historical fiction.
Classification: LCC PS3601.N55441 G46 2018 (print) | LCC
PS3601.N55441 (ebook) | DDC 813/.6--dc23.

For Mom and Dad

Gentleman

Of

Misfortune

A Novel

SARAH ANGLETON

Bright Button Press ● St. Louis, Missouri

1

A single small stone dropped onto the six of spades on the Faro table, drawing the attention of the only two men in the noisy smoke-filled gambling hall shrewd enough to notice. The dealer frowned at the development. All night he'd proven as quick as he was crooked, compensating for his small stature with his cold stare and quick hands, winning the house far more than strict probability allowed.

Equally interested in the stone was the player who sat to the dealer's right with an unimpeded view of each man around the table. Lyman Moreau, more observer than gambler, had played poorly enough all evening to attract little notice from his companions. Now he leaned forward in his chair, his eyes on the unusual token as the dealer indicated the offending object.

"What the hell is that?" Betting and conversation halted around the table at the dealer's words. Startled men followed his gaze to the tiny blue green stone etched with the outline of a beetle. His impatient fingers tapped the top of the box containing the remaining cards. "Get that thing off my table."

But Lyman watched the man who'd caused the commotion, a well-dressed, self-described merchant who'd been bragging and gambling and drinking all night.

"That, sir," the merchant slurred, "is an Egyptian scarab unearthed in the Valley of the Kings."

The dealer sucked in a breath and puffed out his chest. "I don't care what you say it is. If it can't buy a man a drink, it doesn't belong on my table."

"It hardly seems worth slowing the game." Lyman had said little throughout the night, preferring instead to listen. Gamblers of all classes came looking for trouble in this part of the city. Those who couldn't hold their liquor and their secrets usually found it. And now the merchant had presented an opportunity. "I say let it play."

The dealer scowled at Lyman, but gestured toward the table and said, "Any more bets?"

Several men slid coins from one card to another, some placing copper tokens on top to wager on a loss. Lyman placed his bet on the jack to win. Satisfied, the dealer pulled an ace, followed by a four, an empty space on the table, and another victory for the house. The dealer slid his winnings into the bank and play returned to a furious pace.

Lyman suspected the box, or shoe as it was known, contained a mirror that allowed the man to see what cards to expect and how to most advantageously manipulate them. But the cheating didn't concern him, as he had seen the prize he most wanted and felt sure the dealer's indifference would work in his favor.

Three pulls later, the dealer placed the six of hearts beside the shoe and the merchant's shoulders slumped. When the second card, the jack of clubs, hit the table, Lyman fought hard not to smile. The dealer had no such concerns.

Grinning broadly, he slid the scarab toward Lyman. "I think this'll be your winnings then."

Lyman shrugged and scooped up the stone, dropping it into his coat pocket as he pushed back from the table in a single fluid motion.

*****

Like great brick tomes wedged together along a shelf, the line of houses rose around Lyman. No other city he knew swallowed a man as completely as New York.

The sun had just risen over the cobblestone streets and the city began to wake around him as he ascended the steps of number thirty-four. He rapped on the painted door for a full minute before detecting motion inside.

"Who the hell makes that kind of racket on a man's doorstep at this hour?" Lyman would recognize the voice anywhere, gravelly with age and hard living. Horace Laurent ripped open the door and stood with bare feet, unbuttoned trousers held up by one suspender, and a shotgun aimed at Lyman's chest.

"Horace." Lyman removed his hat and bowed, never allowing his eyes to stray from the end of the gun which, after a moment, the man slowly lowered.

"Oh, hell. Come in then, you cussed devil."

Lyman swept through the doorway and settled himself on an ornate sofa. "Thank you for your kind hospitality, my old friend."

Horace leaned the shotgun against the doorframe. "I know I'm in for something when Lyman Moreau knocks on my door. What brings you here?"

Lyman glanced around the richly furnished room. Above the carved mantel hung the portrait of a lovely young woman with dark hair and eyes. He opened his mouth to reply, but stopped when a lilting feminine voice drifted from the top of the stairs.

"Who is it, Horace?"

"Business. Stay upstairs," came his brusque reply.

Lyman's brow creased and the trace of a grin tickled the corners of his mouth.

Horace met his eyes briefly and groused, "None of your blame business." He sat in a chair across the room from Lyman. "Now, would you kindly tell me why you are knocking on my door at this ungodly hour?"

"I've come with an opportunity."

He looked long at Lyman, his eyes bright and piercing. "Just what kind of opportunity?"

In his younger days, before life had brought him to a lower place, Horace had been an adventurer and a scholar. Later, his black market dealings brought him to the shores of America and swept him into a mutually beneficial partnership with Lyman, a young swindler then down on his luck, but rich in knowledge of New York's seedy underbelly.

Lyman reached into his pocket and opened his fist to reveal the small stone.

"What is it?"

"A scarab. Turquoise. Have a look."

Horace stood and took the carved stone, rolling it between his fingers and examining the plain beetle-like etching. "Looks like it's from a setting—a ring or some other piece of jewelry. It's seen better days anyway, that's for sure."

The old man's tone was nonchalant, but Lyman understood that though surely Horace had seen many finer pieces of antiquity in his day, his interest had been piqued.

"And how did you come to possess it?"

"I won it." Lyman reached for the scarab. He let his arm drop again when Horace made no move to return it.

"Well, is it genuine?" Lyman prompted.

Horace nodded. "It's real enough. What do you mean you won it?"

"Won it off a well-to-do merchant in a game of chance at the port."

Horace smiled now, his fingers trembling. He tossed the scarab back and asked, "Is there more?"

Lyman placed the prize in his coat pocket and grinned. "Five crates, I hear. And mummies, too."

"I've no use for mummies." Horace's flushed face glistened with a fine sheen of perspiration, peculiar for the cool of the house on a spring morning. "What is it you hear, exactly?"

The old man's appearance gave Lyman a moment's pause, but Horace's stiff manner at mention of the mummies did not invite polite inquiry about his health.

"There's a ship out of Trieste carrying cargo from an Antonio Lebolo." Lyman slowed at the name, reproducing it as best he could from his recollection of the gambling merchant's drunken babble. "You know him?"

Horace rubbed his whiskered chin. "I know of him. A Frenchman. He worked for Drovetti in the Valley of the Kings."

"Well," Lyman continued, relieved his recently acquired information had so far proven reliable, "evidently he shipped his plunder to America to be sold by Gillespie & McLeod. Then he up and died. All I need is documentation to support my claim as his nephew and heir. Am I right to assume you have connections who are able supply that?"

Horace sagged against the back of the chair and waited a silent beat before responding. "I might know a man. Not a reliable sort, but could make you the heir of the Viceroy of Egypt. If he had a mind to." The old man's cracked lips spread into a smirk that soon faded.

"Now that would be fun, but hardly necessary."

"What would be fun?" The female voice came from a figure of loveliness descending the stairs in a voluminous skirt and puffed sleeves. Lyman watched as the woman from the portrait emerged.

Her fingers tucked a wayward strand of dark hair into a knot at the back of her head, which sat atop a long, elegant neck. Her eyes met Lyman's and she offered the hint of a curtsy before entering the sitting room.

"Mariana, may I present Mr. Lyman…" Horace stood, pushing off the arms of his chair with a low grunt. "I forgot to ask. What name is it you use now?"

Lyman stood as well, bowing to the olive-skinned angel. "Johnson will do."

"Well then, Mr. Lyman Johnson, allow me to introduce my wife Mariana."

"An absolute pleasure." Lyman bowed again and was pleased to see a faint blush rise on Mrs. Laurent's cheeks.

Horace lowered himself once again into the chair, seeming to deflate with the effort.

"And what was you two gentlemen discussing?" She stepped around Horace's chair and settled onto the end of the sofa. Lyman remained standing and thought to answer her, but noticed Horace give a subtle shake of his head.

"Nothing to fret about, darling. Mr. Johnson was presenting a business proposition, but I'm afraid it won't work out."

"Why not?" Mariana patted the sofa, inviting Lyman to sit by her side. "He seems like a good sort of fellow. Did I hear you say mummies? How intriguing."

Lyman sat stiffly on the edge of the sofa, close enough to his friend's wife to detect the faintest scent of lavender.

Horace narrowed his eyes. "Eavesdropping is a nasty habit, my dear."

"Nonsense. It isn't eavesdropping if it's in my own house. And it is a wife's duty to aid her husband when she can. Don't you think so, Mr. Johnson?" She swiveled to face Lyman and to both his delight and discomfort, she placed a hand on his shoulder.

"I have to agree." It was his turn to blush.

"Smart man." She turned to her husband with such a flash of anger Lyman could feel the heat of it, even if he did not fully understand it. He watched Horace wither in her gaze.

"If it's papers you need, Quinn will get them for you."

"Trouble is I don't trust Quinn," Horace grumbled.

Mariana swept away his protestation with a wave of her hand. "You don't like Quinn, Horace. That's not the same as mistrusting. I'm going out this morning. I'll fetch him. You'll send a note with what you need."

Horace said nothing, but he soon rose from his chair and shuffled to a writing table in the corner of the room where he closed and nudged aside a slim book, pushing it against a glass sphere on a wooden frame. Withdrawing a sheet of paper from the drawer, he scrawled a brief note, folded it, and held it out for Mariana.

"There's no reasoning with you," he said with a sigh that implied reserved pride.

"You're a wise man, Horace. Occasionally." She slipped the folded note into the bodice of her dress and leaned toward her husband, kissing him lightly on the nose. The gesture struck Lyman at once both condescending and intimate, and a wave of embarrassment rushed over him.

Mariana straightened, smoothing her dress. "Mr. Johnson, it was a pleasure to meet you. Will you be here when I return?"

"You may depend on it."

Her eyes sparkled as she reached for a wide-brimmed hat hanging by the door. She donned it and re-tucked her disobedient curl before disappearing through the front door.

Lyman watched her exit. "You've done well for yourself, my friend."

"I'm in a lucrative field," answered Horace, settling once again into his chair.

"Lovely girl." Lyman indicated the portrait, which, though stunning, had failed to capture the beauty of its subject. "A bit young for you, perhaps?"

Horace waved a spotted hand in front of his face. "It's not age that matters so much as the experience. She keeps me young."

Lyman settled once again onto the sofa, sizing up his friend. He could still see, in many ways, the vibrant, barrel-chested man he'd once admired almost like a father, but he could not deny that Horace's fire had cooled with age, and perhaps more. Some unnamed illness plagued the man before him, revealed by the careful way he held himself, like every movement demanded a moment of recovery.

"Not sure that's working, Horace. Are you well?"

"I'm well enough. And what about you? Thought you married a zealot and became a farmer or something."

Horace was business first, but with that out of the way, it pleased Lyman to know his former partner had kept tabs on him. Their relationship was a tenuous one, often coated with deception with perhaps genuine concern at the center.

"Were you afraid I'd gone off the crook? Made myself respectable?"

"I wouldn't presume to hope as much as that, but I thought a change in situation might settle you."

Lyman was fourteen when he'd met Horace—the younger man grasping to rise out of the mire of his childhood and build a life for himself, the elder a gentleman turned burgeoning criminal. Lyman ran hustles for Horace, helped him navigate the coarser parts of the city, as he stole and cheated his way into the black markets of New York. In the process, the two men developed if not trust, at least fondness for one another.

"I chose a different path." In truth, Lyman had been in love with a religious woman, but she had turned out not to be as forgiving as her faith might suggest. "Found myself a wealthy widow instead, became a landed gentleman."

"This wife of yours doesn't mind if you hop up to the city to dip your toes in the black market?"

"I doubt she's terribly concerned. She's dead." Lyman had become practiced at feigning grief, but he would make no attempt to deceive Horace.

"I'm sorry to hear that. Was she good for you?"

"Yes. Much too good." Katherine had been his wife for only six months. She was a few years older than he, a widow alone and unwell. She'd put her faith in an untrustworthy trickster who offered her hope, giving him her heart in exchange. If only he'd been more deserving of it.

"And why, if I may ask, does a comfortable widower decide to come back to the city and commandeer a shipment of antiquities?"

Lyman shrugged. "I missed the life, the action of it all. I can't see myself retired to the countryside. It's not in my nature." He changed the subject before Horace could dig deeper. "Who is this Quinn fellow?"

"Martin Quinn, a clerk in the Office of the Collector of Customs. He's an ambitious, conniving cutthroat, but he can be useful when he stands to profit enough."

"How much is enough?"

"Elegant crime takes commitment and capital. I believe I taught you that."

"Will he help us?"

"If you want that shipment, he's the best man in the city to get it for you. Maybe the only one." Horace frowned. "And I doubt he'll say no to Mariana."

"So you don't trust him."

Horace leaned forward, fixing him with a hard glare. "I trust him as much as I trust you."

2

The morning stretched into a breezy afternoon by the time a carriage pulled up to the front steps to purge its passengers. A stately gentleman with a silk top hat and brocade tailcoat emerged first and extended a hand to retrieve his more delicate companion.

Mariana wore a glow of pride as she stepped onto the cobblestone, the dimples of her rosy cheeks visible to the observer at the window of the row house.

"Your wife is back. And she's brought a guest." Lyman spoke over his shoulder to Horace, who crossed the room to see for himself.

"That's Quinn." He turned from the scene; which, to any casual observer, might suggest a closer relationship between Mr. Quinn and Mrs. Laurent than could be considered proper. "You'd be wise to guard your secrets."

"Noted, my friend." It occurred to Lyman that Mrs. Laurent would be wise to guard her secrets as well.

Their laughter reached the house before them, but soon enough the pair tumbled through the doorway, arms intertwined. Quinn at least had the courtesy to untangle his arm from Mariana's, but not before locking eyes with her husband in a silent challenge familiar to Lyman, who felt a wave of revulsion seeing his old friend cower under that gaze.

"Horace, you're looking well today." The man removed his hat to reveal tidy waves of auburn hair; and the fact that he was at least two inches shorter than Lyman. Like him, Martin Quinn was perhaps thirty years in age; and was a man who loomed larger than his physical appearance might suggest.

Without waiting for a reply, Quinn placed his hat on the seat of the chair Horace had recently occupied and stretched his hand toward Lyman. "And you are the gentleman Mrs. Laurent spoke of so highly. Mr. Johnson, is it?"

"Mr. Johnson it is. To know that Mrs. Laurent spoke of me at all is a pleasant surprise." Lyman grasped the offered hand in a firm shake.

"You mustn't be so modest. I hear you are a criminal of the first rate, Mr. Johnson." Quinn walked to the writing table and sat on its edge, a choice that would leave him at least a head taller than anyone else sitting in the room. "A common name, if you don't mind my saying."

Lyman remained standing, tilting his head to his new adversary. "Not at all. My father was a common man."

Tucking his arms around himself, Quinn said, "That's the beauty of this country of ours. Anyone can become someone if he's willing to put in the effort. But I'm sure you must have a French background. I have a gift for identifying nationalities. It's because of my role as a customs agent, you see."

"I wouldn't dream of questioning your expertise, but to my knowledge, I am only American."

"Ah, but the question is, are you capable of becoming Irish?" At these words, Quinn stood and pulled from his coat pocket several folded papers, which he handed to Lyman.

Horace removed the top hat from his chair and sat watching the exchange. Mariana left for the kitchen and soon returned with coffee and a plate of small cakes. Lyman examined the documents now in his hands. The first was a letter addressed to the captain of the *Intrepido*, naming an agent of Gillespie & McLeod as receiver of the Lebolo shipment from Trieste.

The second, appearing aged and weather-beaten, bore a broken seal and was addressed to Mr. Michael Chandler from his uncle, Antonio Lebolo. This letter concerned the bequeathing of certain Egyptian artifacts arriving on the ship *Intrepido*, destined for the merchants Gillespie & McLeod.

The third, marked by the same broken seal and written in the same hand as the second, was addressed to the merchants from Antonio Lebolo directing the shipment to be released to his nephew, should he wish to make a claim.

Lyman couldn't help but be impressed. In a matter of just a few hours, Quinn had convincingly produced the necessary documentation. Only one thing remained.

"What of the duty?"

"Sizable; but not, I believe, unreasonable. This documents that the full duty has been collected by one of my colleagues, and it is yours for the amount, plus thirty-five percent."

A low whistle escaped Lyman's lips as he accepted this last paper. "And what does this thirty-five percent buy me, exactly?"

"To begin, the identity of Mr. Michael Chandler, a recent Irish immigrant. The documents, all very good forgeries, if I may say so. My silence on the matter. And, I might add, Mr. *Johnson*, my indifference."

Lyman looked toward Horace, slumped in his chair, but with his attention focused on Quinn. "What do you think, Horace?"

The old man replied, "Thirty-five is substantial, but you won't do better than Quinn."

Quinn smiled. "That almost sounded complimentary, Horace. Do we have an agreement then?"

Lyman glanced one more time over the documents he held. "Elegant crime takes commitment and capital. We have a deal."

*****

Lyman stepped down from the carriage and drew a deep breath of salty air. Horace followed, dressed now in the silk vest, frock coat, and well-heeled boots of a respectable businessman one would expect to find in the counting houses along the seaport.

"All right, Michael Chandler, remember you're the wayward son of Maria Lebolo and I'm Mr. Peterson."

"Yes, yes, we've been through this." Lyman waved a gloved hand to dismiss Horace's words. "Thank you for your confidence. I can manage very well."

Horace pulled open his coat and flashed the ivory handle of a pistol. "Watch yourself, Michael. I still owe you a hole in your gut for dragging me out of my warm bed in time to watch the sunrise."

"Easy, old man." The sight of yet another gun unsettled Lyman, who rarely carried more than a sharp folding knife. He wondered what kinds of dealings Horace had become involved with since they'd parted, that he'd become so well armed. "I'll fetch your treasure," Lyman reassured him. "Then we'll share a drink to celebrate."

Arriving behind them was a cargo wagon, borrowed from an acquaintance of Lyman's. Horace nodded as it pulled alongside the carriage and told the driver, "Be ready to make a quick exit should this go badly."

In the driver's seat sat Mariana, poorly disguised in an ill-fitting men's suit. She'd insisted on coming and, in the end, Horace had relented. She only shrugged in response to her husband's words and then caught Lyman's eye with the sideways glance of a coquette.

He felt himself flush with pleasure, but he would not spare Mariana another thought. With every careful step Lyman took along the road, past the counting houses of Schermerhorn Row, he absorbed his new identity. No longer was he Lyman, the bastard son of a whore, who had rescued himself from a childhood spent just blocks away from this very spot.

Michael Chandler was an immigrant farmer working to make his way in America, grateful for an opportunity provided by a generous uncle but uncomfortable in the environment of the great Port of New York. Lyman allowed uneasiness to envelop him, shoulder to shoulder with the disembarking poor, sick from a treacherous voyage, in close proximity to the hardened sailors who would take up temporary residence in the brick dormitories and in the arms of the prostitutes on Water Street.

Lyman scanned the East River, known locally as the street of ships, where the packet vessels slipped in and out with regularity; the clippers with their easy loads of tea, spices, and opium sped through the water; the floating icehouses set sail for the Caribbean; and the cargo ships lounged on the water like great beasts whose hides buzzed with fleas.

Men hauled luggage to the street's edge. Mothers clung to small children both to snatch them from danger and to steady their wobbly sea legs. Sailors grunted and pushed against capstans, working great winches, raising and lowering cargo into stacks awaiting journeys to warehouses along the seaport.

This was not the port of Lyman's youth where he'd hid among the freight wagons and watched merchants argue with ship captains.

By 1833, the shipping industry had become more scheduled, more reliable, and more useful to a booming America.

Horace put a hand on Lyman's shoulder, halting him. "There. That's the one." He pointed to the smallest of the cargo ships in port, a three-masted wooden vessel, the name *Intrepido* painted in golden script on the bulwark. "It's Italian."

Lyman scanned the ship. "Not as large as I'd hoped."

"No," Horace agreed. "Larger would be better, but maybe they won't speak much English. That'd help."

The two men approached the ship, heads held high, exuding authority, their eyes following the actions of crewmen forcefully maneuvering a dangling crate into position as it lowered to the pier. As they worked, the ship's crewmen called orders to one another, coordinating their efforts in guttural Italian. The boom of the crate touching down echoed between ships and across the street to the brick of the counting houses.

Lyman caught the arm of one of the sailors nearest him. "Pardon me, but could you tell us where we might find the captain?"

The man wiped his brow on a grungy sleeve and took in the appearance of the two American gentlemen without any indication of comprehension. Then he shrugged and pointed to a man standing on the opposite side of the gangway, his face buried in a leather-bound book. *"Il primo ufficiale."* The sailor turned and regrouped with his fellow sailors, busy releasing the crate from its straps. Lyman and Horace were forgotten, left to approach the first mate without introduction.

"Pardon me, sir." Horace spoke this time, and the officer looked up from his ledger with a start.

"May I help you, gentlemen?" The Italian first mate spoke with flawless, though heavily accented, English.

"I expect so, sir. We wish to claim a shipment from Antonio Lebolo."

The officer dropped his gaze to the ledger with narrowed eyes, running his finger down the page as he scanned. When he reached the bottom, he looked up, his face drained of color. The first mate's voice dropped to a disquieting whisper. "Who are you to make this claim?" His lip curled into an accusatory sneer.

Lyman's heart fluttered. Not yet nine o'clock, the morning was already bright, the sun like a gas theater lamp beating down on him, sending a tingle of nervous exhilaration through his limbs.

Horace did not hesitate. "My name is Mr. Robert Peterson of the firm Gillespie & McLeod. This gentleman is Mr. Michael Chandler, nephew to Mr. Lebolo. We're expecting a shipment of Egyptian Antiquities. May we assume you have it?"

"*Sì*. I have a shipment from Lebolo, from Egypt." He waved his hand over the ledger, "But I am curious what kind of man would wish to claim it." A single bead of perspiration rolled down the officer's temple. His weight shifted subtly forward.

"Ah," Horace pulled open his coat, just brushing the pistol, and pulled out the documents Quinn had prepared. The officer tensed, obviously noticing the implied threat before reaching for the papers, both concern and curiosity etched across his sea-worn face.

With a trembling hand, he took the papers from Horace and studied them for several uncomfortable moments with great interest. Horace and Lyman exchanged looks, and Horace's hand went to his coat where his fingers tickled the pistol's handle.

At last, the officer looked up from the pages and exhaled. Lyman stepped forward, dropping three silver coins one by one onto the ledger. The officer's mouth widened into a satisfied smile. "Everything here is in good order. My men will retrieve your shipment."

*****

The business dealings finished, Horace retreated to the carriage to seek relief from his nerves in the bottom of a whiskey bottle. Lyman remained at the pier as fascinated as he'd been as a boy watching the crane hoisting cargo over the side of the ship to the men waiting and directing below.

The sailors were quick at their work, responding to shouted instructions from the first mate, a man who seemed to grasp from the bribe, the urgency required in retrieving the shipment. Paying little attention to Lyman, the crew unloaded the next five crates in almost rapid succession, each bearing a label for Gillespie & McLeod.

Mariana joined Lyman on the pier to watch the work, her approach earning several startled glances. Breeches or no, there was no hiding the femininity of a woman like Mariana. Her movements were too graceful, her steps too light, but it did not seem to matter. When the sailors—not one of whom spoke even a word of English as far as Lyman could tell—saw that she wished for them to load the crates onto the cargo wagon, they were delighted to do so. Many of them removed their caps and bowed.

Mariana returned a modified curtsy that made the sailors laugh with appreciation. Then she climbed onto the wagon and cracked the reins without a word to Lyman as he walked slowly to the carriage, offering a wave of thanks to the chuckling men.

3

In contrast to the busy storefronts a block away, the building Lyman guided the carriage toward was dismal. It seemed it had once been painted some shade of blue, but all that remained of the color was a few stubbornly clinging strips of peeled paint.

At their approach a wide cargo door slid open, pushed by the gloved hands of Martin Quinn.

"What's he doing here?" Lyman muttered under his breath.

Horace, slumped in the seat beside him, perked up at the question, a half empty bottle in one hand and a scowl on his face. "He must've asked Mariana where you were storing the goods. She would've told him. Too trusting."

Mariana stepped from the darkened doorway and stood next to Quinn, so close she might have leaned into him.

"You're sure as hell not the man you used to be," Lyman said. "You've let that Quinn take over your business and turn you into a blame cuckold!"

Horace's complexion deepened at the words. The muscles of his jaw tensed and his eyes flashed bright with purpose. Before Lyman could brace himself, the punch landed. A shock of pain radiated across his jaw. Mariana gasped. Lyman leaned back against the seat, his fingers probing the stinging flesh of his cheek. He slid his tongue across his teeth to reassure they remained intact.

Horace loomed over him, his breath sour. "There will be no more discussion of my marriage." He dropped down from the seat and retrieved his fallen bottle, leaving Lyman to nurse his wounds.

He knew the old man to be prideful but still, the outburst surprised him. Horace had never shied from threatening violence and no one questioned his resolve to follow through, but he wasn't a man to act on impulse.

Lyman drew a long, slow breath and stepped down from the carriage. After seeing to the horse, he entered the warehouse to find two of the crates already removed from the back of the wagon.

Quinn looked up, wearing a smirk. "Help me with the crates, Mr. Johnson. I'm anxious to see what you gentlemen have managed to achieve."

"What concern is it of yours, Mr. Quinn? You got your fee." Lyman wiggled his sore mandible. It hurt to speak, but his distaste for Quinn provided ample reason to overcome the inconvenience.

"Merely curious, and wanting to offer assistance if I can. It occurred to me you might be in need of another strong back." His eyes slid across Lyman's already bruising face. "But perhaps old Horace has more vigor in him than I'd imagined."

Busy sifting through the contents of one of the crates, Horace remained silent, but Lyman thought he saw a sneer bloom on the man's flushed face as he bent over his work.

"Unload the mummies!" Mariana approached the back of the wagon. She stopped beside Horace, keeping her back to him as she waved her arms at the other two men, encouraging them to get to work.

"The lady wants mummies." Quinn gestured to the crated treasures, and Lyman hoisted himself into the back of the wagon with as much manly strength as he could muster.

Quinn appeared next to him and pointed to a crate longer and narrower than the one Horace pillaged. Lyman stood ready at one end, Quinn at the other. The crate was lighter than Lyman expected, but when he thought of Horace, aged and already deep in the bottle, he felt grudgingly grateful for Quinn's help.

They lowered the crate onto the ground and Quinn picked up a crow bar to pry the lid loose. Lyman grabbed a second to help and the two made short work of it. As the lid rose, his breath caught. Under a layer of straw lay a human form, wound head to toe with crusted beige wrappings.

Lyman heart pounded noticeably in his chest. A cold sweat broke across his brow. He wondered who the fellow might have been and how he wound up so unceremoniously stuffed in a box.

"I think there're more in here." Quinn dug into the packing material and unburied a set of bandaged feet, presumably attached to a second mummy beneath the first. He nodded to Lyman, who clasped the first mummy's shoulders so the two could lift it out of the crate.

Altogether, the crate held the remains of three Egyptians. Two similarly long crates turned out to hold four each. Not one was in a sarcophagus as the kings of the ancient tombs were reported to be, but all were whole, and despite being removed from their final resting places, appeared little damaged in death.

Horace paid no attention as the other men lay out and examined the dead. Instead, he and Mariana, whose eyes wandered occasionally to the younger men and their dead charges, continued to pilfer through the smaller treasures.

Horace shook with glee as he uncovered relic after relic. His deft fingers worked quickly and the pile of valuables grew, as did the size of his already dilated pupils. The treasures included precious scarabs, canopic jars, shabti amulets, and even the painted wood models of an entire army of Nubian archers.

With a string of priceless beads draped casually around her neck, Mariana picked up what appeared to be a reed sandal wound with intricate straps. "Is this a golden shoe?"

Horace reached and wrapped gentle fingers around the delicate object, giving Mariana little choice but to let him take it. He brought it close to his eyes. "Will you look at that? Gold thread laced through the straps. It's got to be." He slapped his knee and handed the shoe to Lyman, who accepted it graciously though he'd have preferred to keep his eye on the mummies.

Just as the drunken merchant had boasted, there were eleven of them, silent and disturbing. One caught Lyman's attention particularly. The crusted linen strips had fallen away from what was once a human face, now frozen in a final ecstatic moment. The mummy's mouth remained open in what might have been a silent scream, yet the sunken cheeks and closed eyes were unquestionably peaceful. Like the other ten, its arms had been folded across its hollow chest, as if the dead man were praying, or singing, or delivering a message from beyond.

"You and your damned mummies." Horace pointed at him, accusing him of some implied offense Lyman couldn't begin to imagine. "There's real treasure to be had here. And the sooner you get your mind off those cursed things, the better."

"I think they're fascinating," Mariana whispered, leaning over the nearest decrepit body, the beads falling across its chest. She still wore men's trousers and a wool shirt, but she had loosened her black hair so that several strands draped across her cheek and brushed the mummy's wrappings.

With no attention to spare, she examined the deceased ancient resting across a makeshift board and crate table as if he'd always belonged in this dreary warehouse. Mariana completed her survey and raised her gaze to catch Lyman's lingering stare. She flashed him a coy simper and tucked the loose strands of hair behind her ear.

"They're nothing but trouble," Horace growled. "Dead men should stay dead, something the ancients failed to understand. And now the world is littered with these restless half-decayed creatures that aren't alive and aren't quite dead enough."

Mariana giggled as she walked around the desiccated remains toward Lyman and the mummy that had so caught his attention. "They look dead to me." She reached out her hand, lightly dragging one finger down the mummy's sunken cheek. From the corner of his eye, Lyman caught Quinn staring at her, his mouth open.

"This one is screaming." A devilish grin spread across her face, her soft features oddly juxtaposed with cruelty. "Wonder how he died?"

"He died before he was mummified. His mouth was opened that way by the embalmer." Horace put down the medallions he'd been examining and searched the face of his young wife as if she were a stranger. "Best not to think on it." Lyman identified pleading in his friend's bloodshot eyes that were suddenly moist at the corners. His friend had never appeared so aged, and Lyman found himself wondering just how old the adventurer was.

"I ain't scared, Horace." Mariana rounded the mummy's head and inched herself close to Lyman until her hip brushed against him, her lavender scent making him dizzy.

"You *aren't* scared, are you?" Horace corrected her, his eye catching Lyman's as he inched away from the older man's wife.

Mariana crossed her arms and scowled. "No *I'm not*," she insisted, emphasizing the last word. "And you *ain't* cursed."

A smile tugged at the corners of Lyman's mouth at her subtle jab and the way she crinkled her nose, lightly sprayed with tiny freckles.

Horace spared her little attention, focused instead on the shrunken face of the mummy. It seemed that he had grown paler in the filtered light of the warehouse, his demeanor affected by some invisible power in Mariana's words. His eyes remained on the mummy as he spoke.

"Don't talk to me of curses, woman. You know nothing of the demons that haunt the waking dreams of men who interfere with the dead." Horace's voice filled every crevice of the vacuous room, absorbed by the dusty crates, the silent deceased, and Lyman, whose limbs grew cold at the candor of his friend's words.

Mariana bent in a fit of laughter, taunting her husband with exaggerated mirth. Quinn joined her, placing a hand on her shoulder, but Lyman did not join them. Instead he stood transfixed by her figure before him—a beautiful young body descending into a writhing heap of callousness.

Horace's complexion purpled and he turned his back to the scene. The moment he did, Mariana's fit subsided.

She steadied herself with one hand covering Quinn's on her shoulder, the other atop the screaming mummy's chest. She narrowed her eyes and bent over the mummy. Pulling her hand back from it slowly, she whispered so that only Quinn and Lyman would hear, "There's something in there."

Horace had turned his attention back to the other open crates, the ones carrying different kinds of treasure. Lyman glanced to where Mariana pointed. How he hadn't noticed it before, he wasn't sure, but she was right. An odd bulge protruded from beneath the mummy's folded hands.

"Let's unwrap it." Mariana's face had become wild, her brown eyes dancing in the low light.

Dread seeping like ice-melt through his body, Lyman thought for the briefest moment of saying no, but watching the way the light played in those seductive eyes, he wondered if he could deny this woman anything in the world.

Quinn spoke up, annoying as a flea, unwelcome and irritating. "I've heard the Egyptians sometimes concealed valuables in the linen strips as they wrapped their dead."

"That's just a pharaoh they might do that to, I think." Lyman offered, though he regretted the words when he saw the excited flush fade from Mariana's cheeks.

"Maybe, but it can't hurt to look." Quinn spoke more loudly, his confidence clearly growing under Mariana's appreciative gaze, attracting the notice of Horace, who approached the threesome. He stopped several feet short of them, his face pale as though he might be ill, but he said nothing.

Mariana's fingers worked quickly, peeling away the wrapping that ripped and shredded on contact. Neither Lyman nor Quinn offered to assist, but they watched her work.

Her eyes reflected wild glee as she tore into the decayed linen. It was as if the mummy were a large Christmas present and she a small child awakened at dawn by the delighted anticipation of its discovery.

Thousands-year-old dust drifted through the air, visible in the beams of sunlight streaming from the high windows. Lyman stepped back and covered his mouth with a hand. Quinn, he noticed, removed his gloves and held them over his nose. Mariana coughed but did not slow her progress. She had successfully unwrapped the mummy's chest, upon which only a thin few straps of linen secured what was evidently a scroll.

She did not stop there, however. She leaned over the face of the silent dead and asked, "What treasures are you hiding?"

"That's enough!" Horace stepped forward. "Let him alone."

Horace's command shattered the silence and drew Lyman from what had begun to feel like an otherworldly fantasy.

Lyman shook his head as Mariana eased a roll of parchment from beneath the mummy's exposed hands.

"Look what we found," she said. "Move this thing out of the way."

Lyman didn't hesitate this time. He stepped forward and lifted the mummy from the table, placing it on the floor before walking around to stand by Mariana's side. Her long fingers worked carefully to smooth the ancient scroll.

Dark with age, it was remarkably little damaged by decay. As they looked, shapes emerged, like a child's stick figure drawings and the scribbled writings of another place and time.

"What does it say?" Lyman had caught Mariana's enthusiasm and nearly forgotten his old partner still standing dumbfounded several feet away.

Mariana looked up at the old man, her expression one of expectation. "You going to read the blame thing or not?"

"Good Lord, Mariana. You're determined to kill us all." Unsteady, Horace approached the mummy, pushing Lyman out of the way to squint at the figures to which Mariana pointed.

"It's hieroglyphs, right? Egyptian writing?" Mariana looked at Horace now with renewed respect and it seemed to soften the old man, who flashed a tender smile toward his wife.

"Yes, these are hieroglyphs."

"Can you read them?" Lyman asked, his interest mounting. Ancient words he deemed to be powerful. To know this script may have sent the person, who had become this decrepit corpse into the beyond with such a terrifying expression may, in his estimation, make them the most powerful words he'd ever encountered.

"Well?" Mariana coaxed as Horace pored over the scroll.

"Course I can read it." Horace bent lower, his eyes inches from the papyrus. After several moments of silence during which Lyman realized he'd been holding his breath, the old man shook his head.

"You can't do it." Quinn did not ask, but rather made a statement dripping in mockery.

"I told you I can." Horace straightened and rubbed his eyes. "It's too dim in here. We'll have to take it back to the house where I can study it properly."

"Are you sure you want to do that?" Lyman surprised himself with the question, but he couldn't shake the feeling there was trepidation in Horace's voice. To see him this off balance—attacking his friends, welcoming his enemies, and absorbing his fears into his own home—disturbed Lyman. Horace was a changed man since last they'd met—weaker, less certain of himself, his vitality fading almost by the moment.

Horace's hands shook as he carefully rolled the scroll. "We'll return for the artifacts tomorrow. Will that work for you, Lyman?"

"Yes. This building is used rarely. As long as we repack and label the crates as belonging to us, a day or two shouldn't raise any alarms."

Horace nodded and turned back to his treasures. The scroll tucked protectively under one arm, his nimble fingers working to secure the smaller treasures back into their boxes.

Quinn cleared his throat. Lyman turned to find him bending to pick up the feet of the screaming mummy now halfway unwrapped, its leathery skin like carved obsidian. Lyman lifted the shoulders, the frightening features sending a shiver of revulsion down his spine.

"Not looking his best, is he?"

"Pardon?" Lyman found Quinn's casual grin distasteful, and he wondered just what sort of man he might be.

Quinn shrugged. "I'm only suggesting that this is not the way I would wish to be remembered, shriveled and slight."

"I'm not sure anyone remembers this man."

"No, maybe not. How about you, Mr. Johnson?"

"What do you mean?" Lyman asked as they hoisted another mummy back into its crate.

"How is it you'd want to be remembered?"

"I've never given it a thought. I prefer to live in this moment."

"A wise philosophy. The current moment may be all you have." Quinn's cold eyes conveyed danger.

Lyman almost could have admired the man's calm demeanor, even while issuing a subtle threat, had that threat not been directed at him. There was no reason for him to fear this man, but yet, something about Martin Quinn put Lyman on edge.

4

"You'll stay in New York a while I hope, Mr. Johnson?" Mariana brought him a glass of whiskey as he settled onto the sofa. "Or should I call you Mr. Chandler?"

He had returned to the house with Horace and Mariana. Martin Quinn did not. He'd made his excuses and, after demanding a future report about the contents of the mummy scroll, tipped his black brimmed silk top hat and slithered off to whatever business shady customs agents must attend. Lyman sincerely hoped he would never see the man again.

"No," Lyman answered Mariana's question, receiving a pout in response. "I'll leave in the morning." He stretched his stiffening jaw, adding, "And you may call me what you like, Mrs. Laurent." At least the next time his old friend tried to punch him Lyman's own actions would be to blame, rather than those of Martin Quinn.

A small dimple appeared on her left cheek when she smiled. She perched on the edge of the sofa and faced him. "You're leaving so soon? Do you not like the city?"

He rested his outstretched arms on the back of the sofa, appearing far more comfortable than he felt. "I love this city, but my fortune lies elsewhere. I've already booked passage for myself and my dusty friends."

Mariana turned her attention to her husband, his nose buried in a worn leather book as he entered the room.

She stood and crossed the room toward him. "Horace, wouldn't it be nicer if Mr. Johnson stayed for a while? It'd be good to have a houseguest, especially one so interesting. I've hardly gotten to know him at all."

Horace closed the book and looked up with a start, as if he'd only just realized there was anyone else in the room. His eyes met Lyman's, who lifted a hand to his swollen cheek. He could already feel his eye beginning to blacken.

"I'm sure Lyman has somewhere else he needs to be." Horace placed the book on the corner writing desk next to the scroll and carefully unrolled the ancient message.

"Don't be rude." Mariana's sharp reprimand failed to penetrate the old man's concentration.

"But you'll stay with us tonight. I insist. Let me get to know you a bit before you disappear from our life again."

Heat rose on Lyman's neck and he wondered if he'd have the fortitude to fight back if Horace really did decide to hit him again, this time for succumbing to Mariana's flirtations. Hoping he wouldn't have to find out, Lyman approached the desk, peering over his friend's shoulder to the faint figures on the ancient parchment. As he stared, colors emerged in the dim light of the room. Shades of yellow, brown, and red filled in bits of the pictures that Lyman knew formed some sort of words. There were several columns of text as well, easily identified as such but meaningless to his untrained eye.

Horace reopened the book he'd carried into the room and ran his finger over a page of handwritten notes. Glancing from the journal to the flattened scroll, he scanned the images and muttered to himself, nodding. Next, he turned his attention to the text, his trembling fingers hovering just above the delicate material.

"What does it say?" Mariana's question came as a frantic whisper. She leaned over the table, her elbow resting next to Horace's, her right hip pressed into him, causing Lyman to experience a pang of jealousy followed by what he might have identified as shame if he were a different sort of man.

Many a pretty girl had turned his head, and this one was exceptional, but entanglement with Mariana, the wife of his most learned and slippery friend, would not serve him well. Then there was Quinn to consider, a man with a certain power and reach—possibly her lover—and a stark reminder to Lyman that a beautiful woman could be dangerous.

Horace brushed Mariana's question aside with a glance. She straightened, taking a step back toward where Lyman stood. Her lower lip protruded slightly in an angry pout that was simultaneously childish and tantalizing. "Thinks he knows everything."

"Your husband is a smart man." At his words, the desire dropped from her expression and he felt the bottom fall out of his stomach. He hoped he hadn't revealed to Mariana how her disappointment affected him. He cleared his throat. "How do you know about interpreting hieroglyphs, Horace? Did you learn from that explorer you worked for in Egypt? What was his name?"

Horace scoffed at the question. "The man I worked *with* was Drovetti. But that sorry excuse for an Egyptologist wouldn't know a hieroglyph if it danced off a stele and kicked him in the nose." Mariana laughed and Horace's lips formed a smirk before he continued. "Before I made my way to America I met a Frenchman in Italy, a young language expert named Champollion who came to evaluate some of Drovetti's pieces. He had this theory about deciphering Ancient Egyptian hieroglyphs using Coptic."

Lyman stared at his friend in wonder. "What's that?" It was easy to forget at times that before Horace became the gentleman of crime who'd taken a delinquent boy under his wing, he'd first been a gentleman scholar.

"It's an Egyptian language, more modern than the ancient hieroglyphs and written in figures similar to Greek. It's still spoken in some Orthodox pockets." Horace's eyes brightened as he spoke, and Lyman glimpsed the man his mentor once was before the ruin that had brought him to the shores of America with few prospects.

"And while others were wasting their time trying to interpret Egyptian pictures, Champollion thought instead the pictures could be read like letters, as precursors to Coptic. He was right."

Lyman smiled and shook his head. Out of the corner of his eye he saw Mariana's dimple return as she gazed at her husband, pride spreading across her features.

"What does it say?" They spoke in unison.

Horace pointed, his finger stalling above the images on the scroll. "This standing figure here is performing rites for the resurrection of the god Osiris. It's common enough. Shows up in temples all over the blame place in Egypt. What we're looking at is *The Book of Breathing.*"

Lyman leaned in and squinted at the papyrus. He couldn't read Coptic any more than he could have read Greek, but as he looked at the ancient drawings, he could begin to imagine he was seeing the representations of sounds.

"It's a book of funeral rites and spells to guide a spirit into the afterlife," Horace continued as Lyman stepped back.

"Spells?" Mariana leaned in to take her turn squinting at the ancient figures. Her nose hovered mere inches above the musty papyrus, her breath slow and heavy as though she were inhaling its meaning.

"Ancient Egyptians believed that man is composed of both an individual personality, or *ba*, and a life force, or *ka*. When he died, if a man were wealthy and important enough to have all the rites performed, the two parts would unite and form a glorified *akh* and experience the next life."

"Or haunt the living." Mariana didn't look at the men as she spoke, but stared into the air, her attention captured by something unseen.

"Do you know what this other text says?" It surprised Lyman that his question escaped in a whisper, the air seeming to grow denser around him than it had been a moment before.

Horace nodded, pointing a gnarled finger at the scroll. "These three columns here," he began, indicating the text to the right of the illustrations. "This is what tells us whose funerary texts we're reading."

"Whose it is? You mean who the mummy is?"

Mariana's head snapped to attention at his words, and Lyman could see that her forehead had become damp with perspiration.

"Most likely. Much of this is just a collection of standard incantations and hymns, but parts appear personalized, perhaps commissioned specifically for the deceased. I believe this says it belonged to a priest of Amon-Re, a prophet of Min who massacres his enemies."

"Sounds ominous." Lyman commented as lightly as he could manage, though his heart pounded wildly in his chest. "Anything else?"

"It gives us a bit of the man's lineage. He was the son of a priest named Osoroeris and a priestess named Chibois." Horace hesitated, bent lower over the scroll, and Lyman had to crouch next to him to hear the next whispered words of his friend.

"And his name was Horos."

Mariana's scream shattered the stillness of the room and then ended as abruptly as it had begun, replaced by an uncomfortable laugh. "Horace? The mummy's name is Horace?"

Lyman joined her, laughing at Horace's joke, relieved at the release of tension in the room and perhaps between the people within it.

However, Horace did not smile, instead gazing stony faced and serious at the scroll.

"Oh God. You're not joking." Mariana's giggles subsided. She placed one delicate hand on Horace's shoulder and he shrugged it off as if the touch of a beautiful woman were too much burden to bear.

Lyman shuddered. "I could use a drink. Horace?"

The man turned in the chair to face Lyman and nodded without a word, but it was Mariana who spoke. "Well, I sure as hell need a drink."

5

Lyman awoke unsure initially where he was, his nightmares escaping in a noxious mist, leaving him drained rather than refreshed. Silence pressed on him like the walls of a tomb, but the smell brought him back. He was fully dressed, minus his coat, and from his rumpled clothing wafted the sweet, oaky scent of whiskey, mingled with a hint of lavender, of Mariana.

Memories from the previous night swirled in his mind, indistinct images which faded as the shapes in the dark room emerged, his vision adjusting to the gray morning light. Rising from the bed, he draped his coat over his arm. Lyman's head throbbed. His left eye ached and was slow to open. His stomach churned and threatened to expel its contents, reacting to a familiar pain. More sleep would have done much to ease the symptoms of his poor decisions, but he feared that if he remained in the house and faced Mariana, fresh and beautiful as the morning, he would find it difficult to leave at all.

He steadied himself and walked softly out of the room and down the hallway toward the stairs, his movements made clumsy by fatigue. Faint light forced its way through a small window, painting dim rectangles along the hallway. The features of the space jumped into Lyman's vision. At the top of the stairs, the door to Horace's bedroom stood wide.

Lyman glanced in as he passed and thought perhaps he would utter a farewell to his friend, one last attempt to soothe any ill feelings. Perhaps, he thought, they would meet again, when enough time had passed for Mariana to fade from Lyman's thoughts.

He crossed the room and stood next to the bed, remembering the press of Horace's shotgun on his chest and wondering whether he should reconsider. But he'd been feeling uneasy about Horace. Malevolent forces had entered the man's life and Lyman's mentor had transformed under the pressure. He had the impression that the two might never meet again.

Though he confided this to no one, Lyman believed fervently in premonitions, even if he himself rarely experienced one. He'd seen evidence that others had and now he feared for his mentor. Or fear may have been the wrong word, as his confidence in Horace's own ability to contain the chaos of life felt still intact to Lyman, just perhaps threatened. What Lyman felt might more accurately have been described as protective. This is what compelled him to Horace's bedside, to inform the man of his leaving and to see whether he might be begged to stay after all.

The room was quiet and dark behind thick curtains drawn against the dawn. Faint light drew a perimeter around them. Thin lines of gray engaged in a feeble attempt to illuminate the room's furnishings and, slowly, Lyman's vision began to adjust. Looming shapes—washstand and wardrobe by day—stood shadowy watch, silent guardians, or threatening demons.

Lyman detected the outline of only one figure atop the high four poster bed. He reached toward it, his arm brushing against the clutter piled on top of a nightstand he had not seen. He attempted to set right the objects—several books, a pipe, a bottle of pills.

Setting the bottle gently on the table, he reached a hand to Horace's shoulder. The man didn't budge. Lyman held his breath, bracing for an angry reaction and then it occurred to him that his was the only breath in the room. Only silence issued from the sleeping man—not a moan, not a snore, nothing.

Lyman slipped his hand across Horace's chest, bare beneath a loose nightshirt. It was unmoving and unnaturally chilled. He removed his hand, bringing his clenched fist to his mouth to muffle the anguish he felt in that moment. There could be no uncertainty. Horace was as dead as the eleven Egyptians awaiting him in a warehouse by the port.

Lyman ran from the room and sank onto the top of the stairs, but he did not remain for long. He could do nothing about dead. The man who had taken him under his wing and taught him his very mode of survival was gone and the world would be a dimmer place without him, but it would not stop spinning.

He pulled himself to his feet to descend the stairs, slowly, cautiously. He had no interest in waking the house. As he reached the landing on the bottom of the stairs, he thought to look into the sitting room, his attention drawn by a slight rustle in the corner where the writing desk stood. His eyes now well adjusted to the dark, he saw her shape leaning against the desk, her head resting on her arm. As she was still dressed in loose men's clothing, he might not have recognized who she really was except her hair hung loose, cascading in tangled curls off the edge of the desk. On the floor next to her lay a top hat with a wide, dark band.

His first thought was that Mariana might also be dead, but the illusion faded as she mumbled something incoherent. Lyman crossed the room toward her, though he wished not to wake her. He did not want to be the one to deliver the news that her husband was dead, perhaps fearing she already knew.

This thought struck him like a knife. Perhaps she would not grieve at all, was in fact the cause of Horace's demise and would soon seek solace in the arms of Quinn, the owner, he realized with another stab, of the top hat. He knew he'd had a lot to drink, his pounding head told him that much, but Lyman was not prone to drinking so much he blacked out.

He pushed these thoughts from his mind, unwilling to indulge them. The left side of his face still ached from Horace's well-placed punch, and even if Mariana or Quinn were guilty, the knowledge would do nothing to bring Horace back. Nor would it honor his memory. The only way Lyman could do that was to continue to carve out a life for himself, using the very lessons Horace had taught him.

Lyman approached Mariana and saw that she had fallen asleep studying the scroll. It lay partly unrolled beside her on the desk alongside the glass ball on its stand and a candlestick in which a candle had burned itself into a cold puddle of wax.

Careful not to make contact with Mariana, Lyman brushed a lock of hair aside and rerolled the papyrus. He donned his coat, tucked the scroll under his arm and crossed the room to let himself out the front door, not pausing to bother with the lock.

Death had already arrived and let himself in.

*****

A late night rain shower had left the cobblestone slick and dotted with murky puddles, soaking Lyman's brogans as he wound his way through the busy streets toward the docks. He stopped and gazed into a collection of water reflecting both the rising sun and the distorted face of a gentleman who had overindulged the previous night. Removing his hat, he quickly pulled his dark hair forward, concealing his swollen eye, and then replaced the hat off-kilter.

A consummate showman, Lyman always found appearing unkempt in public disconcerting, but without the benefit of a looking glass and the application of cosmetics, he could do no better. The city was waking, throwing off the night in favor of the business of the day. One more man in a wrinkled suit and cockeyed hat would draw little notice.

Within the hour he had arranged for the delivery of his ancient companions to the docks and secured passage on the steamboat ferry to South Amboy, where he and the mummies would board a train bound for Camden, New Jersey. If all went well, he would arrive in Philadelphia before nightfall.

He settled into a seat on the steamboat and let his throbbing head drop to his chest, readjusting his hat low over his bruised eye and drawing a long, slow breath. Grief swept over him, his hands recalling the chill of Horace's lifeless body. Lyman shuddered and wished for a glass of whiskey to dull his senses, though he knew his roiling stomach would have rejected it.

Passengers filed past him, conversing with one another, ignoring the man slumped in the corner, withdrawn into his coat and his thoughts. One voice, however, caught Lyman's attention with its authoritative resonance.

"Is there a Mr. Lyman Johnson on board this vessel?" A murmur spread among the passengers at the sharp sound of the lightly accented voice.

Someone, a woman to Lyman's right, whispered, "It's the watch."

Lyman's heart pounded and with it pulsed the pain in his head. He didn't move, but kept his head down, feigning sleep and silently praying he wouldn't be noticed.

"What are you wanting with him, detective?" a man asked.

"Sorry, Cap'n," came the reply. "I don't mean to delay ya. I need to question him as part of a murder investigation. We were told we might find him here."

"There's no one on this boat by that name."

"But maybe someone's seen him at the dock somewhere?" His voice swelled, clearly addressing the crowd. Someone shifted near Lyman, brushed against his leg. He didn't dare stir. "Tall, dark hair, well-dressed, and pretty beat up in the face?"

No one spoke.

"Looks like no one's seen him. And you're wreckin' my schedule, detective." The captain sounded the whistle. "Now pay a fare or get off my boat."

Lyman barely moved all the way to South Amboy, stirring only when he heard the whistle blast signaling the boat's approach to the dock. He hadn't slept for fear he might shift and alter his careful arrangement that concealed his identity as the man sought by the police, and because he had too much on his mind.

A murder, the detective called it. Lyman pictured his friend's body peaceful atop the bed as though he'd been only sleeping. The room was dark and Lyman had not seen what Mariana must have that caused her to send the watchman to chase him.

Lyman couldn't have killed Horace, he knew, but then, never before had he recalled so little about a night of drinking. Never before had he awakened with the lingering scent of another man's wife on his clothes and not remembered how it had gotten there.

Shuffling amidst the other passengers, Lyman disembarked from the steam ship, pushing his way toward the captain to arrange for the unloading and reloading of his crates onto the train bound for Camden.

He opened his mouth to speak and the captain scowled. "You're Chandler, the one with all them crates."

"Yes sir," Lyman replied, trying to smile in the face of the man's obvious disdain.

"You got quite a shiner there underneath that fancy hat o' yours."

Lyman coughed. "Yes, I'm afraid I had something of a rough night."

"I'll just bet you did, Mr. John-son." He drew out the name. "I hear murder can be hard on a man's soul. His face, too."

It occurred to him that he might try to deny the boat captain's meaning, but to do so would likely prove futile. Instead, he stared the man full in the face. "I did not kill anyone."

The captain ran his hand over his peppered beard. "But you didn't want that detective asking you any questions."

"Do you, in general, relish talking to the law?"

"My testimony ain't never been sought after in a murder case."

"You are indeed fortunate." Lyman chanced a smile and this time, the man returned it. "Thank you for your understanding, sir. May I see to the unloading of my crates now?"

At this he put an arm across Lyman's shoulder, pulling him close. "Let's see about that, because I've got to wondering just what it is you're hauling out of New York with a murdered man in your wake."

Lyman pulled back, standing tall, and straightened his rumpled coat as best he could. "I'll show you."

The steamboat captain led the way and soon the two men stood before the crates, the last of cargo remaining in the hold. It was Lyman who took a pry bar from a dockhand and wrenched open the lid to the first crate.

"Oh Holy Mother of God." The captain stepped back, crossing himself, his eyes wide with fear, locked on the desiccated features of the screaming mummy. He turned to Lyman. "What in the hell do you mean by bringing this cursed thing on my boat?"

"Actually there are eleven," Lyman replied with a casual shrug.

"You," he pointed a grimy finger at the deck hand, then at Lyman. "Get these monsters off my boat. And then you, Mr. Chandler or Johnson or whatever your name is, I ever see you again and I'll take you to the jailers myself."

Lyman removed his top hat and bowed his head. "You have my word, sir."

6

From the moment he stepped off the stagecoach and spotted the wharves of Penn's Landing, Lyman missed New York, with its seedy underbelly and dingy façade. In contrast, Philadelphia gleamed. Brick buildings with polished marble stoops rose steadfast above the oft-washed cobblestone streets, crisscrossed in a precise grid. It seemed the entire city existed only to remind the rest of the world what perfection might look like if one possessed the courage to demand it.

Philadelphia was a place for proper behavior, its citizens expected to improve themselves just as they improved and maintained the structures surrounding them. This was not a city that screamed welcome to a man like Lyman, but it was a city in which minds desired improving, and curiosities about natural history abounded. He may not have felt particularly comfortable with what Philadelphians offered, but he felt sure they would be a willing audience, anxious to see what he had for them.

Lyman arranged transportation for himself and his crates to the Mansion House Hotel on Market Street—an elegant choice, not as extravagant as he may have chosen, but one that would lend him credibility in the eyes of the city's high society as he arranged for the exhibit of the mummies.

After settling his belongings into a lavish room, and tending to his bruises, Lyman spoke with the proprietor briefly before taking a cab to the University of Pennsylvania on Ninth Street.

"Thank you." He bowed to the driver as he exited the cab in front of twin marble-trimmed, two-story brick buildings, practical in design and pristine in appearance. "Could you tell me which building houses the medical college, please?"

"The one on the left is Medical Hall." The man touched his low cap before slapping the reins, urging his two horses forward and leaving Lyman to size up the structures.

Surrounding them was a low wrought-iron fence with a narrow pedestrian opening leading to a wide, pleasant walkway, shaded by mature trees and separating the two buildings. A distant church steeple peeked above branches.

Lyman approached the arched doorway at the front of Medical Hall. As he did so, the door flew open and a young man rushed out in a flurry of coattails, bumping into Lyman and nearly pushing him off the walk.

"Excuse me, sir," Lyman spoke forcefully, taken aback as he struggled to maintain his balance.

"I beg your pardon, sir." The young man offered him an embarrassed grin and an exaggerated bow, sweeping his hat from his head full of greasy, brown hair, but didn't quite meet his eye.

"Think nothing of it." Lyman stood straighter, brushing imaginary dirt from his coat. "Are you a student here?"

"Why else would I be here, sir?" the young man replied.

"Then you could help me. I'm looking for someone with an interest in ancient human remains."

The student's eyes widened. He replaced his hat and said, "Oh, it's Dr. Morton you want. His office is on the second floor, at the top of the stairs. You can't miss it."

Lyman watched the young man hurry off, clearly in a hurry to be somewhere, perhaps anywhere, other than the medical college.

He entered the building and found himself in a hallway between what looked to be the entrances of two auditoriums, mirrors of one another. The low mumble of a distant lecture drifted through an open door, the sounds accompanying a wafting, sickening smell like one encountered after stumbling upon a deceased animal in the woods.

He covered his mouth and nose with his gloved hand and hurried up the stairs. As the medical student suggested, Lyman found a door at the top labeled with block letters spelling "Dr. Samuel George Morton." His knock nudged the unlatched door.

"Enter, please."

"Pardon me, Dr. Morton. I do not wish to interrupt."

"Not at all, sir. Come in."

The man sat behind a large oak desk. Books lined the walls. The only window in the small office caught the spring breeze that carried with it the scent of daylilies, a welcome mask to the offensive odors rising from the auditorium.

Lyman took a deep breath and introduced himself to the doctor as Chandler. Dr. Morton rose, offering a hand to shake and indicating the empty chair beside the desk. Morton had a kind, slim face, with bright blue eyes and receding gray hair that hung limp to just above his ears, but when he stood, Lyman swallowed his surprise as the man's large belly appeared above the desk.

"So, Mr. Chandler, what can I do for you?"

He sat, startled to discover next to him at eye level a glass case containing a blackened human skull.

"I apologize, Mr. Chandler," said Morton, pointing to the skull. "We are men of science in this building. I'm afraid some of the items we surround ourselves with have the tendency to shock."

"Oh, no," Lyman explained. "Well, surprise perhaps, but it's quite all right. In fact, this represents the very type of thing I came to discuss. I have recently come into an inheritance of a rather unusual variety."

"Oh?"

"My uncle was an adventurer who excavated Egyptian tombs in the vicinity of Thebes."

"Is that so?" Morton licked his thin lips, his attention clearly captured.

"Yes. He worked often with Bernardino Drovetti, the famed Egyptologist sent by Napoleon Bonaparte to excavate the treasures of that land. And now he has willed to me eleven mummies from his most recent expedition."

"Eleven! How wonderful." The now animated and eager doctor shifted forward in his chair.

"He was very generous, my uncle. But Dr. Morton, I must admit I know little of mummies and would be grateful to have a man of knowledge to help determine their importance." Lyman reached into his bag and pulled out the rolled papyrus, placing it on the doctor's desk. "This was found wrapped with one of them."

"You unrolled them?"

"Only enough to loosen the scroll. Are you able to understand it?"

Dr. Morton smoothed the papyrus across his desk and gave it little more than an unenthusiastic glance. He rolled it again, handing it back to Lyman. "I doubt there's a man alive who can interpret Egyptian Hieroglyphs."

Lyman's heart fell at the words which, as far as he knew since Horace's untimely passing, might have been true.

Morton's eyebrows arched and a grin spread across his lips. "But if you would permit me to examine the mummies, I may be interested in purchasing their heads."

"Their heads?" Lyman shifted in his chair, revulsion rolling over him as he pictured lopping the heads off the preserved bodies.

"It's only the heads I need. For years now I have been studying the theory of polygenism." The doctor paused as though his statement explained everything.

Lyman's stomach churned. The odor of putrefaction and the floral sweetness of the springtime air mingled in the close office and he swallowed a wave of nausea.

Dr. Morton seemed to mistake Lyman's silence for encouragement to continue. "What I suggest is that there were a number of simultaneous creations, one for each race of human on the planet."

"I see." Lyman did not wish for the man to launch into his theory but saw no way around it once begun. He'd come to the medical college hoping to recruit a doctor's assistance in setting up an exhibit, but if there were also the possibility Morton would simply purchase the mummies, then Lyman would have to let him go on.

Though he'd not planned to rid himself of his traveling companions so quickly, for the right price, he might be persuaded.

"It is a fascinating study, based on the cranial capacities of the various races." The doctor droned. "I have conducted careful measurements of many skulls. As one would expect, the skull of a white man is significantly larger than that of the colored man, the lowest of the humans on the scale of intelligence. But of course, one understands Negro behavior much better when one considers his limited cranial capacity."

"I had no idea." This seemed to Lyman a difficult beginning to any kind of business deal. The more Morton spoke, the more enthusiastic he became, reminding Lyman of religious zealots he'd known, determined only to prove the truth of their own opinions. "It always seemed to me that oppressed people appear less intelligent than their oppressors simply because that is how their oppressors would have them viewed."

Morton fixed Lyman in a steady gaze from behind his desk. He continued in a lower, more cautious tone. "Mr. Chandler, are you an Abolitionist?"

"Certainly not." Lyman spoke the truth. He had never been terribly concerned with the plight of American slaves. That was an issue for others to puzzle out. "I'm just fascinated by your theory. The evidence you've collected supports it?"

"Oh yes. The average white man's brain has a capacity of eighty-seven cubic inches. The Negro brain is nearly ten cubic inches smaller, and the Indian cranial capacity falls between them. I'm hoping next to study the ancient skulls of the Egyptians. I have a young partner working on collections for me, but it seems providential that you should seek me out."

"I am no man of science, but if I understand you, your theory relies on the understanding that a smarter brain need be a larger one."

"Yes, but that is only logical."

"Perhaps, but then I've seen plenty of black men and even known a few, none of which would have had difficulty fitting my hat upon his head."

Morton chuckled. "Sir, may I assume you are confessing yourself no brighter than a Negro?"

"To suggest that would be foolish, but as I think about it, there may be some outliers you're not considering. What about this free black Walker who stirred up such trouble in Boston a few years back? He put together a treatise that threatened to change the way his own people thought of themselves. I suspect he would have to be somewhat intelligent to do that."

"Dead, I believe, and likely for his efforts that displayed neither intelligence nor wisdom. If I could gain access to his skull, I am confident it would tell more of his unfortunate tale."

"Then perhaps it's the purchase of his skull you should pursue." Lyman had come across his share of unsavory characters in his lifetime, but none struck him quite as this Morton. He carried the air of power, a manufactured smugness particular to academia that lent him the illusion of both rightness and invincibility.

"Mr. Chandler, I think we have gotten the wrong impression of each other. I should very much like the opportunity to examine these mummies of yours. I have not yet placed the Ancient Egyptians with all their great advancements in the scientific fields, on the scale of human intelligence. To do so would yield great insight into the questions of racial origination."

Lyman sighed. "What on earth would I do with eleven headless mummies?"

"Of course. I see your dilemma." Morton shuffled papers across his desk as he spoke, an attempt, Lyman assumed, to appear too important to be bothered with details of a deal, but Lyman understood that no man was too important to be bothered with such.

The academic and the burner were not so different, each playing a careful and well-rehearsed part, positioning himself to exert influence over his audience. The difference was that whereas the burner won his power through flattery, misdirection, and trickery, the academic claimed his with stubbornness and conceit.

Lyman waited, wearing a mask of calm assurance, knowing the power would soon shift in his direction.

"Well," Morton began, once again shuffling the papers on his desk. "This is a medical college. I'm sure we could make use of mummified human remains. What price do you ask, bodies and all?"

"Dr. Morton," Lyman began his address in a deferential tone. "I am not a salesman, nor am I a wealthy man and I am certainly not the intellectual that you are, but my uncle was a highly respected Egyptologist. I could not in good conscience take less than nine hundred dollars for each."

It was an exorbitant amount, a fact Lyman read clearly on Morton's face. The doctor swallowed, the papers on his desk forgotten as he sank back into his chair, his hand on his chin.

"I hardly think that a fair price," he said at last.

"My uncle was a brilliant man, Dr. Morton, and generous as well. I could not dishonor his generosity."

40

"I see," Morton said with a furrowed brow. "I do see, of course."

"It would, however, please him to know that his hard work would contribute to the education and understanding of the next generation of brilliant men. Perhaps eight hundred and fifty dollars would do."

Morton set his hands on the desk and frowned. "I can see you are a clever man, Mr. Chandler. I can give you eight hundred and fifty per mummy, but I will only purchase two. I expect my source will come through soon and two will provide a fine start to my study. You understand I'll also need to authenticate the specimens."

"I would expect nothing less," Lyman replied, never more satisfied to gouge a man. "You may have first pick of the lot. One has been partly unrolled. I assume you will not wish to take that one. If you have respected colleagues who might also lend their authority to the collection, I would be pleased to have the word of as many as are willing."

"I know several men who would be delighted to study them. I'm curious, what are your plans for the other nine?"

Lyman stood, as did Dr. Morton, signaling the end of the meeting. "I plan to display them for the general interest and education of the public, if I can find an appropriate location. Peale's Museum seems a likely possibility."

The academic frowned. He shook his head and sat, pulling a piece of paper from his desk and writing upon it. "Peale's would be a worthy choice, but special exhibits are planned far in advance. Have you considered the Masonic Hall? That would do very nicely." He stood again and handed the paper to Lyman. "Take this note of introduction. The Freemasons love this sort of thing."

"Thank you, Dr. Morton." Lyman offered a slight and insincere bow.

"You're most welcome. I embrace any opportunity to better the great minds of Philadelphia. I expect I will see you again before too long, Mr. Chandler."

7

Morton's word was good. His name carried weight with the Freemasons. Soon Lyman had not only a proper location in which to display his deceased cargo, but also audiences with some of Philadelphia's most prominent scientific minds, many of them willing to sign a statement of authenticity once they'd seen the ancient dead.

An imposing Gothic structure on the north side of Chestnut Street, the building stood out among the neighboring row houses. Like everything in Philadelphia, the building was well-maintained. There was a freshness to it as well as a sense of stubborn pride. An eager Mason explained to Lyman that after a fire destroyed the original building almost fifteen years before, the new temple had been built with less fanfare. No longer adorned with a steeple to rise above the city, the effect was that the building stood sturdy and substantial, daring onlookers to question its importance. In that way it reflected the Freemasons themselves, a secretive society of leaders, suspicious to outsiders but driven by ordained purpose.

To Lyman, it resembled a mausoleum, a testament to time and to the ingenuity of man, the perfect place to lay the dead amidst compass, star, and all-seeing eye. The symbolism of the Freemasons rivaled that of the ancient pyramids, making their temple a place he imagined the mummies felt at ease.

Lyman's advertisement ran in the *Gazette*:

> The largest collection of Egyptian mummies ever exhibited in this city is now to be seen at the Masonic Hall, in Chestnut Street above Seventh.
>
> They were found in the vicinity of Thebes, by the celebrated traveler Antonio Lebolo and Chavelier Drovetti, General

Consul of France in Egypt. Some writings on papyrus found with the mummies can also be seen and will afford, no doubt, much satisfaction to amateurs of antiquities.

The exhibit opened on a clear Saturday morning in the middle of April. Nine mummies lay waiting in the banquet room of the Masonic Hall, locked inside eternity as the living stole moments from their busy schedules to ogle them.

The public streamed in, the line rarely slowing. For twenty-five cents they came, the good people of Philadelphia, wealthy business owners, working men, and women, their skirts tugged by children admitted for half price.

They came to view the mummies, but they stayed for the tales spun by Lyman, as the Irish showman Michael Chandler, who described with relish the dusty tomb of Thebes, the honeycombed walls, and in some cases, even the floors covered in the remains of the dead.

"Many of the poor old souls were so badly disintegrated one could barely imagine them as ever having been made of living flesh. The explorers exercised great caution, not wishing to dishonor the deceased, but many of the desiccated bodies wound up pulverized to ancient dust beneath their boots."

"So it's ashes to ashes and dust to dust," shouted a tall man in plain dress near the back of the crowd. While the faces of most displayed rapt interest and vague surprise, this man revealed only disgust. "These old bones can't escape the fate that awaits us all."

"Indeed, sir," Lyman continued. "But that didn't stop the ancients from trying. They were cheating death in a way, outlasting its effects so they could be remembered forever."

"And can we say that happened?" It was the man in the back again. "I ask you, do we know the names that once referred to these shriveled bodies? Can we make out their features, imagine the skin plump and supple with life? It seems to me they have been forgotten as we all will be."

"It's true." Lyman gritted his teeth, his patience worn thin by the heckler. "We may not know their names, but we know something of their social ranking and their wealth. There may have been mummies stuffed into corners, strewn across the floor unceremoniously, but these were gently and respectfully placed in special niches within the burial chamber. These were the ones whose rank in the world mattered, whose lives were admired, who were beloved."

At these last words, Lyman noticed a pretty young lady in the front row whose big blue eyes locked with his before dropping. She hid a rising blush behind a fan. He couldn't help but smile before moving on.

"You see, there are different degrees of burial," he began to explain, but the man in the back would not desist.

"Dead is dead. It's a fate we all encounter, and we all must confess our sins to seek the redemption that comes only from God. These heathens died outside of the grace of Christ and so they attempted to cling to earthly life. In the end, it only failed them. All that's left are these shriveled corpses gawked at by strangers in a land of which these formerly exalted people never dreamt."

Lyman had lost control of the crowd's attention. As the nodding picked up, accompanied by alarmed murmurs, he slipped away annoyed, but satisfied in the knowledge that every one of them had already paid their twenty-five cents, even the tall preacher who now held spellbound the attention of the pretty blue-eyed girl.

He crossed the length of the unoccupied room behind the banquet hall, thinking he might close the exhibit for the day to enjoy an early supper. Perhaps he would spend an evening at some local rum-hole spinning tales of mummy curses to gullible topers who would buy a man a drink to hear a good chiller or to a wanton adventuress likely to seek comfort in the arms of the storyteller.

Just as he reached the hallway that led toward the back of the building, Lyman heard the door from the exhibit hall slide open and shut again behind him.

"You should try Moses."

"Pardon me?" Lyman stopped and turned toward the deep clear voice. The words had come from a man he did not recognize, but whose fine dress implied importance. The last thing he wished to do was debate the theological implications of his mummy exhibit, but something in this gentleman's demeanor caused him to pause. Lyman accepted his outstretched hand in a firm shake. "Mr.

Chandler, my name is Titian Peale. I am the head curator and naturalist for Peale's Museum here in Philadelphia."

"Of course," stammered Lyman, swallowing a lump in his throat. "Thank you for visiting my exhibit."

"I wouldn't miss it." Peale smiled warmly as though the two men were longtime friends. "They're all alike, these sanctimonious preachers, the bane of the exhibition business. Can't let them get to you. Are you familiar with the story of Moses, Mr. Chandler?"

"Not particularly," Lyman admitted. He had only a passing knowledge of the Good Book, its lessons never aligning with those that had always served him best.

"God saved baby Moses from Pharaoh's decree that all male infants of Israel were to be slaughtered. The daughter of Pharaoh found and adopted the baby. So Moses was an Israelite who grew up as an Egyptian before he became the great liberator of his people. Read up on it. You tell that preacher these mummies of yours are related to the story of Moses and he'll not say a word against you."

"Clever. Thank you, Mr. Peale."

"Don't mention it, and please, call me Titian. Your collection is impressive. How did you come by it?"

Lyman's voice faltered for a moment as his mind searched for the strands of his carefully woven story. If Peale noticed, he gave no indication. "My uncle uncovered them near Thebes," Lyman explained, catching the ends of the threads. "And graciously willed them to me."

"That's right, your very generous uncle. I remember hearing the tale." Peale drew out his words, tinged in the intonation of disbelief, but Lyman had not even a moment to reflect on the implications of this, as his new acquaintance continued. "Thebes has been a source of much discovery of these strange ancients. I've thought a time or two that I might try my hand at Egyptology. My primary interest has long been with the preservation of animals rather than humans, but I suppose the processes involved might be quite similar."

The curator might have traveled to another realm as he spoke, his enthusiasm swelling to such a pitch Lyman almost hated to interrupt, but he did want to leave behind his encounter with the preaching heckler and catch a moment of fresh air. Lyman coughed.

Peale's head snapped to attention and he smiled. "But I didn't follow you to discuss butterfly preservation, though it is a fascinating topic."

"I've no doubt," Lyman responded, to which the naturalist returned a smirk.

"I was hoping you might consider moving your impressive collection."

"To your museum? That would be an honor, sir." Lyman hesitated. He had initially believed the Philadelphia Museum to be the best location for the mummies, but seeing the steady response to the exhibit, he wasn't anxious to share his profits with the Peales.

"You're hesitant," said the curator. "Worried about profits, I imagine."

Titian Peale's conspiratorial smile caught Lyman off guard, a sensation he never enjoyed. Perhaps this naturalist was a businessman as well.

"Not to worry, sir. We are capitalists, all of us. I was raised by a man who tried to make his fortune gathering and displaying collections. Sometimes he was successful. At times he was not. A man has to make a living."

"I'm glad to see you understand my predicament."

"I do. And I hope you understand mine. I have no space currently for mummies in my museum. But I do see their broad appeal and think we Peales must reevaluate the possibility of including them. I have some thoughts about your exhibit, about where it might find a home that could benefit us both. The museum is currently housed on the second floor of the Arcade building. Are you familiar with it?"

"I have often seen it," answered Lyman, picturing the large building just down the road from where they stood. He'd walked past its four stone archways numerous times. "I've not yet had the pleasure of visiting the museum."

"It's a beautiful space, designed by the great Haviland. The museum takes up the entire second floor. I'd like you to be my guest. And we can discuss the future of your fascinating exhibit.

46

Join me once you've tidied up here. Perhaps by now your zealot has worn through his audience's patience."

At Peale's words, a scream pierced through the low mumble filtering from the banquet room. The thrum grew louder and Lyman's head snapped toward the noise, dread seeping through him.

"Sounds like you'd better see to that."

"Pardon me," Lyman grumbled as he stepped back toward the banquet room.

He didn't get far before Peale caught his arm and Lyman stopped to look over his shoulder at the man, who held an embossed calling card in his outstretched hand.

"I'm afraid I must be going, Mr. Chandler, but I do hope you'll consider my suggestion. Come by the museum any time. I'd be delighted to show you the place."

Lyman took the card with a bow and watched as the respected curator hurried out the back door. He felt a pang of jealousy that he could not follow. Instead, he turned and rushed to throw open the banquet room door.

The crowd had dwindled somewhat since the preacher had commandeered the exhibit. Of those who remained, none examined the mummies or the papyrus scroll. Instead, they stood in a packed circle in the middle of the room. Lyman pushed his way among them. "What's all this?"

"Please, sir, he's collapsed." The answer came from the girl with the striking eyes who pointed toward the convulsing body of the preacher.

"My God, what happened?" Lyman dropped to his knees beside the man who looked at him with unfocused eyes, silently pleading for help.

"Someone fetch a doctor!" He tilted the man's head so he might at least not choke on his own spittle. As he held the preacher, he surveyed the frightened crowd until his eyes lit on a familiar face with a mop of greasy brown hair.

"You!" He pointed to the medical student, who attempted to duck away. "Can you help him?"

The student's shoulders slumped and he shook his head.

Lyman sighed. "But you know people who can. Bring someone!"

The student offered a curt nod and turned to go.

"It's them mummies what did this."

Lyman didn't see who had spoken the words, but the sentiment was echoed in whispered murmurs.

"Don't be ridiculous." Lyman attempted to maintain a steady calm in his voice, though the words reached him far more than he'd have believed they could. He felt the life drain from the preacher as the convulsions subsided with a final shudder and his eyes turned glassy.

The crowd exited after a time and, with the exception of only a few of the Freemasons themselves, who seemed to be intentionally avoiding the room, Lyman found himself alone in the building with now ten dead men.

Lyman laid out the body and retreated from it. He waited until the sky had grown dark for the physician to arrive and finally stepped out to the street to find a patrolling police officer to whom he reported the situation. The officer scurried away and soon returned with a coroner.

"A stroke, I feel sure," said the short, round man. He wore a wrinkled brown coat, the hem stained dark with blood. The coat reached almost to his feet, as though it had been tailored to fit a much taller man.

He stood to speak to the police officer, who remained dutifully attentive to the fresh body, and raised his voice so that Lyman, withdrawn to the far side of the room where he pretended to be in deep contemplation of the papyrus, might also hear.

"You say he was preaching when he collapsed?"

"I had stepped out of the room at the time, but that is what I was told."

The short man nodded, wiping his hands on his filthy coat. "There appears to have been no foul play." He looked at the officer. "Help me get him out of Mr. Chandler's way."

With a nervous glance toward the displayed mummies, the officer bent to pick up the dead man's feet as the coroner gripped under the arms and the two were out the door at last.

Lyman drew a long breath, looking at the largest piece of papyrus unrolled on a table beside where the preacher had fallen. Among the distinguishable images, Lyman noticed particularly the incomplete figure of a man stretched across a platform, much of his upper body lost to the weathering of time. The memory of Horace's cold body laid out on a bed fluttered into his mind, but now the shadowy image transformed into the preacher, dead on the banquet room floor.

Standing above the figure of the dead man, the scroll depicted a second, looming figure, this one with the body of a man, the head of a canine, and skin as blackened as that of the desiccated mummies. He surveyed the nine remaining, long-deceased men and shuddered.

8

Ablaze with artificial light, the four large marble entry arches of the Philadelphia Arcade were a welcome sight against the growing gloom of the evening. Lyman hurried inside and walked through the long colonnade. Above his head, starlight attempted to penetrate the cloudy night to shine through several large skylights that during the day would serve to flood the arcade with sunlight. Around the edges of the opening, Lyman could see a hint of the wonders on the second level.

Most of the small shops lining the first floor were darkened, closed up for the night, the Arcade largely empty of the public. Lyman's steps echoed as he walked across the marble floor toward the stairs leading to the second floor.

He explained at the museum entrance that he'd arrived at the personal invitation of Titian Peale and a bored clerk waved him through the gate. For a moment he simply stood in the grand hall, the gigantic bones of a prehistoric creature on a raised platform towering over him. The complete skeleton of a mouse at its feet accentuated the enormity of the creature. Also present were the taxidermic remains of a male elephant labeled "Columbus." This pachyderm had certainly been large, but its enormous prehistoric counterpart dwarfed it.

A detailed mural of the imagined natural habitat of the giant served as backdrop to the display, which also included an oil painting depicting the excavation of the bones in Ulster County, New York.

Lyman had just turned away to proceed to the art gallery when Titian Peale approached him from behind.

"Mr. Chandler, thank you for coming."

Lyman turned with a wide grin and stretched out his hand to his new benefactor. "I'm sorry it took me so long, Mr. Peale. There was an incident at the exhibit. It took me a little time to extricate myself."

Peale pumped Lyman's hand. "No need to apologize. I myself am often held up by the unforeseen."

Lyman wondered just how many men had suddenly dropped dead among the exhibits of Peale's Museum.

"And the curious public can be irritating," Peale continued. "But then, men like us must be tolerant of the incessant questions if we are to make a living doing what we love."

"And just what is it that men like us love, Mr. Peale?"

"Science, Mr. Chandler. Science. The wonders of the natural world, preserved in such a way as to be available for study long after we ourselves are dead. That's what I do it for, and one could argue that is exactly what those specimens of yours were doing as well— making natural science of themselves, dedicating themselves even long after death to the learned. And to the masses."

"Forgive me, sir, but I doubt the Ancient Egyptians had the education of the masses in mind when they entombed their dead."

"And yet here they are in America, educating the masses." Peale placed a hand on Lyman's back and indicated a hallway to the right of the mastodon skeleton. Lyman followed his host as the man continued to speak. "Tell me of your intriguing collection, Mr. Chandler."

Lyman launched into his rehearsed speech about his uncle the great explorer, making sure to include plenty of impressive names and details for the benefit of the gentleman curator, who nodded along as they walked, occasionally asking a thoughtful or clarifying question.

"And when were they found?"

"The excavation began in 1828 and employed more than four hundred men. They dug for months around Thebes and eventually stumbled on a large system of catacombs filled with hundreds of mummified human remains, some in better condition than others. My uncle salvaged eleven for himself. He died soon thereafter and the mummies were sent to me, as per the instructions found in his will."

"Only the mummies?" Peale stopped in front of a large display case filled with sparkling minerals, each neatly identified on a small accompanying plaque.

Lyman could hardly mention that the shipment had contained other treasures but that they had been part of the spoils given to another criminal, one who was now dead under curious circumstances.

"Only the mummies," he replied, adding, "and hieroglyphic writings found with them."

The men began to move again, past a long display of preserved fish and other ocean-dwellers, the likes of which Lyman had never seen. Large gas chandeliers cast soft light reflected off iridescent scales, creating the illusion of fluid movement. A handsome couple strolled arm-in-arm through the hall in the opposite direction, pausing to gasp at the effect. Lyman would have been pleased to join them in their observations, but the curator's pace never slowed.

"I only counted nine," Peale said.

Lyman stole another glance at the shimmering display before answering. "Yes sir. Two were sold to Dr. Thomas Morton at the medical college."

Peale winced, but offered no further comment, stopping at a door on the far end of the hallway. He took a full ring of tinkling keys from his coat pocket and opened the door to a set of poorly lit stairs which he did not hesitate to descend. "What do you intend to do with the rest of the collection?" The question floated disembodied up the stairwell as the curator faded from view.

Lyman swallowed and trailed his host down two flights, to emerge once again on the first level of the Arcade. "I hope for a time to continue placing them on exhibit."

"Good. That's good. I wish we could place them in the museum, but I'm afraid the management of our special exhibits is handled by my brother Franklin, and he's been busy. The space is spoken for, but there may be an elegant solution to that."

Peale crossed the wide hallway and arrived at the entrance to a darkened storefront, blinds pulled tight, blocking any view into the space. "As you must have noted when you entered, there are a number of rooms in this building, most of which are occupied by shops or small businesses of one type or another. My workroom is in one as well, only a few rooms down from where we are now. But this one here is vacant at the moment. I thought it might be a perfect location for your mummies if you're interested."

The curator withdrew the ring once again from his pocket and examined the keys before selecting one to open the storefront door. Peale stepped through the entrance and pulled open the blinds, allowing light from the colonnade to spill into the space. From the gloom, shapes emerged on the papered walls—diamonds in rich shades of red and gold. Spread across the floor, a thick, lavish rug waited to be seen in contrast with the dullness of preserved death.

Lyman surveyed the room, calling into existence phantom mummies in the space.

Peale pushed past him and spun, his arms outstretched. "If we move in a few display tables, nine mummies could be very comfortable here, I think. I have some influence with the manager of the Arcade. If you wanted the room, it could be easily arranged."

"That's an intriguing possibility, Mr. Peale."

"Please, call me Titian. There are too many Mr. Peales running amok in Philadelphia."

The easy informality of the man took Lyman aback, and he was genuinely moved by it.

"Thank you, Titian. I truly appreciate your interest my collection." Lyman was sincere. For a criminal to be aided so much by a respectable businessman was a rarity, and it lent a legitimacy to Lyman he could not express to his new friend who believed him to be Michael Chandler, the nephew and heir of another respectable man.

"We museum men must stick together. And I think it might serve us both well. I have nothing against the Freemasons. Your type of exhibit works well in their building, but if you were nearer the museum, it would lend your collection more authority and have the added benefit of bringing us each more customers."

"You might be right about that, but I never thought of myself as a museum man before. I'm not sure I qualify as such."

"I'm not really a museum man myself, only a member of a museum family. I'm an artist, an explorer, and a naturalist. I just work in a museum. And what are you, really, Michael Chandler?"

Lyman's breath caught. Logically, he knew Titian could not know Chandler was a nom de plume, that he was in truth an imposter who had orchestrated an elegant crime. But for just an instant, he wondered if the man had somehow discovered his secret. He paused, looking into the empty shop. "I'm not sure I've ever figured that out."

"Ah, you are a museum man, I think." Titian laughed. "A man of varied interests with a fascination for objects of intrigue. Do you intend to remain in Philadelphia indefinitely?"

"This is a fine city, but no, it is not my intention to settle here."

"I don't wish to offend you, but I thought not. You appear knowledgeable enough, and you've rehearsed your story well, but you are not a scholar."

"I'm not offended in the least," he replied, though he was disappointed that the man had seen through his attempt at high-minded discourse. Still, it spoke volumes that Peale didn't seem to mind dealing with him as an equal in spite of their difference in backgrounds. "What you say is true. There's a limit to how much I can do with the collection in an academic center like Philadelphia."

"Then when you travel on, it will be with the added advantage that you have exhibited your collection if not at Peale's Museum, at least in the vicinity of it."

Lyman stepped out of the shop, his eyes sweeping across the stately marble pillars lining the long hallway toward the front entrance of the Arcade. Peale pulled the blinds, stepped out behind him, and locked the door. He returned the keys to his coat pocket and, wearing an expectant smile, turned to face him.

"Thank you, Titian," Lyman said. "I'll speak to you again soon."

"Excellent. I look forward to hearing from you either way."

9

Lyman emerged from the imposing building to warm night air and a sky full of twinkling stars. Delighted by his success in conversation with an influential member of the first family of the museum industry, the common criminal turned amateur Egyptologist drew a long breath and decided to take a walk.

He passed a small theater and a busy restaurant, its windows spilling light onto the walk, and continued another two blocks lined with closed shops. He took in the sounds of the freshly fallen night—the clopping of hooves and the crunch of carriage wheels as the nightlife emerged against the backdrop of hissing street lamps.

But it was a different sound that pulled him from his contemplations as he approached the darkened Masonic Hall. A side door flew open, crashing against the stone building. Someone uttered a curse.

The hall, bordered on both sides by brick business establishments, stood at this hour shrouded in shadow that afforded him no clear view, but his sense was that all was not as it should be. The Freemasons were a private and well-mannered group, not prone to skulking in dark places swearing.

Lyman reversed direction and slipped along an alley to the back side of the row of buildings, well beyond any illumination the streetlamps offered. The sky was clear and the night still young. He hoped he might see well enough to determine the cause of the disturbance. He stopped at the end of the alley to peer down the street toward the source of the crash, several voices replacing the sound.

Three human shapes hovered by an open door at the rear of the Masonic Hall. These were not men who carried themselves with the self-assured stature of Freemasons.

Two of the figures carried something between them, with the third directing them toward a carriage, its horse tied and calm at the side of the road. None of them turned toward Lyman as he spied from his hiding spot. He couldn't determine what the two carried, but as they loaded their burden into the carriage, he strained to hear and their words became clear to him, as did the gist of their unlawful plans.

"Oh God, the thing's oozing," came the first voice, the frightened whine of an effeminate young man.

"That's the sweaty slime of your fear, you ignorant coot." The second voice was deeper, its owner clearly in charge. "Leave it here and help me with the others."

Lyman heard a cough, then a new voice. "It? Shouldn't we show some respect?"

The leader responded, "Kline, you ignoramus. It's just bodies, no different than any other. Dead is dead."

"Yeah, dead is dead." Another cough. "And cursed is cursed. I ain't particularly interested in being either one."

The effeminate voice piped up. "Who said anything about being dead? I ain't risking my neck for no corpses."

"You're both imbeciles. These are the best score we ever got."

"What's anyone want mummies for anyway?" asked the cougher, who cleared his throat and spit a fine collection of phlegm onto the street.

The figure Lyman had pinpointed as the leader stepped over the nasty puddle at his feet and led the other two back into the building. He couldn't hear what this potential buyer might want with mummies—with *his* mummies.

Lyman burned with anger. That someone would have the nerve to steal from him, and in such an unsophisticated way was, in his mind, a source of shame among the criminal element. He would not stand for such indecent behavior after he had so successfully stolen the mummies himself. If these new thieves expected a curse, Lyman would give them one.

The moment the door closed behind them, Lyman crept from his hiding spot and approached the carriage. He reached inside the buggy, his probing hands counting three bodies wrapped in brittle linen, and despite the effeminate man's fears, as dry as the bones contained within them.

Quickly he withdrew his hands and slid next to the horse, waiting patiently in the dark. Lyman grabbed hold of the beast's bridle and held a hand to its muzzle to which the horse balked, throwing back its head and letting out a loud whinny.

Lyman lost no time lest the noise alert the three thieves. He loosened the animal's tie and climbed into the driver's seat, snapping the reigns and sending the startled horse into action. The frustrated shouts of the would-be burglars echoed through the alley and vanished as he rounded the corner to a lighted roadway where he sought an officer of the law.

It took some time for the befuddled man to understand Lyman's predicament and to overcome his horror at the silent passengers stowed in the carriage, but he agreed to join him on the driver's seat and return with him down the dark street to the back of the Masonic Hall.

"The door's standing open. That's unusual," the officer unhelpfully observed.

Lyman was grateful that, in the dark, the officer could his not see his contempt for the man's slowness of thought.

"Yes," he replied. "This is the door through which the scoundrels were removing my exhibit, loading it piece by piece into their waiting carriage. This waiting carriage."

The officer held his lamp to the door frame, examining it. "I see. Piece by piece. That is, mummy by mummy, I suppose." He drew out his words, so thick with disgust Lyman thought he might be able to see it if more light was available.

"That's correct. They're quite valuable, I suppose, on the black market. If one can believe such things."

"Just so." The officer peered into the darkened building, holding his light in front of him at his arm's full length. "Yes, I suppose the right sort of criminal could make a profit off just about anything these days."

"What is the world coming to?" Lyman offered, wishing only that the man would hurry his investigation into the building, so that if the robbers remained, there might be any chance of catching them.

"Indeed." The officer was clearly in no hurry.

"Should you search the building?"

In the warm glow emanating from the lamp, Lyman saw the officer give a curt nod, as if gathering his nerves about himself. When the man at last entered the building following his trembling light, Lyman unhitched the horse from the wagon and slipped back around the corner to his alley from which he had first observed the would-be thieves.

Just as he'd hoped, not five minutes passed before three figures crept out of the shadows toward the carriage. He couldn't be sure from which way they had come, but it was clear to him they had not been hiding inside the building and that they thought both of their pursuers were now inside and safely out of the way.

They uttered not a word, but one of them climbed into the driver's seat while the other two piled into the carriage compartment. And then one screamed.

It wasn't a loud or particularly long scream, but it pierced the otherwise quiet night air like a knife puncturing an air-filled bladder.

"Oh, God, they're still here!" It was the cougher and the realization sent him into a fit.

"Shut up or I swear what I'll do to you is worse than any old mummy curse."

Lyman admired the leader's commanding tone. His partners seemed to respect it enough to follow his command, but their fear was palpable, and Lyman would use that to his advantage. He crept along the side of the carriage, knife in hand, and stood to give the horse a slap on the rump that sent it down the dark street without the buggy in tow.

"What the?" and then the leader saw the form of Lyman emerging from the darkness.

"Now you can tell me why you are attempting to steal my mummies."

The two in the carriage took the opportunity to jump out and run without a backward glance. The third, the leader, Lyman already held tight by the collar before he'd even have time to think about escape.

"Look, Mister," the leader began and Lyman realized he recognized the voice.

"You're the young man from the medical college. The one who ran into me."

"Yes, sir." Pride, rather than fear, filled his voice and Lyman found his admiration for him grow.

"So I'll ask you again—why do you, a medical student, wish to steal my mummies?"

"It's an impressive collection, sir. Very educational."

Lyman drove his arm across the thief's chest, pinning him against the buggy and with the other hand held the knife to the young man's throat.

"You need to understand that there is an officer of the law inside that building, and that if he were to catch you, the law would be the least of your concerns. This building is the sacred meeting place of the Freemasons of Philadelphia and if they were to get wind of this, there'd be nothing left of you."

Lyman had no idea what the Freemasons may or may not do to an unauthorized person caught in their halls, but the rumors of their absolute control of the city and their cruelty in dealing out swift punishments to the unfortunate souls who crossed them was, he hoped, enough to strike fear into the scoundrel's heart.

Instead, the thief laughed. "I'm not fool enough to cross the Freemasons."

"What do you mean by that? Did a Mason send you to do this?" Lyman shoved him harder, smashing his head against the hard side of the carriage.

"Please, I'm only trying to make a little money. You can understand that."

"And are you in the habit of stealing to make your living?"

"Nothing anyone needs anymore, I swear, at least not usually. I steal bodies, fresh ones, just buried. I sell them to the college for their dissections. It's a public service, you understand. You'd be amazed how many bodies they go through. It's an endless source of revenue for someone like me. For someone who's good, I mean."

"Good enough to get caught. And I'm sure I don't need to tell you that my bodies aren't fresh. They're more than three thousand years old."

"I know, I know. This was a special job. There's a single buyer, wants them for his research."

"Morton? Did he set this whole thing up with the Masons to get hold of the rest of my mummies?" Lyman gripped the knife tighter, considering how he might best procure a confession.

"I swear I don't know anything about that. I was just hired to do a job. I take orders from a third party. I'm not hired directly." Panic edged his voice, as did the ring of truth.

Lyman pulled back, allowing the thief a breath before punching him in the gut and watching him crumble with a grunt. It was clear that this young man was nothing more than a petty grave robber, perhaps even a skilled one whose luck had run out this night.

But if Morton had been behind the attempted burglary, and if he held sway with the Freemasons, that concerned Lyman very much. He'd have to move his exhibit to a safer location, one to which Morton wouldn't have easy access.

"Very well," Lyman said as the grave robber pulled himself to a stand and drew slow, deep breaths.

"You're letting me go?"

"I'm letting you go. But if I see you or your friends anywhere near my mummies again, I'll shut down your operation and see that you are never able to steal, or take a deep breath, again. And if my collection is molested in any way from this night forward, I'll assume you are the guilty party and I will find you. Do you understand?"

"Yes, sir." The young man paused.

"The police officer will finish searching the building soon. You'd be wise to be gone when he does."

"What about the carriage?"

"I assume it's stolen as well. If not, then you may feel free to explain to the police how they came to acquire it."

With that the young thief ran and Lyman watched him go, barely a shadow in a dark alley.

10

The next morning, Lyman gave notice to the Freemasons and posted a sign that the mummy exhibit would temporarily close, to reopen soon in another location. To his delight, would-be patrons approached the entrance in steady waves, only to turn away disappointed. Speculation swirled that the curse of the mummies had struck down a preacher who dared blaspheme them. Rather than repel the public, the tale had ignited its morbid curiosity.

He considered admitting small numbers, perhaps charging more for the privilege of viewing the mummies while they remained off-exhibit to the general public. That might serve to further entice a certain segment of the population, but the burglary attempt had left the exhibit damaged. He could only hope that by keeping the mummies out of sight for a time the rumors and excitement might grow.

"Grave robbing evidently doesn't require great care," Lyman mumbled as he sifted through the wreckage. Linen wrappings had been rubbed away in places where rough hands grabbed at the desiccated bodies, and scrolls had been torn by carelessness. The mummy Horos, with the gaping mouth that had so captivated Mariana, was now missing a leg.

Lyman found the ghastly appendage and disentangled it from the pile of delicate linen and bone he'd carried from the carriage the previous night, presenting it to his maimed companion. "I finally know why you're screaming, my old friend." He smirked at the joke, but as he gazed at the mummy's distorted features, he felt a spreading cold seeping through him and quickly turned his back on the oddity stretched across the display table.

As much as possible, he averted his eyes from the shrieking mummy the rest of the morning as he collected, separated, and packed the other pieces of the ruined exhibit, hoping the damage could be repaired. By early afternoon, Lyman sent word to Titian that the mummies would move into the Arcade as soon as possible. He arranged for transport of the collection and placed advertisements in the Philadelphia newspapers about the new venue, set to open in a few days' time.

Finished at last, he found a nearby doggery and ordered a whiskey.

"Yours is a face I haven't seen before." The man behind the bar filled a glass from a dark bottle. He was slim and middle-aged, wearing dingy clothes and a cheerful smile. It was the grin that distinguished him from the dozen or so patrons that had hardly looked up when Lyman entered.

He sipped the strong liquor. "I'm new in town. Thought I might visit one of the city's fine drinking establishments."

"You sure you're in the right place?" The man who spoke settled onto a stool a few feet from Lyman. The bartender passed the newcomer a tall glass filled with dark ale that the man had ordered with no more than a head nod as he approached the bar. Lyman watched him take a long swig and wipe his mouth on the back of his hand. The man wasn't finely dressed, and had an overworked sternness about him, but his eyes were wide and interested, and that was all Lyman needed.

"It's close to my work. Name's Chandler." He reached down the bar and clasped the man's calloused hand.

"I'm Edwards. What's your work, Mr. Chandler?"

Lyman sighed and swirled the whiskey in his glass. "I was a showman. I displayed mummies, but now, I don't know."

"What do you mean you don't know?" His brow furrowed with suspicion. "Hey, barkeep, how much you give this man to drink? You either have mummies or you don't."

"I do." Lyman threw back the rest of his drink and signaled for another, savoring the burn in his throat.

"And do people come to see them?" Edwards prompted as the barkeeper filled the glass.

"I was showing them at the Masonic Hall, but then disaster struck."

"Well what in Sam Hill happened, Mr. Chandler?"

The man's questions had grown louder and other tavern patrons had begun to take notice of the conversation, as Lyman hoped they would. "A man died," he responded in a whisper. "A preacher. And then a group of grave robbers tried to spirit the blame mummies away in the night."

He paused to make sure anyone with the inclination had leaned in sufficiently to hear the rest. "There's a curse."

The gray-eyed man coughed into his ale, sloshing a good bit of it onto the bar. "Oh, hell. barkeep, you better get Mr. Chandler here another drink."

*****

It was only after a long, liquor-soaked night of tale-telling that Lyman stumbled through the front door of the Mansion House Hotel and his unstable legs wound a path to the stairs.

"Mr. Chandler?"

Spoken by a man whose voice Lyman couldn't have placed, the words reached him as if through a long tunnel. He sensed the address was meant for him. He turned abruptly and slipped down two stairs before catching himself on the banister, a jolt of pain radiating through his right ankle.

"Mrs. Chandler arrived earlier this evening."

Lyman tried to question the hotel proprietor, now standing at the foot of the stairs addressing him, but his thoughts moved more slowly than his reluctant legs and all he wanted to do was sleep. A rush of determination not to blackout in a heap on the stairs pushed him up the remaining distance. Unsure whether he'd responded appropriately to the proprietor, and certain he didn't care whether he had or not, Lyman clumsily placed his room key into the lock and crashed through the door, relieved to be alone at last.

"I was beginning to think you weren't coming back." The voice tugged at Lyman's memory. He tried to focus on his surroundings, the room familiar, but filled with the soft glow of lit oil lamps when it should have been dark. His stomach churned.

"Pigeon-eyed, like the last time I saw you." A woman with indistinct edges crossed the room and slipped beneath his arm to steady him. She smelled of lavender, familiar and comforting. Lyman fought to make sense of the words spilling from her—soft and gentle, but containing barbs he could almost feel.

"Not long before you failed to say goodbye, stole a valuable artifact, and left me to wake alone in a house with a dead man."

"Mariana." The name escaped his lips without thought, as if he'd been always prepared to say it.

She urged him toward the bed and he limped along with her and sat. She lowered herself next to him and lifted her arms, rotating her delicate wrists and arched her back like she'd been waiting for him for some time.

Her presence in his hotel room, after he'd assumed he'd never see her again, felt exhilarating and dangerous and so overwhelmingly sad he wanted to cry. He lay back on the bed and fought to keep his eyes open as the room spun around him. "How did you get in here?"

Finished with her stretch, she stood and appraised him before answering. "I know a few tricks. The hotel proprietor was pleased enough to allow Mrs. Chandler entrance when I showed him the letter from my husband summoning me to join him in Philadelphia."

"How did you know where to find me?"

"I simply used the note you was kind enough to leave when you slipped out of the house where my dead husband lay in our marriage bed." She nudged his shoulder in a gesture that struck Lyman as inappropriate and lovely. "Not as hard to find as you think you are." She grinned and pulled away, sending a glance to the desk behind her. Lyman followed her gaze to a glass ball, pale blue and cradled on a wooden stand. He'd seen it before, in Horace's house in New York.

"You found me by scrying?" Lyman knew of the powers some possessed to gaze into reflective surfaces and interpret signs of the future, but he'd never known anyone to use the ability to track a person.

"Well," Mariana sniffed. "I knew which port you were leaving from, a man traveling with mummies. That's not exactly inconspicuous."

Lyman pulled himself slowly into a sitting position, steadier than a man in his state had any right to be. Fuddled as he was, the anger and grief he felt over Horace's death was sharp enough to penetrate the whiskey fog in his mind, allowing the details of his escape from New York to flood his thoughts.

"You sent the detectives. You accused me of murder."

She turned her back to him, hugging herself as she took a deep, halting breath. "I did no such thing. I told them you might have information about my husband's death."

"I found him before I left. If he was murdered, I didn't do it."

"He was murdered." She turned to face him, her cheeks streaked and glistening. "But I know you didn't do it. You never would. You loved him." Her words sounded genuine and they flooded him with dizzy relief.

"Mariana, I remember so little of that night. What happened?"

She reached a hand to his face and caressed his cheek, teardrops gathering on her lashes. "You and Horace were celebrating. You'd both drunk a lot. Quinn came and behaved the way Quinn does, as gentlemanly as a snake. You told Horace you'd had enough and if he wasn't going to throw the man out, you would.

"Horace couldn't take that kind of assault on his character. He thought so much of you, you know. He told you to sleep it off and he'd handle his own business. You went upstairs to bed and Horace tried to fight Quinn."

"Tried?"

"I loved my husband, but he wasn't a match for a man half his age. It took Quinn hardly a minute to get him around the throat and less time for Horace, as drunk as he was, to pass out."

"That was it?"

"Quinn said he wasn't dead. He called him a lucky son of a bitch and swore if he ever..." Mariana shook her head, her eyes downcast. "Well, he said terrible things."

"But Horace died?"

She nodded. "He was moaning a little and I asked Quinn if he'd help me get him up to bed to sleep off the drink. He grumbled but he did it, just slung him over his shoulder and took him up the stairs. He came back down with an evil look in his eye. Scared me to death."

"Did he hurt you?"

"Not in any important way. He grabbed me and shook me, left bruises on my arms and threatened me, too. Said I was a fool to be with such a man."

"But you didn't see the murder?"

"The doctor looked at the bruises on his neck and said he died from his injuries. I told the watch it was Quinn and that you were a witness. That he'd been there and that they'd argued. They caught up with Quinn, but without your testimony, he wouldn't have stayed locked up for long. He has too many allies, people he holds secrets over."

Mariana sniffed and Lyman reached into his breast pocket for a handkerchief that wasn't there.

"I was so scared," she said. "I didn't know where else to go."

"You don't have friends?"

"Not outside of the city, and Quinn has more. I'm scared he'll come after me now, for revenge. And you. He won't like having the threat of you hanging over him." Now the tears really rolled, down her cheeks and onto her neck with no handkerchief to stop them.

Lyman moved to her. He draped his arm around her and pulled her close. "I'm sorry, Mariana." The warmth of her body seeped into his liquor-soaked brain and in that moment, he felt there was no place else he could ever want to be.

She nodded. "You were already so drunk, and when you went to your room, Horace and I fought. I'd asked him why he attacked you in the carriage."

"I called him a cuckold," Lyman admitted. "I deserved what I got."

"He asked me if it was true."

"And what did you tell him?"

"The truth, Mr. Johnson. I loved my husband."

"Did he know that?" Somewhere in the fog of his thoughts he wanted to scold her for her behavior, the way she had danced around Quinn like he was the earth and she his moon, but as she leaned into him, and Lyman felt her uneven breaths, he couldn't bring himself to do it.

"He knew." She pulled away from him then and her dark eyes focused on him. "The truth is, Quinn frightened me. He was a man who didn't like to take no for an answer. He'd worked hard, he said, to get where he was, and he always got what he wanted."

"He wanted you?"

She nodded, and the tears began to fall again. "It's my fault Horace is dead. I as much as killed him myself."

11

Lyman awoke the next morning with a sour taste in his mouth and a persistent pounding in his head which was amplified the moment he opened his eyes. He closed them again, long enough for his other senses to awaken, only to be assaulted by the persistent scent of Mariana. She might have been no more than a dream if her essence did not linger so convincingly on the barely disturbed bed linens beside him.

Lyman sat up to survey the remains of whatever poor decisions he'd made in the night, releasing an unmanly groan. He still wore his full set of rumpled clothes from the day before, a realization for which he was grateful. Beautiful though Mariana may be, the painful memory of Horace still clung to her, and Lyman was not anxious to invite more ghosts into his life.

Mariana's glass ball was missing, along with its stand, but an unfamiliar carpetbag sat in the corner of the room. Of course she'd left no note. He wouldn't have expected one. But she had not left him, and for that he was grateful, too.

Lyman splashed water on his face and changed clothes quickly. He begged a cup of milk and dissolved ash from the hotel proprietor's wife to settle his roiling stomach and vowed to keep his wits about him the next time he ventured into the night.

He arrived shortly at the Arcade, asked after Titian Peale, and was directed to a first floor shop just a few spaces down from the one in which his mummies would soon be displayed. The shades were drawn over the large front window, but through the closed door, he could distinguish the muffled sounds of movement.

"Titian," he called, knocking as he pushed his way into the room. The room itself was similar in most ways to the one Lyman would be renting, but its cluttered shelves and stacked keg barrels in the corners served to shrink the space considerably.

The walls were nearly concealed by framed sketches of every manner of creature, some of which Lyman could not have identified. From shelves, rabbits, birds, and a collection of several bats stared at him through glassy eyes.

Lyman's own eyes began to water and he drew shallow breaths. The close air in the room swirled with the effluvium of hundreds of animals, an odoriferous soup that threatened the uncertain control he held over the contents of his stomach.

"Come in, my friend. Welcome to my workroom." Peale crossed the room, wiping his hands on a stained apron that covered him from shirt to the tops of his shoes. He offered Lyman a warm smile, but no hand to shake. "I was delighted to receive your message. I trust the room will serve your purposes?"

"I'm sure it will do nicely."

"I have something for you." Titian turned and searched the shelf behind him, pushing aside several small jars containing crabs suspended in a clear liquid. When he turned back, he held a book. "I wondered if you'd read any of Belzoni's writings?"

Lyman shook his head and took the book, *Narrative of the Operations and Recent Discoveries in Egypt and Nubia*. He flipped open the front cover to find a sketch of the author, an imposing, dark figure with a black beard, flowing robes, and thick turban. In the background stood distant pyramids dwarfed by the man who dominated the portrait. Belzoni held his right hand, palm up, directing attention to discoveries yet to be made. In his left hand he grasped a staff. This man carried himself as a prophet prepared to call forth the miraculous.

"Giovanni Belzoni began much like you, a humble performer. And he became as fine an Egyptologist as ever was known. I thought perhaps his writings might be a useful supplement to your pool of knowledge when you reopen your exhibit. When do you think that will be?"

Lyman thanked him and slipped the book into his coat pocket. "Two days hence, but I'm afraid some of the mummies didn't fare well in the burglary attempt." He explained to the curator the damage the relics had suffered. The man listened intently, his stained hand rubbing his sparsely whiskered chin. After Lyman finished his tale, Titian clapped him on the back. "You've come to the right place. I've something of a penchant for preservation. We'll sort them out."

Lyman took stock of the workroom. If anyone could piece together the bodies of the ancients, Titian Peale was certainly the man to do it.

His gaze fell on a large wooden frame containing rows and rows of brightly colored insects behind thick glass—beetles, grasshoppers, and wasps, all so lifelike they might have been resting before scurrying off to do whatever insects do.

"Are these all your work?" Lyman gasped, running has hand gently along the top of the frame.

"Oh, yes," Titian responded. His tone was humble, but the corners of his eyes crinkled with his delight.

"They're stunning."

"Thank you. I have always been good with insects, ever since I was a small boy. This is a newly constructed case, but there is much more to the collection upstairs in the museum. You should see what I do with butterflies."

Lyman turned then to his right and was met with a strange sight. On a long table sat at least fifteen varieties of lizard in various stages of disembowelment. He brought his hand to his mouth and nose.

"Does it bother you? I'm sorry. I sometimes forget not everyone has the stomach for this kind of work."

Lyman recovered himself. "It was a tad alarming at first, but truly I find it all fascinating. How do you do it?"

"Between you and me, it's largely a process of chemical trial and error. And of course it depends on the outward anatomy of the animal. All animals are quite similar on the inside, you know."

Lyman hadn't known, but he nodded.

"Different shapes and sizes offer different challenges. But the basic principle is that the parts most vulnerable to deterioration must be removed and what remains, dried. It's much like your Egyptian friends."

"Is it?"

"Of course," a delighted Titian explained. "That's why at excavations they find small jars among the mummified remains. Brains, intestines, any soft organs have to be removed because they'll be the first to putrefy and spoil the body. Have you ever seen a decomposing corpse?"

"Certainly not," Lyman said, faintly sick at the thought. It occurred to him that the young men he'd looked down upon when he caught them trying to rob him had handled many decomposing corpses and he wondered if they'd ever spoken so candidly about them.

"No, I suppose not. Most people don't wait long enough before burial to see the truth of nature."

"The truth?"

"The truth that while 'ashes to ashes and dust to dust,' is so, it also skips over a great deal of unpleasant putrefaction in between. Within very little time, a human body bloats and breaks down, the juices in the intestines leaking and devouring tissues. It's not a pretty process, though in a way it does possess a certain beauty."

Lyman doubted that, too.

"What the ancients discovered is no different than what the taxidermist of today knows—how to dry out the body and rid it of all the decomposition agents."

Lyman pointed to the lizards on the table, one of which was posed as though it were about to climb a tree branch. "So you remove the organs."

"That's the first step. Then I apply drying agents."

"Such as?"

"I've tried a variety of mixes." Titian gestured to the stacked barrels. "Generally I work with turpentine, camphor, lavender oil, saltpeter, mercury sulfide, and arsenic."

"It sounds like imprecise work."

"Not always. I've developed standard techniques through the years. I imagine the Ancient Egyptians were remarkably precise. Wouldn't wish to accidentally dissolve a pharaoh." He picked up the posed lizard and Lyman could see that the body only appeared lifelike and was in fact completely stiff. "These little creatures don't mind much if a few of them fall apart."

Lyman tried to smile. He was disgusted by the process Titian described, but he also couldn't entirely quell his curiosity. "So as a taxidermist and artist, you believe you could preserve a human body as the Egyptians did?"

"I see no reason I couldn't, but my good man, what I am saying is that I could do it better. In the museum we do not display wrapped and shriveled lumps of flesh that were once animals. Begging your pardon, but what kind of person would want to see that? We display creatures as God created them, lacking only the breath of life.

"Our animals are seen as they would have been in the prime of life, as they scurried and hunted and grazed. I see no reason I couldn't preserve a body much better than the Ancient Egyptians ever dreamed. Whereas they dried and wrapped and encased, I could dry and stuff and pose."

"Has anyone ever asked you to do such a thing?"

"My goodness, you are an odd fellow, Chandler. I don't expect that anyone would ever ask me to do such a thing. If they did, I would refuse. But," Titian leaned in close, as though to prevent judgment from the taxidermic animals gathered in the room. "Between you and me, a good washing in an arsenic solution would be just the thing if one wished to create a modern mummy."

Lyman examined the youthful countenance just inches from his own face and wondered what kind of darkness lurked behind it. He recalled Peale's earlier words, *all animals are quite similar on the inside*, and he couldn't help but wonder if the same held true for all men.

12

Lyman arrived at the hotel to find Mariana in the room with curtains drawn and a single candle burning brightly on the table, her body bent low over the glass ball nestled on its wooden frame. Rather than reflecting light, the glass seemed to absorb and then transform it into a swirling convolution of glowing shadows.

She did not so much as turn in Lyman's direction when he closed the door behind himself, but as his eyes adjusted to the low light, he saw that she was dressed in a fashionable scarlet gown not well suited for a widow, nor indeed for a modest wife traveling with her husband. When he leaned in to peck her cheek she flinched, startled as if she'd not previously detected his presence.

"I didn't mean to frighten you. I thought you'd heard me enter." He gazed at the magnetic pattern churning beneath the smooth surface of the ball and could just detect the faint reflected curve of Mariana's cheek. "What is this?" he asked.

Close enough to smell the powder on her skin he could see the glint of a tear streak. Her eyes narrowed. A small crease formed in the middle of her brow, and he had the sudden urge to kiss her right then. He might have done so had he not caught movement out of the corner of his eye.

The shadows shifted within the ball, twisting and writhing with a new insistence Lyman felt more than saw. The movement was fluid, like waves licking at a shore, then building and curling, becoming grasping fingers.

"Did you see that?" The tremor in Lyman's voice shocked him, but not as much as the vision playing out before him.

"Did you?" Her voice could hardly be described as even a whisper, but Lyman detected the surprise in her question.

Maintaining his gaze on the glass proved difficult, as the shadow images refused to remain steady. They floated not just within the sphere, but through the air, like ash might fly from a fire, difficult to track and gone soon after it's glimpsed.

Several moments passed in silence before Mariana sat back in her chair. Lyman watched her bosom rise and fall above the snug bodice of her gown.

"Do you understand what you saw?" she asked with a quavering voice.

He glanced at the ball. The candle flame still danced on its surface, but the swirling shadows had vanished.

"It doesn't matter what I saw. I don't even know what to seek."

"But there was movement in the glass, enough that you, with no talent at all, couldn't help but notice it. There's urgency in the message."

He bristled at the comment on his lack of talent, but the rest of her words fell over him like heavy air before a storm. "And what is the message?"

Mariana dropped her head into her hands. "It's not that simple, Lyman. The future is fluid, and the signs of it open to interpretation."

"Then what am I, a man of no talent at all, to make of this, oh great mystic?"

"You're mocking me." She pulled open the curtain. Early evening light spilled into the room. Crossing her arms, she dropped back into her chair and waited for his reply, deep melancholy emanating from her.

A sudden wave of compassion moved him to respond more honestly than he would have liked. "I would not mock you. I did see something I can't explain. Perhaps you can."

She sighed. "There were bodies, eleven, which must represent the mummies. They were fading, in and out, small numbers of them, two and three at a time."

"That doesn't seem so ominous. I do intend to sell them eventually and have already rid myself of two. What else?"

"There were other shapes, darker ones, swallowing up the bodies. I think it means you are being pursued."

"By Martin Quinn? I assure you no one will swallow up my mummies without giving me a tidy profit in exchange. I'm not afraid of Quinn. I already foiled a burglary attempt. The mummies are mine until I choose to let them go."

She shook her head. "I don't think it was Quinn. He'd be after you, not your precious mummies. I saw an image of a man accompanied by beasts devouring what's yours. Does that make sense?"

In Lyman's mind flashed the scene in the workroom, the disemboweled lizards and glassy-eyed bats. "I suppose that could be Titian Peale. He works with a fair number of animals, but he's the man who invited me to exhibit at the Arcade. I don't believe he means me or my property any harm."

"Is he a good man?"

Lyman tended not to ask such questions, or categorize people in such terms, knowing that he himself would so often fail the test of goodness. Then, too, he thought over Titian's frank discussion of taxidermic corpses and wasn't sure how to answer Mariana's question. "He's an agreeable sort," he ventured.

Mariana pursed her lips. "Well, like I said, the future is fluid. Images in the glass can be hard to interpret. This man Peale, does he seem unusually interested in the exhibit?"

"Of course he's interested. There's nothing unusual about that. He's a museum curator, a student of natural history. And, I believe, a man of integrity."

"Does he know you stole the mummies?"

"Certainly not." But reflecting on his first encounter with Titian, Lyman recalled the scrutiny in the man's eyes as he listened to the story of Antonio Lebolo, the generous deceased uncle. He added, "I may not have any talent in seeing signs of the future, but I've always been a good judge of character."

"I'd like to meet him." Mariana stood, smoothing her dress. "I'll go with you tomorrow. I can help set up the exhibit. I'd like to see the scroll again and get a look at this Mr. Peale of yours."

Lyman hesitated at the mention of the scroll. Recalling the fascination she'd expressed in it on the night Horace died, he pictured himself brushing against her curls as he removed the papyrus from the desk where she'd fallen asleep poring over it. Perhaps, like with the shadows in the glass ball, she could glean some understanding from the strange characters only Horace could interpret. The thought sent a shiver through his spine that made him want to change the subject.

He stood and faced her. "Where did you go this morning?"

"I would hardly call it morning," she answered. "It was nearly noon when I left you in a drunken stupor. Imagine my surprise when I returned and discovered you'd pulled yourself out of bed and made your way into the day."

Mariana lifted the ball from its stand and placed it gently into a bag at her feet. "Can't a lady explore a new city when she finds herself in one?"

"A lady about Philadelphia without an escort?"

Mariana laughed as she picked up the wooded frame, collapsed it, and placed it in the bag next to the orb. "You're concern is sweet, but don't think I'm some delicate thing you have to protect. I'll go where I wish, no matter whose wife I'm pretending to be."

"Then I am grateful that you are not truly my wife."

"Are you? I wonder." She pulled her wrap from the back of the chair, settling it around her shoulders. "So, what am I to call you, dear pretend husband? Michael?"

"When we're in public, if you please."

"And what is it in private? Johnson doesn't suit you at all."

"Chandler suits me fine."

She pulled her wrap tight about herself and shook her head. "Very well, Mr. Chandler. It's time to take your wife to supper. And tomorrow, we'll go to the Arcade together."

*****

"Darling, why would I look like a widow if I'm your wife?"

The point was appropriate, but the cut of Mariana's dress was not. Genuine grief, Lyman felt, could be seen on a countenance as well as in a clothing choice. Subdued colors would have met his expectation rather than the emerald she now wore. What troubled him most was how comfortable she seemed, how carefree walking next to him, a man she hardly knew. She was nothing short of enchanting, and her presence made him feel things he didn't want to feel about the recent widow of a dear friend.

Mariana tucked her arm through the crook of his elbow as they walked through the front archways of the Philadelphia Arcade and into the marble colonnade, past the shops just beginning the day. When he opened the door to his own room, she gasped.

"Oh, my. Just look at them." She released his arm and stepped wide-eyed toward a row of tables in the middle of the room. On them lay the mummies, in as perfect state of preservation as they had been when Lyman first pried open their shipping crates. His eyes drank in the peaceful scene, the respectful poses of the long-deceased, and marveled that Peale had performed nothing short of magic.

Mariana stood alongside the smallest of them. From the bottom of its feet to the crown of its head, the mummy was no more than three feet. "This one is only a child," she said, stretching her hand over the shriveled corpse, resting her fingertips on the center of the tiny chest where a beating heart once resided. When she looked up at Lyman, her fallen countenance caused his breath to catch.

He cleared his throat. "I'd forgotten you'd not seen so many of them laid out together. It can be a shock."

"They're magnificent. Is this how the public reacts to them?"

"Some do. Others are more disgusted, but all are solemn. They ask a lot of questions."

"What sort of questions?" She leaned over the child mummy again, her face inches from the shriveled cheeks.

"They're curious about how they were found, of course, but mainly they want to know why and how they were made."

She withdrew her hand from the withered body. "People fear death. They fear what the future holds for them, even after death. Some small part of them wonders whether the Egyptians got it right, whether the secret to eternity is found in the body. They wonder if there's the glimmer of a soul still trapped within this dry flesh and whether or not they should be gawking."

Lyman had no idea whether the people who came to see his mummies thought about such things, but she had exactly identified what he himself had wondered. "I'm afraid I'm under-qualified to answer such questions."

"And that's why, Mr. Chandler, you need a partner who can handle concerns of a more spiritual nature."

"He's already had one of those, a fanatical heckler." Smiling, Titian Peale knocked lightly on the door frame and walked into the room. "I'm afraid it didn't end well for the man."

Lyman walked toward the curator, his hand outstretched. "Good morning, Titian. The mummies are perfect."

"They're not, but I have mended them as well as I can. It's more difficult to work with desiccated flesh than with more recently deceased specimen." Peale spoke to Lyman, but his eyes wandered to Mariana, and a blush rose on his cheeks. "Not even open and you have a visitor, I see."

"Ah, Titian Peale, this is my wife, Mariana Chandler. She has only recently joined me."

"It's a pleasure, Mrs. Chandler. Your husband has stumbled headlong into a fascinating field. I'm curious what you think of his mummies."

"I'm delighted by them, of course, but as I was telling him when you entered, he needs to add a more spiritual element to the exhibit."

"And what would you suggest?"

"When brought face-to-face with death, most people are more concerned with the spiritual than with the scientific. The exhibit should have an element of both."

Seeing Titian's mystified expression, Lyman interjected, "Mariana fancies herself an accomplished crystal gazer."

The words dripped with condescension, designed to draw Titian's approval as a man well above such superstitions, but the curator's response to Mariana carried no more than polite curiosity. "Is that so?" His wide smile soothed Mariana before she could express anger at her supposed husband. "I'm afraid I don't know anything about that art. It would be a delight to see you in action. Both for me, and for the patrons of the exhibit."

He gestured to the mummies. "What do you say, Chandler? Will you let your talented wife inject some spirituality into this disturbing display?"

Lyman tilted his head to indicate his defeat. "I could never say no to my beloved."

Mariana brought her gloved hands together and pushed up on her toes in obvious delight at his response. Had she been standing closer to Lyman, he felt sure she would have kissed his cheek. Instead, she turned her attention to Titian Peale. "There is parchment as well, did he show you?"

"Yes, and in fact, there is more than the single scroll. After the burglary attempt, the wrapping fell away enough to expose another on a second mummy, along with an additional smaller piece of papyrus."

Titian stepped to the side and Lyman's gaze fell on the shelf behind him where he saw three rolls of aged papyrus. Mariana rushed forward, reaching out to touch them.

"Please be careful, madam. They are delicate, and, I'm sorry to say, already heavily damaged."

Mariana stopped short of touching the scrolls, but her fingers continued to hover just above them as she asked, "Can you read them?"

The hope in her voice was palpable to Lyman, as if bringing to life whatever ancient words might be held within the scrolls would somehow resurrect Horace. It was only grief, overwhelming him in the moment, but when Titian shook his head, Lyman's breath caught in his throat.

"I can't make them out," Titian admitted. "Egyptian hieroglyphs are outside my scope of knowledge, but I'm sure there are scholars who can. I could make inquiries if you'd like."

"Thank you, Mr. Peale. I would be most grateful if you could." Mariana stepped closer to Titian, placing her hand on his arm.

Peale tensed. Had he not experienced a stab of jealousy, Lyman might have felt sorry for the man.

A consummate gentleman, Peale extricated himself from Mariana's grasp, but replied, "I cannot deny assistance to a lovely and curious lady."

"In that case, Mr. Peale, since my husband will be occupied today by preparations for the exhibit, I would very much like to see your museum. Would you show it to me?"

"Of course." He was smiling again even as Mariana slipped her arm through his. She glanced over her shoulder and smirked at

Lyman before allowing herself to be led out the door, leaving him alone once again with his corpses.

13

At the Arcade, Lyman observed, impressed, as Mariana held her head high, and became the wife of Mr. Chandler, the curious new tenant brought in by the curator of the museum. She toured the colonnade admiring the wares and befriending the shopkeepers who might send business his way. In Mr. Kerr's tea shop, she discussed the reading of tea leaves, an art she had never attempted, but that sparked interest in her powers with the orb.

When the mummy exhibit opened two days later to a large crowd whispering rumors of a curse, Lyman procured for her a small table set to the side of the exhibited mummies all looking their best, repaired with a generous supply of well-camouflaged wire and the skillful touch of the world's foremost expert on taxidermy. In her corner, Mariana gazed into her orb and drew out for the crowds well-imagined details of the lives of the ancient kings and holy men displayed beside her.

With the precision of an expert at deception, she wove together intricate plots of scandal, murder, and betrayal, leading in one instance to the mummification of a disgraced pharaoh while he still lived, screaming his curses as he slipped into the beyond, though not once did she mention the name Horos.

Her legends were chilling, if somewhat unbelievable, but the public was drawn to them all the same.

The changed venue, too, breathed new life into the exhibit, and the morbidly curious clamored to see the mummies, usually staying to also look in at the museum with its prehistoric bones, model trains, and portraits. Children and their parents marveled at both Lyman's withered human remains and Titian's magically life-like animal carcasses.

No patrons connected the two collections, or if they did, never found the courage to remark upon it. But they did ask plenty of questions. Lyman grew increasingly adept at answering, armed as he was with the authority lent him by his association with the Peale family and by the writings of Giovanni Belzoni, a man whose real adventures fed the tales of the explorations of Lyman's alleged uncle. He offered his visitors science and history, while Mariana gave them magic. In the presence of three-thousand-year-old mummies, it seemed they wanted both.

For nearly a month the people came, the crowd rarely thinning throughout long days. In the evenings, when the exhibit closed, Lyman dropped his head to one shoulder, stretching the muscles in his neck. Talking for hours to the public, regaling them with heroic tales of archaeological discovery, took a toll. He was adept at slipping into another man's skin, enjoyed it when he brought out a smile of trust he'd never deserved from an unsuspecting crowd, but after more than three weeks, Lyman's stamina had begun to wane.

Mariana had returned to the hotel and Lyman was finishing up for the night, straightening the exhibit pieces and dousing the lights, when an unfamiliar voice addressed him from just beyond his door.

"Mr. Chandler, might I have a word?" The owner of the nasal voice wore a dark suit and pair of spectacles. Short in stature, he was in every way a respectable looking man who held a card out to Lyman. The card identified him as Francesco Bertola, Professor of Veterinary Medicine.

"Certainly, Mr. Bertola. What can I do for you?" Lyman stepped into the hallway, closing the door behind him. He slipped the card into his pocket and withdrew a key, but before he could insert it in the lock, Bertola placed a hand on his arm to still it.

"I would very much like to examine your mummies."

Lyman paused a moment to wonder what particular interest a veterinarian might have with mummies, but recalling the unsettling conversation in Titian's workroom, decided he wouldn't ask. He placed the key in the lock and turned it, letting Bertola's hand slide from his arm. "I'm afraid the exhibit is closed for the night, but if you'd like to return in the morning, I'll be happy to show them to you and answer any questions you may have."

The man opened and closed his mouth, as if he'd thought of arguing, but then decided against it. Lyman began the long walk down the colonnade toward the exit, his footsteps echoing in the marble-lined walkway. Bertola followed.

"Thank you, Mr. Chandler, but I have a few questions right now, if you don't mind. It is Mr. Chandler, isn't it?"

Lyman stopped, exasperated. Exhausted from a long day with the public, he longed for a drink and supper and bed. "Yes, that's correct."

"How many mummies do you have, sir?"

"Nine." Lyman hoped the brevity of his answer might discourage further inquiry. It didn't.

"But were there only nine originally, or have you lost some along the way?"

Lyman began walking again, anxious to slip away. The question unnerved him, but he answered. "There were eleven. Two have gone to the medical college."

"I see." Bertola trailed him. Lyman increased his pace, causing the shorter man to walk briskly in order to keep up. "And they were discovered by your uncle, Antonio Lebolo?"

"Yes." Lyman tossed the answer over his shoulder.

"Please, sir, I'm a friend of the heirs to Mr. Lebolo's estate, and I was unaware of a nephew Chandler who might lay claim to any of it."

Lyman drew up short and spun on his heel to face Bertola, who nearly ran into him. "Are you accusing me of something?" He loomed over the wiry man, his heart thumping in his chest. He'd begun to sweat despite the pleasantness of the evening.

Bertola reacted to none of his discomfort, however, and seemed only to calculate the size difference between them. He took a step back and stammered. "I-I only meant, sir, that I'm unfamiliar with the Chandler branch of the family. Did you know your uncle well?"

"My relationship with my uncle is none of your business, Mr. Bertola, family friend or not."

"No, I suppose it's not."

Lyman turned again and exited the Arcade into the night which was peaceful despite the presence of a good amount of traffic. Bertola, still in pursuit, broke the relative quiet.

"Except that I've been legally authorized to investigate the whereabouts of certain pieces of the Lebolo estate and to arrange the sale—"

Lyman pushed him back into the shadow of the archway and pinned him to the building with an arm pressed across his throat. Bertola's eyes widened with fear behind delicate spectacles. Releasing him with a shove, Lyman caused the man to lose his balance and crumble to his knees, gasping.

"You don't want to be here, do you?" Lyman heard the pity in his own voice, the honeyed words that made false promises of safety to this weasel of a representative, a veterinarian sent to do the work of the police.

Bertola caught his breath and slowly stood, shaking his head as he crept down the steps toward the street where any further violence would be witnessed. "Look," he said, "I don't know who you are, but I do know you are no relation to Antonio Lebolo. And you're right. I don't want to be here. I'd rather let you go your way, but I feel a responsibility to the family, to my friends."

"Friendship is a burden." Lyman's sincere response elicited surprise from Bertola, whose magnified eyes appeared to glow in the yellow light from the streetlamps.

Emboldened, the man continued, "My instructions are to sell them and send the money to the family, but maybe we can come to an agreement."

Lyman considered his options. If he refused to deal, Bertola would surely go to the police. To keep him quiet, Lyman would have to kill the man, a prospect both messy and thoroughly unappealing. It meant something, however, that Bertola had not simply begun with the law. Either he wasn't confident that Chandler was an imposter, or he really did want to dispense with his unfortunate responsibility quickly.

"Very well. I will not begrudge my uncle's family a portion of my inheritance."

Bertola's shoulders dropped and he visibly relaxed. Lyman pressed on in his role as the aggrieved nephew. "Even though Uncle Antonio bequeathed the mummies to me alone."

Bertola offered the slightest of bows, not daring to take his eyes off Lyman.

"Come to the exhibit tomorrow afternoon." Lyman sighed. "I will be fair."

"I've no doubt you are a gentleman of your word." Bertola reached for a handshake that Lyman didn't engage. Instead, he turned and walked down the street toward the hotel. He had to let Mariana know it was time to leave Philadelphia.

*****

He rushed up the stairs two at a time. Inside the door to his room, Mariana waited for him, evening gloves in hand and dressed in a modest blue gown that, for once, didn't strike him as lurid. She'd swept her curls into a bun on the back of her head, leaving wispy tendrils to kiss her cheeks, rosy with anticipation.

"You took long enough. Are you ready to go to supper or do you intend to wash off the filth of the day?" Her lower lip jutted slightly, indicating that perhaps he needed to take the time.

Lyman looked down to scrutinize his appearance. His hands passed inspection, soft and clean as always, but his shirt tail peeked from beneath his coat, and the boots he'd worn through the day were in great need of blacking. Under normal circumstances his disheveled appearance would have demanded his attention, but this was not the time.

"Mariana, I have to leave as soon as possible." He withdrew Bertola's card from his pocket and handed it to her.

She glanced at it before dropping it onto the desk behind her with a sigh of resignation. "This is the man I saw in my vision. A veterinarian from Philadelphia that wants to swallow up our mummies?"

Her response gave him a moment's pause. In truth, he'd dismissed her vision, but he couldn't deny that she'd seen signs of Bertola, even if she'd interpreted them to mean that Titian was a danger to them. In the future, he would have to give her words more credence.

"He could be dangerous." Lyman described to Mariana his encounter with the man who'd claimed the authority to seize the mummies. She listened without interruption before offering an unexpected response.

"If he's the kind of man you think he is, then you should pay him off."

85

So surprised was he that Lyman couldn't formulate a response before she continued.

"He's been put in a bad position by the family and he doesn't know what he's doing. You said yourself he didn't even care whether or not you were a Lebolo."

"But he could still decide to investigate. Even if I could maintain my alias, Michael Chandler is no nephew to Lebolo. It won't take a great deal of inspection to reveal that."

Mariana placed a gloved hand on his arm. "Then don't give him a reason to inspect. Give him some money, like you told him you would. He will have done right by the family, and we can go on our way."

Her plan made a kind of awful sense. The notion of so easily giving up hard-earned money fought against every part of Lyman's criminal instincts, but he still had nine mummies. A man could make a good living if he owned nine mummies, especially if he were free of competing claims to them.

"I'd still have to leave Philadelphia."

Mariana shrugged. "Of course we have to leave. And once we're gone, the veterinarian will go back to his business and stop interfering in ours."

Lyman noted her deft inclusion of herself in his plans. With skillful lies, she had insinuated herself into his life in Philadelphia, but if he were to leave this city, he could separate himself from her. Perhaps it would be wise to do so.

"You are coming with me, then?" he asked.

"Mr. Chandler, you can hardly expect to travel without your wife. As you are a gentleman of your word, you can meet with Mr. Veterinarian tomorrow and there's no reason we can't enjoy supper tonight." Mariana placed her folded gloves on the desktop. "If you clean yourself up. Those boots are a disgrace."

14

Francesco Bertola looked as surprised to receive the $1700 from Lyman as Titian Peale appeared at the announcement that Lyman and his mummies would be moving on from the Philadelphia Museum.

"I wish you good fortune, my friend. I've penned a letter of introduction." Peale handed him a sealed envelope that Lyman tucked into his pocket. "My name can be useful as a reference. Please don't hesitate to contact me if I can be of further assistance."

"Thank you," Lyman responded. "Thank you for everything."

The two men voiced their stoic farewells and that evening Lyman saw his nine mummies, tightly packed and boxed, loaded onto a steamship on the Delaware River.

"We're lucky to be away." Mariana snaked her arm through his. In the fading dusk, her olive skin made her appear more shadow than human. That is what she had come to represent to Lyman—a shadow that threatened to overtake him.

"You are right, Mrs. Laurent." He patted her hand as if she were the pitiful widow he wished she really were.

She turned her head to look at him. "You shouldn't call me that in public, Lyman."

"And you should call me Michael."

"I don't like using a name that's not yours."

"I paid good money for that name. It most certainly belongs to me." He untangled himself from her. "We needn't keep up your marriage charade once we leave the city."

Her bottom lip protruded in a small pout and for a moment, he believed his words had hurt her. He experienced only a twinge of regret, replaced quickly by resentment at her attempted manipulation.

She responded, "We are less noticeable traveling as husband and wife than as an unmarried couple."

"Mummies are noticeable. If Martin Quinn wishes to pursue me, I'll not be hard to find regardless of whether or not I am traveling with a pretend wife. Once we leave here, you should go your own way. We are nothing to each other."

He meant the words, but when she backed away from him with a sharp intake of breath, he regretted his callous tone. "Mariana—"

"No. Don't." Her voice trembled, but she didn't cry. "Only I thought you was a different sort of man. Horace loved you like a son. I assumed you felt the same way about him, but of course not. Criminals are all the same. It's a lesson I should have learned a long time ago. I know I was wrong to think you might help protect me. Or that I might have something you need, too."

Lyman surged hot with anger at her insinuation that he hadn't cared about Horace, or that because he had, he should feel an obligation to her. "You have nothing I need, Mrs. Laurent."

"Don't I?" she returned. "Your mummies are no more than dust without me and my orb to give them life."

Lyman didn't respond, but settled himself far from her on the steamship so he might be alone with his thoughts. Her point was a good one, but he'd have to think about it. Where women were concerned, Lyman hadn't always demonstrated good judgment, and a woman like Mariana Laurent, cunning and lovely, could as easily be a great asset as a terrible liability.

*****

Late that night, the ship docked in New Castle on the Delaware. Weary travelers wandered into the town to find rooms for the night. Still barely speaking, Mariana and Lyman found their way to a small house with a sign identifying it as an inn.

"Welcome," chimed a man behind a small desk. "Caught a late steamer from Philly, eh? Name's Miller. You and the wife need a room for the rest of the night?"

Lyman extended a hand to Miller, who shook it firmly. "We would be much obliged if you have two rooms, please."

Miller nodded. "I see. She ain't your wife. I have rooms for both of you. And," He put his hand over one side of his mouth, leaning close to Lyman with his next words. "I can send you some companionship for your room, if you'd like."

Mariana, who clearly heard Mr. Miller, gave a haughty "Hmph."

"A little warm companionship could do a man some good," Lyman answered, making no attempt to hide his words from Mariana or anyone else who might wish to hear them. "Is there a stagecoach stop nearby?"

"Yes, sir," Mr. Miller answered, a happy conspirator now. "The coach stops right here. You can catch it in the morning if you're ready to leave so soon. You enjoy a little of our hospitality and you might not be in such a hurry to leave."

Lyman didn't look at Mariana as he accepted the key to his room.

*****

They boarded the stagecoach early the next morning, along with five other travelers toward French Town, Maryland. Lyman was grateful for the full coach. Mariana didn't acknowledge him and said little, but the other passengers provided plenty of distraction. Included in their party were one couple with a nearly grown son, headed to Baltimore, and drummers working across the Eastern states to hawk their wares.

From them Lyman gleaned stories of the many small towns popping up along the Pennsylvania Canal System—not as established as the Erie Canal of further north, but still with plenty of debauchery to offer. Lyman determined this was the route his mummies would take. Curiosities would play well, he felt sure, among the superstitious, heavy drinking canawlers, and those who tended their mules, served their drinks, and provided their whores.

These would not be the same caliber of learned patron he'd encountered in Philadelphia, but their money would be just as good. After paying off Bertola, Lyman was anxious to find a lucrative engagement, and he grudgingly came to the conclusion that traveling with a pretty young seer might be advantageous after all.

It wasn't until they pulled into French Town late in the day that Lyman broached the subject with Mariana. They saw the mummies safely unloaded and checked into an inn called The Buck, run by a man named Powers.

Lyman informed Mr. Powers he and his wife would require only one room for the night and nothing extra as they would be leaving on the first boat they could catch down the Chesapeake to Baltimore.

The man grunted and handed Lyman a key. Out of the corner of his eye, he caught the sight of Mariana's dimple on her flushed cheek.

Only when they were seated in the dining room to a dinner of roasted dove did she speak to him. "So it's to be Baltimore then? For both of us?"

"I think we should give it a try. It's a manufacturing town—maybe not as clean and suspicious as Philadelphia, but just as hungry for educational diversions, I'd wager, and perhaps a bit of the macabre. I think we can blend in well there for a time."

"And what then?"

"Have you ever traveled on the canals?"

She shook her head and poked a forkful of meat into her mouth.

"It's a colorful way to go. A rough crowd, but I'm tempted to try it. There are a number of little canal towns where a display of mummies would be viewed with a strange interest."

"And when we run out of little towns?"

"I was thinking I might try to sell the remainder of the mummies as a group. Showing them together has been lucrative, and I wouldn't object to someone else trying their hand at the business, if they will offer me a high enough price. Then we can both have a tidy sum to start over. Separately."

Mariana cleared her throat, as though the words she wished to say had gotten caught. "You think you can find an interested party traveling on the canal?"

"No," Lyman said, reaching for his glass of ale. "But there's someone out there who will welcome the opportunity to display a group of mummies. I'll find them, if not on the canal, then at the other end of it."

"If we make it to the other end. We haven't had the greatest luck so far. I wonder how our dead friends will like being transported like cargo across Pennsylvania."

"I'd ask them, but I'd be too afraid they'd answer." Lyman smiled at his jest. Mariana did not. She picked at her food and sighed.

"Please don't joke about them. I don't think they like it," she said.

"Now who sounds superstitious? I thought Horace was the one afraid of the mummies."

"Maybe he was the smart one."

"We know that of all of us he was the smart one, but I refuse to be afraid of the dead."

"You don't think they communicate with us?"

"You might have had me convinced a time or two at the Arcade with your talk of murderous pharaohs, but I've never received a message from a dead person. Have you?"

"I don't know, maybe. Don't you ever get the impression that you're not alone, even when you know you are?"

"My dear, I do not welcome uninvited guests."

Her eyes locked on his, and in them he could almost see fire swirling like the ominous fog in her orb. She waited a beat, the silence between them growing ominously. "Is that what you say I am?"

Lyman set down his fork. "You did show up uninvited, claiming to be my wife."

"I wanted to warn you about Quinn. Horace thought a lot of you." She spoke with a sincerity he felt in the pit of his stomach. The corners of her eyes were moist.

"I cared for the old man, too. And it warms my heart to finally see distress in your countenance when you speak of him."

"Listen here, Mr. Johnson, or Chandler, or whoever you really are, I'm not a woman who is going to sit around in a mourning dress and cry all the time. But I am now a woman all alone, without friends, without a husband to protect me. That doesn't give me many options."

He reached across the table and placed a hand gently on top of hers. "I know. You're a strong and brave woman. Horace would have settled for nothing less. Despite my misgivings in Philadelphia, I'm glad you're with me."

"Are you?" she asked, one eyebrow raised.

He admired her skill. Since they'd left Philadelphia, she'd managed to guilt him into an invitation and now a compliment.

"Yes, I am." He meant what he said. No matter how intrusive she'd made herself, Mariana had been the beloved wife of the man Lyman admired most. Perhaps he did owe it to Horace to look after her and to protect her, at least for a time.

Mariana had won this small battle.

"You know," he said, hoping to demonstrate the strength of his commitment by offering something of himself, "I'm a grieving widower myself."

"You have a funny way of grieving." She sniffed. "And if that's so you have no right to judge my behavior."

"Yes, well, the circumstances are different. You didn't kill your husband."

He let the words sink in. Neither said more on that subject or any other as they finished their supper.

*****

"Look at that." Mariana stood beside Lyman on the city dock, the two having just disembarked from the large steamship *Chesapeake*.

"You're impressed with the fair city of Baltimore?" he asked, surveying the gently sloping cityscape before them.

"It's like we're on display."

"Yes, in a great amphitheater. And the city is the audience." Lyman laughed and Mariana turned angry eyes to him. He held up his hands. "I didn't realize you were so poetic."

"There's a lot you don't know about me, Mr. Chandler." She turned her back to him and the waiting carriage.

"I've no doubt that's true, Mrs. . . . . Chandler."

She smiled and accepted the hand he offered. He supported her into the vehicle and followed, settling onto the seat beside her.

The driver slapped the reins and they lurched forward, following a city street uphill. "I gather you've never visited Baltimore before?" Lyman asked.

She shook her head, sending the dark curls beneath her hat bouncing across the nape of her neck. "I've not been a lot of places."

Her words should not have shocked him. Even dressed up as a pampered wife, Mariana did not carry herself as a woman of advantage. Still, Horace had been a man of the world, bearing the marks of a learned gentleman well beyond the years he lived as one.

"May I ask how you came to be married to Horace?" The question was an indelicate one he knew, but then, Mariana just now didn't appear to be a delicate woman.

Her posture stiffened, and it was as if a curtain that had been previously thrown opened had now been quickly drawn shut again. "Because I'm not good enough for him, is that what you think?"

"I don't know you well enough to make such an assessment, but you do appear to come from very different backgrounds."

"That's a careful way to say it." She scooted closer to him on the bench. Part of her skirt bunched onto Lyman's pant leg. Her hand slid from her own lap onto his, her long gloved fingers finding the inside curve of his thigh. "Is it such a surprise that a lonely man would desire the company of a young wife?"

Lyman took firm hold of her hand and guided it away from himself. "I'm sure you made a beautiful couple. Pardon my curiosity." He scooted toward the carriage window and gazed out at the city scenery. Baltimore was more to his liking than Philadelphia had been, built with less precision and more determination. The city's population was growing along with its dedication to its emerging railroads, fed by the desire to outcompete New York's canal boom.

The city had become a center of travel early in the history of the United States, playing host to political conventions and catering to that clientele by raising fine hotels and numerous remembrances of its trials and triumphs. Former president John Quincy Adams called it "The Monumental City," a moniker Baltimore had embraced with pride.

The carriage stopped in front of the Fountain Inn—smaller and quieter than the more extravagant Barnum's or Eutaw House Hotels, but still a respectable establishment. Lyman eyed the yellow brick façade dotted with windows at regular intervals, each featuring a stone lintel and decorative keystone. Only two blocks from the hotel stood the red brick building that housed the Baltimore Museum.

Inside the inn, they found a parlor furnished with mahogany and overlooking an interior courtyard of flowers in full summer bloom. Mariana grabbed his hand and squeezed. Lyman introduced himself to the proprietor as Chandler, and Mariana as his wife.

"Sir," Lyman said to the man who checked them in, "can you tell me much of the museum?"

"That depends on what you'd like to know."

"Do you know the curator?"

The proprietor rubbed a hand over his chin. "Only that he's a Mr. J. E. Walker. That's what I see in the papers. Haven't met the man myself."

"And what can you tell me of the museum?"

"Not a lot, I'm afraid. It burned down six months ago."

15

The Municipal Museum of the City of Baltimore bore its blackened scars with dignity. It sat at the northwest corner of North Calvert and East Baltimore Streets, one block south of Battle Monument Square and the courthouse. Lyman paid the carriage driver to wait and entered the building, hurrying to the second floor entrance of the museum. No attendant impeded him, and Lyman walked through the wide galleries that smelled of fresh paint. Framed cases, with glass gleaming, lined the walls, but contained scarcely any exhibits. A few paintings decorated the walls, spread out to give the illusion of a larger collection. Lyman's footfalls echoed through the sparsely furnished room, and when he reached the last, he distinguished voices drifting through an open office door.

"I don't know if I can be of much help to you, Colonel. We're only now recovering from a fire ourselves. As you can see our exhibits are still underwhelming in number."

Lyman took a few more tentative steps and knocked. A man with wild black hair and a long mustache leaned out of the doorway to eye him.

"May I help you, sir?"

"I apologize for the interruption, but I am looking for Mr. J. E. Walker."

"You've found him," the man with the mustache replied and waved Lyman into the room before turning to a second man sitting behind a desk. "Perhaps you'll find him more helpful than I have."

The man behind the desk rose, brushing imaginary wrinkles from his brown suit. Wisps of determined hair clung to his mostly bald scalp, and he had the deeply creased forehead of one who spends a great deal of time in thought. "I'm Walker."

Lyman took Titian's letter from his coat pocket. "It's a pleasure to meet you. My name is Michael Chandler." He handed him the envelope. "Please accept this introduction from Titian Peale of Philadelphia. He's been a good friend and suggested you might wish to exhibit an Egyptian collection that was recently on display at Peale's Museum in Philadelphia."

Walker sat back down in his stiff wooden chair and read over the letter with a curious expression. Beside him, lining the walls of the small office, numerous shelves stood bare but for a few books, as if Walker had not yet taken the time to fully inhabit the space. Lyman counted the seconds as he awaited the curator's response, but it was the other man who spoke, his voice tinged in barely contained excitement.

"Sir, you are an acquaintance of the Peales of Philadelphia? Why, I am headed to meet with them myself."

Walker set the letter on his desk and gestured toward his colleague. "Mr. Chandler, may I present Colonel David McKinstry of Detroit. He's planning to open a museum in that city and is here seeking consultation."

"And I'm collecting as well. It's an honor to meet any acquaintance of the first family of the museum industry." Lyman found McKinstry's demeanor as flamboyant as his oversized mustache, which struggled to obscure the strong jaw of a man one would expect to be in charge. His peacock blue tailcoat and matching cravat bespoke of an entertainer. Lyman liked the man immediately.

He smiled and asked, "What are you looking to collect, Colonel?"

"Any oddities the public may find amusing."

Mr. Walker rounded his desk and sat on its edge, causing the buttons of his coat to strain despite his slight figure. "Mr. Chandler is in the mummy business."

"Is that so?" the colonel looked Lyman up and down, his eyes wide with interest.

"Yes, my uncle was an Egyptologist and willed a portion of his collection to me. I was hoping to display them here for a time, assuming the good people of Baltimore would be pleased to see them."

"I think there can be no question of that," Walker offered. "You may have heard we experienced a fire earlier this year and are still working to recover much of the former glory of the collection from the days when Rembrandt Peale ran the museum. I would be delighted to see your exhibit. I've little doubt we can find space for it amidst our humble displays."

McKinstry licked his lips. "How many mummies did you say you have?"

"The collection includes nine mummies, as well as several scrolls of ancient text," Lyman replied.

"Would you be interested in parting with any? People do love mummies."

Lyman thought of Horace and the dead preacher, the steamship captain from New York and the police officer in Philadelphia who shuddered at the sight of the ancient bodies. He wondered if the colonel's words were true. People found mummies intriguing, but to go so far as to say they loved them seemed an overstatement.

He glanced at Walker, whose expression might have been stone, and then back to the giddy McKinstry. "I think I could be convinced to part with some of the collection, for the right price."

The colonel leaned back on his heels and rubbed his chin. "I'll tell you what. Let me have a look at the creatures and if I like what I see, I'll give you $1,200 for three of them. That ought to leave enough for old Walker here."

Mr. Walker nodded his bald head in agreement.

"Follow me, gentlemen," replied Lyman. "We'll take a look."

The two men followed him to the waiting carriage and helped Lyman unload the crates into the museum.

"Just look at them," gasped McKinstry, his smile almost penetrating his mustache. The men had unboxed the mummies and spread the collection on the floor of one of the museum's emptier galleries Walker had been using as a workspace.

Despite the hurried travel from Philadelphia, the bodies of the dead had held together well, and Lyman admired, once again, the workmanship of Titian Peale.

Walker paid them relatively little attention, instead turning to the papyri which he had placed gently on one end of a long table holding a small collection of colorful geodes. He leaned over them and, wearing a pair of soft leather gloves, slowly flattened each one, poring over the ancient sketches as one would examine a precious stone.

"Are you able to read them?" asked Lyman, hope fluttering in his heart that Horace's knowledge had not died with him.

Walker didn't look up, but only shook his head. "I'm afraid I can't, but wouldn't it be wonderful to know what they said?"

Lyman couldn't help but be swept up by the enthusiasm in Walker's words. "I believe these are funerary texts, specific to the man who died, describing the way his soul might live on in eternity."

"You think it's the Bible, Mr. Chandler?" the colonel laughed. "In Egyptian?"

"It stands to reason." Walker straightened, one gloved hand still resting on a curling papyrus. "I don't believe Mr. Chandler's point is that this is a representation of the Christian Bible, but that this is a religious text depicting the Ancient Egyptian understanding of eternal life seems plausible."

"You both sound like that prophet Joe Smith with his Golden Bible." McKinstry slapped his knee to accentuate his grand joke, though the punchline was lost on Lyman, and, it seemed, on Walker as well.

"Oh, come on. You've heard of him. He's the one's sent missionaries all over the blame place with his *Book of Mormon* he claims was given to him by an angel and then interpreted from Egyptian. There's the man who'll tell you what your scrolls say."

Walker shook his head and removed the gloves. "Colonel, you surely don't believe in heretical teachings, do you?"

"I'm surprised that a man of science such as yourself would worry about heresy, but no, since you asked, I don't believe him. I think he invented the whole thing as a money-making scheme. What about you, Chandler?" He clapped Lyman on the back.

"I couldn't say, Colonel. I'm not a religious man myself."

"Nor am I." McKinstry gestured toward the mummies. "But these men must have been. How old would you say they are?"

"At least three thousand years, I should think," Walker answered before Lyman had the chance.

"That was the assessment of my uncle as well," he added, which seemed to satisfy both men.

"I'll take these three." Colonel McKinstry pointed with a crooked thumb to three mummies of varied sizes and closed mouths. "Is that acceptable to you, Mr. Walker?"

"If Mr. Chandler is pleased with that arrangement, then I am as well. The museum would be delighted to engage the remainder of the collection for a special exhibit."

Lyman shook hands with both men and planned to take Mariana out for a special supper to celebrate their good fortune.

16

Walker wasted no time in assembling the Egyptian display in a side room off the main central space of the museum. The six mummies he'd lined against one wall. In front of them, the papyrus scrolls lay unrolled on a table, flattened beneath a large sheet of glass.

"Good morning, Mr. Chandler."

Lyman returned the greeting to the bedraggled curator. "You've been hard at work, sir."

"I have indeed," Walker replied. "I will place an advertisement in both the *Gazette* and the *Daily Advertiser* beginning tomorrow." Walker reached into the pocket of his coat which was draped across the end of a display table and handed Lyman a piece of paper filled with scrawled notes, the words difficult to decipher among the numerous editorial scratches.

Lyman squinted at the block of handwritten purple prose:

> *The citizens are respectfully informed that the manager has received from the vicinity of Thebes, that celebrated city of Ancient Egypt, six strangers, illustrious from their antiquity, count, probably, an existence of at least one thousand years anterior to the advent of our blessed Savior, and contemporaries; if so, of the first sovereigns of Israel, viz: Saul and David. They are by no means insignificant aspirants to public patronage. In the present day, in a country unknown, and where transatlantic ancestors, at that period wrapt in the gloom of idolatry and paganism, what singular and interesting points of history could they not unfold, connected with those early periods of the world, where the vital spark, so long at rest, permitted to resuscitate their slumbering remains. But surely none could view these truly singular remnants of Auld*

Lang Syne, without being carried retrospectively to those far distant periods of antiquity.

Lyman looked up to find Walker staring at him expectantly.

"It's magnificent." Thinking back to his first conversation with Titian Peale about using scriptural references to keep the zealots at bay, he added, "Mr. Peale himself could not have written better."

Walker smiled and reached for the paper Lyman extended. "Yes, I expect it will bring the crowds," he replied. "Your collection will open as a special exhibit. Along with the mummies and the scrolls, we'll post your certificate of authenticity from the Philadelphia experts and perhaps a copy of the H. Smith poem, 'Address to the Mummy at Belzoni's Exhibition.' We will resurrect this museum yet, Mr. Chandler."

"It sounds like you have it well in hand, sir."

Mr. Walker stepped back from the table and stood in the middle of the room, surveying his work. "Oh, yes, Mr. Chandler. We'll set the entry fee at the customary twenty-five cents and the people of Baltimore will emerge."

And they did. The same day the advertisements began to run, the public lined up to return to its newly remodeled and reopened museum at last to see what the fire had left them and to wonder over the mummies from the era of King David.

Again Lyman told the patrons stories of the wondrous discovery, growing ever more impressive in his mind. He answered all questions, whether he understood them or not, borrowing pieces of Mariana's well-imagined tales and weaving together science and lore so seamlessly he'd begun to believe himself.

He took note of every person who entered, wary of those who appeared overly religious, delighting in those with wide eyes and fearful expressions. In Baltimore, he wielded more authority than he had at the Philadelphia Arcade. There he'd been the sideshow to Titian Peale's main event. Here he and his mummies were the stars, the saviors of the museum.

Because of this status, however, Mariana's addition to the spectacle was unwelcome. Mr. Walker had felt that to invite the occult into the museum would render it more spectacle than enlightenment. Her ego bruised, she'd remained away, spending her time in a manner unknown to Lyman.

*****

Gray clouds had rolled across the Baltimore sky bringing with them a dense anticipation of relief from the stifling summer heat. Lyman stepped out of the museum as evening began to dim the city. Loosening his coat, he welcomed the swirling air currents that cooled his damp skin and revealed the pale underbellies of leaves dancing on the branches above the sidewalk.

A crack of thunder jolted his senses, followed by the nose-stinging odor of the lightning-streaked atmosphere. Fat raindrops assaulted his shoulders just as he reached the hotel.

He pushed into the room, announcing himself by calling out Mariana's name, but only silence within the darkened space greeted him.

While the storm thrashed against the world outside, the hotel room was thoroughly shut against it, curtains drawn, air heavy with a sweet, sickening scent.

Lyman turned up the lights, his eyes seeking and, at last, finding her, a heap of skirt in the corner of the room.

"Mariana?" He rushed to her, dropping by her side and gathering her into his arms. "Are you ill?"

The soft light of the gas sconces reflected off the streaming tears on her cheeks. He drew her head against his chest, allowing a silky curl to slip through his fingers. Heat radiated from her and seeped into him.

"Darling," he whispered, "what's happened?"

She relaxed against him and when she spoke, her voice was barely audible above the rain battering the window. "I'm so scared," she said, burying her face in his shirt.

"It's only a storm, my dear. It will blow away as quickly as it appeared."

Mariana pulled away from him, sniffling. She rose from the floor and perched on the edge of the bed, attempting to smooth the wrinkled folds of her skirt. "It's not the storm." Her words came more clearly, edged again in the icy tone with which he was more familiar. "You're right. I'm ill and in poor spirits. I'll be better by morning."

Lyman sighed and rubbed his eyes. "If you are to travel with me, Mariana, you must be honest with me."

"How can I be honest with a man who won't even tell me his real name, Mr. Johnson?"

He drew a sharp breath and stood, hovering above her where she sat, calm and cunning. Her flushed cheeks bore the evidence of her tears, but her dark eyes were dry and appraising. He wanted more than anything to know what wicked thoughts lay behind them.

"I will tell you my name. But first you must tell me what has upset you."

She dropped her gaze. Her explanation came out in choked words. "I saw Martin Quinn today."

Alarmed, Lyman lowered himself onto the bed beside her. "Here? In Baltimore?"

Mariana dabbed at her nose with the back of her hand. "Yes. That part was very clear. I saw it in the orb." She pointed to the glass ball atop a wooden stand on the desk.

Lyman sighed in relief as thunder rumbled long and insistent across the sky. "You really believe he's still coming for me? For us?"

"I know he is, Lyman." Her agitation grew with each word, as did her volume.

Lyman pushed a finger against her lips to quiet her and again was struck by the feverish heat emanating from her. "There's no reason to suspect he's found us here, no matter what you believe you've seen. Your mind is overwrought. When you're better rested, you can face this fear more logically."

"Don't you see? It doesn't matter whether he's here right now. He's coming. You and I are a threat to him." She had lowered her voice, but still she spoke with a conviction Lyman found troubling. "A man is not appointed as a customs agent without placing himself among people with power. You can be sure he flattered, bribed, and blackmailed his way into his position. He will have called in every favor to secure his own release from jail, to cast suspicion somewhere else if he can."

"Yes, but then why would he come after us himself? He is the better known man. You and I might look as guilty as he does. Why is it not the authorities you see in your orb?"

"Because we are innocent, and he has a reputation as a man who can accomplish unsavory tasks without getting dirty. He won't take the chance that his claims of innocence might not stand scrutiny. He'll kill us and be done with it." Her slender shoulders slumped as she spoke, drawing Lyman's eye to the twin hollows above her collar bone.

"And you saw all this, gazing into your glass ball?" Lyman sighed. He couldn't reason with the paranoia now overtaking her, as wild as the wind howling at the window. He thought, as he stood, he should perhaps send for a doctor. "Just when should we expect the arrival of Mr. Quinn, then?"

"I don't know." She squeezed the words between halting breaths. "But he's coming. He murdered Horace. And now he's going to kill me."

"Mariana, I saw the way Mr. Quinn looked at you. I don't think he has it in mind to harm you."

She rose from the bed and fell into him, her head settling against his chest with a thud. "You don't know him like I do. He's the kind of man who would slay a grieving woman. He's the kind of man who'd enjoy it."

Lyman wrapped his arms around her trembling form. "Martin Quinn will not hurt you as long as I am here."

"I want to believe that." She raised her eyes to him and, in them, he saw a vulnerability he would not previously have thought possible. "I want to believe in you, Mr. Johnson."

The hope shining behind her lovely gaze was almost more than he could bear, and he wondered whether he could deserve her trust. He owed Horace nothing. Their relationship had always been one of mutual benefit and, as far as Lyman could see, Horace held no more claim upon him. But then he thought of their final job together—of Horace's revulsion at the mummies, of his lifeless body, and of abandoning Mariana to discover the death he might have prevented. The image of Martin Quinn flashed into Lyman's mind, slick, ambitious, and ruthless. Lyman pulled Mariana close, losing his train of thought in her scent. He wanted to believe his words as much as she did.

The storm had quieted, leaving freshness in its wake, felt even in the confines of the hotel room and providing Lyman with a momentary belief in redemption.

"It's Moreau," he whispered. "My name is Lyman Moreau."

17

Lyman's confession had made life simpler with Mariana. He wasn't sure what the future held for the two of them once the memory of Horace had become less painful, and the lingering threats stemming from his death fell away with time. For now, he trusted her and believed she trusted him, too. Lyman didn't yet relish the thought of further complicating their relationship, but perhaps he had begun to look forward to the day when he might.

Even more than his evenings with Mariana, Lyman enjoyed his days at the Baltimore Museum, which suited him well. Greeting the characters arriving to see the mummies filled him with fresh stories to report to Mariana over their evening meal, which served as a great distraction from her anxiety about Martin Quinn.

One morning, two weeks into the agreed upon three weeks of the exhibition, Lyman noticed a sullen young man with dark hair and circles beneath his eyes to match. As Lyman watched, the patron eased his way around the room, stopping at each mummy in turn, as though he might absorb some knowledge from them. When he'd scrutinized them all, he leaned over the accompanying documents, giving each one rapt attention.

Sadness clung to the unfortunate man, and Lyman found it difficult to look away even as other patrons entered the exhibit hall. The final stop on the young man's careful tour was the framed copy of "Address to the Mummy," and as he bent to read it, a sharp chuckle escaped him. The action was such a stark departure from his air of melancholy that Lyman couldn't help but approached him.

"Pardon me, sir, but I wonder if you might tell me what's so delightfully funny."

The young man paled and backed away from the display, turning to leave. As he did so, he bowed his head and spoke quiet words almost into his shirt collar. "Forgive me. I meant no offense. It's an impressive display."

"I didn't mean for you to go," Lyman insisted, catching the man's coat sleeve. "I only wondered. These have been my companions for many months and not once has one been kind enough to offer me a joke."

Life sparked into the man's eyes at the words, and he indicated the nearest mummy, its mouth gaping. "Perhaps they have, only you haven't been listening."

It was Lyman's turn to laugh, and he was pleased to see when he did so the young man met his gaze.

"I'm Michael Chandler, the proprietor of the exhibit. What is your name?"

"Poe," the young man answered, and then shrugged. "Edgar."

"It's a pleasure to meet you, Mr. Poe." Lyman pointed to the poet's words. "The manager of the museum introduced me to this work. It's certainly appropriate alongside an exhibit such as this, but I must admit I never found it particularly amusing."

The poem was exactly as it purported to be, an address to a mummy asking it to reveal the secrets of its ancient world—a rather dull piece of work in Lyman's opinion, though he'd never claim to be a poet himself.

"It's not the address itself I find amusing, sir," Poe answered, "but rather the idea it deposited in my head."

"Please elaborate."

"Well," Mr. Poe took a slow breath, seeming to gather his thoughts. "I wondered what the mummy would say in return. What he would think of the time in which we live."

Lyman thought for a moment. "I imagine he might find us impressive."

Poe's lips stretched into a sardonic grin, and it struck Lyman that he'd somehow gotten the odd hypothetical question wrong. "Do you think so?"

"I do," Lyman stated, his words sounding more defensive than he'd meant. "For instance, I wonder sometimes about their comfort. Being desert-dwellers in life, they must all be terribly cold, scantily clad as they are in strips of old linen. Don't you think they'd all enjoy a nice suit? Perhaps a good cigar or a glass of fine wine?"

Poe's smile widened and he shook his head. "Your suggestion is that they'd be impressed with our clothes and our fineries?"

"Well, why not? I'm certainly most impressed by the fine things in life."

Lyman had drawn him out. Poe's eyes danced, his entire being came alive. The conversation had clearly caught his imagination.

"Very well, then," Lyman added, determined to adequately illustrate his point. "How about the railroads in constant construction in this very city? That would surely impress even the most arrogant of Ancient Egyptians."

"I don't think so," Poe said, wringing his hands. "Consider all those great stones moved across the desert to construct pyramids and monuments. They must have developed some method of moving heavy cargo efficiently."

Lyman shook his head. "So you believe we've nothing to offer them. I wonder then, what questions would you ask of them, if you could?"

"I'd ask about the practice of embalming, of creating an artwork of oneself, that might be as appreciated in death as it was persecuted in life." A shadow fell once again across the young man's demeanor. Lyman shivered at the thought of one with so much life ahead entertaining such darkness.

"I think that's not a secret they'd likely reveal," he answered. "But if we can take a hint from the modern practice of taxidermy, I'd say they used a mixture of strong spirits and corrosive sublimate."

"Bichloride of mercury? You think that would work?"

"I have it on good authority."

The young man glanced back at the poem and seemed to lose himself once again in it. Lyman watched him as he read and was just stepping back to speak with another patron who'd caught his eye when Poe began to cough. He pulled a handkerchief from his pocket and held to his mouth as the convulsive fit subsided.

"Sounds as if you could use some of those strong spirits," Lyman said to the back of Poe's head as he cleared his throat. Lyman reached into his own coat pocket and withdrew one of the lozenges he'd grown accustomed to carrying as an aid for his voice since traveling with the exhibit. He handed it to the young man, who took it with a grateful nod.

Lyman turned to speak with the other patron who wished him to recount the tale of the tomb excavation by his imagined uncle. As he spoke of the degrees of embalming and of rumored curses, Poe clasped his arm.

"I'm sorry to interrupt, Mr. Chandler, but I have to go and I wanted to thank you for your interesting conversation, and for the lozenge. You know, I think if the mummies were to talk, they'd tell us with all the years of dust and fragrant oils what most impressed them about our age would be our lozenges."

With that, Mr. Poe walked out of the exhibit room. Lyman watched the young man go and then turned back to the other patron to continue his story. Engulfed as he was in the tale that kept growing larger, he failed to notice another man, just outside the entryway to the exhibit, a man with wavy auburn hair and steely eyes.

For an hour the man barely moved but only watched, his gaze following the showman as he worked his way around the room, welcoming the curious of Baltimore, sprinkling their already romantic minds with dark details.

Lyman felt the eyes of the man in his periphery, but when at last he turned to inquire of him who he was or whether he had questions about the exhibit, the steely-eyed man was gone.

18

"Something is wrong with you." Mariana appraised him, absent-mindedly pushing her food around her plate.

"You're the one who's not eating," he reprimanded her gently, placing a forkful of flaky fish into his own mouth.

"I'm not hungry." She slid her plate away to illustrate the point.

Lyman dabbed at his mouth with his napkin and dropped it on the table. "You must stop this fretting. You gaze into that crystal all day and you expect the worst at every turn. You're wasting away."

It was true. Since they'd arrived in Baltimore she'd lost weight, her youthful cheeks grown hollow. She slumped against the back of her chair, rubbing furiously at her bare arms, and did not answer him.

"I'm becoming concerned, Mariana."

She closed her eyes before answering through clenched teeth. "If you're concerned, then let's leave this place before it's too late."

"I'm making a good deal of money here and the exhibit is engaged for another week. I can't break my word."

Mariana's eyes flew open and she leaned across the table to grasp his hand. "Yes, because thieves and swindlers must be known for their word." She tried to pull back from him, but he stopped her, catching her fingers in his firm grip.

"Do not use such words in public, darling wife."

"They aren't paying attention to us," she hissed, indicating the roomful of diners. No one looked their way, engaged as they were in their own dinners, their own conversations.

"Perhaps not," Lyman admitted. "But we must be careful. If Quinn is the threat you believe him to be, rumors and whispers are all he needs in order to find us." He loosened his grip and Mariana pulled away. She rubbed her fingers and scowled. "A trail of mummies might prove more dangerous."

"The mummies travel with me at my invitation. As do you. If you'd like to revisit the arrangement, I'd be happy to do so." Lyman stood, straightening his coat. "I need some air."

*****

Choosing to head north past the museum and toward the imposing Cathedral of Mary Our Queen, Lyman stepped into the growing darkness of the night. He was far from alone. Baltimoreans bustled about him. Carriages rushed by, bearing merry souls on their way to or from a fine meal or an evening's entertainment. Lamplighters, too, went about their business, splashing the sidewalks with circles of yellow light.

Lyman walked on, captive to his own worries, lost and angered by his jumbled thoughts. Mariana's exasperating and obsessive attitude couldn't distract him from his growing concern she might also be right.

Perhaps it had been no more than his own imagination, but in Philadelphia he'd seen the shadowy visions materializing inside the glass and, increasingly, they haunted him. He caught himself, in quiet moments, stealing furtive backward glances, sizing up those around him, searching their faces for traces of malevolence.

There had been the stranger at the museum, which he had not mentioned to Mariana. He wouldn't do so because, as far as Lyman knew, what he had seen might not have been a man at all, but a phantom presence lingering at the edge of his psyche, an embodiment of his own nightmares.

For if any man alive deserved to be haunted, it was Lyman Moreau, though never before now would he have admitted he was frightened by the possibility. His closest companions of late being the ancient dead, he'd become uncharacteristically contemplative about his own life. Even in the sweltering heat of the August night, the cacophony of his thoughts chilled him.

In this distracted manner, he'd walked nearly six blocks before he registered the footsteps of a pursuer, drawing close upon him. Lyman reached into his pocket, his fingers finding the knife folded there. He'd just begun to withdraw it when he distinguished his assumed name among the breathless words coming to him in a familiar voice.

"Mr. Chandler, may I have a word?"

Lyman spun on his heel to find an exasperated man, his shaven face the picture of relief at having caught up to his prey at last.

"Mr. Walker." Lyman made no attempt to hide his surprise at seeing the museum curator in this strange manner. "I apologize, sir. I was lost in thought and did not hear your approach."

Walker bent forward over his paunch, which bespoke of his success as a respectable gentleman. Lyman waited while his companion regained his breath. Once composed, Walker began to spin an alarming tale.

"I saw you walking past the museum as I stepped out, but I failed to catch your attention. There is something of utmost importance I must discuss with you."

Lyman crossed his arms. "You've piqued my curiosity, Mr. Walker. What could have been so urgent it would require you to chase me down a dark street?"

Walker pulled a handkerchief from his coat pocket and dabbed at the gathered moisture on his high forehead. "I would've called at your hotel, of course, but perhaps it is best to have this conversation away from your wife. I would not wish to worry her."

"Now you worry me. Please, tell me what has gotten you so upset."

"A gentleman, though I hesitate to call him such, arrived in my office earlier this evening and relayed to me some disturbing stories about you."

"Disturbing stories?" Lyman arranged his face into his most shocked and innocent expression. "Who was this gentleman? May I ask what he said of me?"

"He was a Mr. Quinn, claiming to be a customs agent from New York who knew you to be in possession of stolen goods. Egyptian goods, to be precise."

A finely dressed couple ambled by, momentarily blocking the glow of the nearby lamp illuminating Walker's face. As they passed, he leaned toward Lyman and whispered, "He said you'd been implicated in a murder."

"A murder!" Lyman repeated loudly, infusing into his response as much incredulity as he could muster.

Walker grabbed Lyman by the arm and pulled him to the dark edge of the sidewalk, shushing him.

Lyman allowed himself to be guided. More quietly, he added, "Who is it I am to have murdered? The entire notion is ridiculous. I know no man named Quinn."

"I thought as much, Mr. Chandler."

Relief flooded through Lyman, and he resisted the urge to embrace the easily manipulated curator.

"You've behaved as nothing but a professional and a gentleman in your dealings with me and my museum. Your exhibit is of the highest quality and the truth of your claims substantiated by respectable men. You arrived with the recommendation and trust of Titian Peale, a man renowned for his commendable contribution to the museum industry. I do not doubt you."

"Then why chase me through the streets?" Lyman's words carried a hint of anger he was surprised to feel. His credentials, though impressive, did nothing to argue against Quinn's accusations, and he knew escape would be the only option left to him and to Mariana. Still, he'd worked hard to win Walker's trust. That the curator would entertain suspicions about him filled Lyman with disgust he had no right to feel.

"Because you must understand that I cannot have the museum embroiled in scandal. We've only begun to reemerge in the consciousness of the city. I don't know who this man is or what he may be about, but I will protect my museum from him. And, I regret to say, from you, Mr. Chandler."

"You regret it, you say. You believe in my complete innocence? You don't sound to me like a man with any deep regrets." Lyman took a long breath to calm his rapid pulse as Walker only stood, his eyes downcast, wringing his hands.

At last, Lyman spoke. "I do understand, Mr. Walker. You are a man who must defend what is his, as I would do were I in your position. What do you need me to do?"

Walker sighed and placed a hand on Lyman's shoulder, an almost fatherly gesture. "You must leave. You must pack up your exhibit and go, tonight."

It was the response he'd hoped for. Still, Lyman felt the sting of being turned out like a criminal by a man who'd claimed to have faith in him.

"Thank you, Mr. Walker, for your generosity. It has been a pleasure to work with you, educating the people of this great city."

"That it has, Mr. Chandler." Walker offered Lyman a firm handshake and the two men began walking toward the museum, this time at a more comfortable pace.

They moved in silence for a time, and then Lyman ventured the question that weighed most heavily on his mind. "And what will you tell this customs agent? Surely he'll return to the museum."

"Yes," Walker replied. "I expect him first thing in the morning, by which time I'm sure I will have discovered that the mummy exhibit unexpectedly disappeared. The only clue I'll be able to offer is that Colonel McKinstry of Detroit had expressed interest in the collection."

What the man proposed was most ungentlemanly and, Lyman realized, most generous. "Thank you, sir," he said, "for your discretion."

The cathedral loomed before them, a silhouette against the night sky. Walker stopped in its shadow. "As I thank you, sir, for yours."

19

Lyman returned to the inn late that night, exhausted and relieved. With Walker's help, the six remaining mummies had been safely stashed with the scrolls into two crates. Baltimore had been good to Lyman, but now he'd felt the hot breath of an enemy on the back of his neck. He was anxious to return to the road.

He'd not been thinking of his earlier argument with Mariana, but when he opened the door to the room they shared, it was clear she'd been thinking of little else. She stood at the foot of the bed in a thin linen nightgown that clung to her sweat-dampened skin and slid off one shoulder when she turned to look at him. Her unbound curls fell soft around her face, and even in the dim light of the oil sconces he could see that her flushed cheeks bore marks of illness.

On the bed before her lay two dresses, a stack of neatly folded undergarments, and a carpetbag, its wide mouth open and expectant.

His shock at finding her in such a state, and not already long in bed was, he feared, evident in his voice. "How did you know?"

"That you wanted me to leave?" she interrupted. "I don't require a vision in a crystal ball to know that. You told me you would prefer the company of three thousand year old dead men to that of me. I'll leave in the morning." She pulled a silky something from the stack on the bed and placed it into the bag.

He crossed the room in two steps and stayed her arm with a light touch. "Mariana," he began, "I didn't mean to imply you are unwelcome."

Her jaw jutted forward, and without looking at him, she peeled his fingers from her arm, dropping his hand from her grasp. "Your meaning was quite clear."

Lyman thought to protest, but as Mariana leaned over her packing, something slid from the neck of her nightgown and caught his attention. A long string of small, dangling beads cascaded from her neck to the bed. He reached for them, letting them slide between his fingers. "I've seen these before. They were part of the shipment. I didn't know you still had any of it."

Mariana snatched the beads from his hand and pulled the necklace over her head, flinging it into the bag. "These are all I have. All I kept of the last antiquities Horace stole." She turned and dropped, slumping onto the bed, the neck of her nightgown sliding further off her shoulder.

"But you haven't worn them. I haven't seen them since the day we sorted the shipment."

She shrugged, tugging at the neck of her gown, though it immediately fell back down, exposing her slim shoulder again. Lyman's breath caught in his chest.

"I haven't always worn them, but I keep them with me. I guess I was just missing my husband tonight. I am allowed to grieve for him, am I not?"

Her response took him aback, flooding him with guilt for noticing the curve of her collarbone. Her eyes remained dry, but sad, and in them he could see what might have been grief. He'd become accustomed to thinking of Mariana as a woman without feeling. Now he wondered if he could've misjudged her.

"I miss him, too." He pushed the bag out of the way and sat beside her.

"Do you?"

"Yes, of course. He was my mentor. Had it not been for Horace, teaching me how to navigate the world as a gentleman, I don't know what would have become of me."

"Was it really that bad, your childhood?"

He'd not expected the question and wanted to probe the depth of her grief, to ask her about Quinn and their relationship, but in this moment, she was so fragile and so lovely, and he couldn't bring himself to do it.

Instead, he found himself answering her, revealing parts of himself he'd long hidden. She nudged him out of kilter in a way no one had in a very long time.

"In part," he began. "My mother was a woman unfit to be called such, and my father, a stranger. Still, there were good things, too. A neighbor woman in the same tenement befriended me. She had a gift for seeing beyond what was right in front of her. In that, you remind me of her. She looked in on me in my most desperate times and kept me fed when she was able."

Mariana shifted so she was face to face with Lyman. She clasped his hand. "You had a guardian angel."

He squeezed Mariana's hand, grateful for the weight of it. "I doubt she would have thought of herself in that way, but yes, I suppose I did.

"She was married to a failed businessman turned failed musician. I'm sure she could have done better for herself, married, if not a gentleman, at least a man more capable of caring for her. But as I said, she saw things others didn't. Her husband was a kindhearted man. He eventually took notice of me, as she had, and taught me to read alongside his own children.

"I even lived with them for a time after my mother's inevitable disappearance. That lasted for a little more than a year before I decided I'd imposed on them enough and struck out on my own."

"What did you do?"

Lyman squeezed Mariana's hand, still holding fast to his. "That's when I bumped into Horace, a lost soul like me. I taught him the ins and outs of the city, and he taught me a new trade. He took me under his wing."

Mariana exhaled a long, heavy sigh. "That might have been my story as well, except without the kindness of neighbors." Her mouth became a grim line across her face. "When I met Horace, I hadn't known how it feels to be adored. I'm afraid I never understood it. Not before it was too late."

"For a criminal, he was a good man."

Mariana's chin dropped to her chest and she brought her hands to her face. She released a long moan. Lyman said nothing for a time, looking on helpless.

At last he gave her hand another gentle squeeze. "We have to go. We can leave separately if you prefer, but I would very much like it if we travel together."

She raised her face to him, her eyebrows arched. "You're leaving? What made you change your mind?"

He considered telling her of his conversation with Mr. Walker on the dark streets and of the alarming reappearance of Martin

Quinn, but this version of Mariana struck him as so utterly delicate, he couldn't bring himself to darken her countenance with further worry or to risk shattering this new vulnerability.

"I realized you were right. If there's any chance Quinn is coming for us, we must keep moving. The sooner we depart, the better."

"And you want me to come? Are you sure?"

"My dear, a man is always more trustworthy when traveling with his beautiful wife. And I suspect with your peculiar set of skills, my showmanship, and our silent friends, this could be a beneficial relationship."

"Very well." Withdrawing her hand from him, she stood and straightened her nightgown, bringing the neckline to rest squarely atop her shoulders. "We must pack. What is your plan?" It was as if a curtain had fallen over her, obscuring any previous hint of helplessness. She had become a woman of business, of single-minded purpose. Whether she had ever truly been anything else, Lyman couldn't be sure. Her performance had been nothing short of masterful. Her transformation struck him as both hurtful and impressive.

"We'll catch the stagecoach at first light and be long gone before Martin Quinn can hear so much as a whisper of our presence."

She nodded, pulling the bag toward herself, preparing to place another folded silky something inside. "And where will we go?"

"North. I plan to backtrack into Pennsylvania. When it's safe, we'll set up our display again and perhaps take out that orb of yours."

Mariana scowled. "To remain so close seems foolish to me. What makes you think Quinn won't find us?"

Lyman was fairly certain they wouldn't be discovered because he had found, in J. E. Walker, an unexpected ally who would soon send their pursuer to Detroit chasing nothing more than the rumor of mummies. This information, however, he wasn't willing to share with Mariana.

At last, he'd begun to see her more clearly, to understand her manipulations as well as his own susceptibility to them. She would be more manageable when frightened and more trustworthy when dependent. He knew an honorable man would not falsely maintain the shadow of such a dangerous threat as Quinn, only to keep a business partner under his thumb.

And though he enjoyed the challenge of her company, admired her charms, and had confided in her secrets few others knew, Lyman was not an honorable man.

20

They caught the morning stagecoach, Lyman grumbling about the high fee for shipping the two remaining crates of mummies and scrolls in the freight wagon to follow. By nightfall they found themselves in Lancaster, Pennsylvania, at an inn on East King Street.

Lyman was relieved to be off the road as Mariana was obviously ill. What began as nervous scratching at her arms had grown more severe throughout the day of travel until she developed welts on her skin where she had torn at it as if brushing off an invisible army of insects. When Lyman pointed out sights along the road, she seemed to barely register them.

He guided her into the brick inn, she leaning heavily on his arm. Had he not known better, Lyman might have assumed she'd been drinking.

The innkeeper was an imposing figure named Roher. Tall and broad, he had a wide, serious face framed by closely trimmed muttonchops.

"Good evening, sir." Lyman pulled off his hat. "Do you have a room available for the night?"

Roher studied them, his eyes lingering on Mariana long enough to make Lyman feel defensive. Even unwell, she was a fetching vision in the scarlet dress she wore, wholly inappropriate for a day of travel.

"I don't house libertines, nor harlots."

"I'm grateful to hear it, sir," Lyman offered. "It makes a gentleman and his road-weary wife feel easier in a place to know it is morally run."

Lines on the man's furrowed brow deepened and he pointed to Mariana, still leaning against her escort. "What's wrong with her?"

"My wife is a delicate creature. Travel is difficult for her, but it is nothing a brief stay in a fine establishment won't cure." Under different circumstances, Lyman might not have chosen to refer to Mr. Roher's inn as a fine establishment, but he hoped his words about Mariana's health proved true.

The man grumbled indecipherable words as he turned to slide a key from the wall of cubby holes to his left. More clearly he asked, "What is your name?"

Lyman hesitated at the question. Mariana had asked him not to use Chandler until they could be sure Quinn was well behind them, but Johnson was known to their pursuer as well. Lyman's own name, he only rarely used.

"Henry."

The innkeeper dropped the key onto the registry log in front of him and shook his head. "Do you always have such trouble coming up with your name, Mr. Henry? I won't suffer a liar, either. I think you and your companion might be more comfortable down the road."

"No. Please, sir." Lyman felt his panic rising. Mariana pulled away from him to rub at the welts on her arms. "My wife needs to rest. I'm sorry I was untruthful."

Roher picked up the room key, which tinkled against its ring. He closed his fingers around it and eyed Lyman with suspicion, but he made no move to turn away. The man at least had been willing to listen.

"This morning we left Baltimore where I was exhibiting artifacts at their highly respected museum. It was a very popular exhibit and we had to leave quickly on account of my wife's health. I just thought we might have more privacy if I used an assumed name. It was foolish of me. My name is Chandler. Michael Chandler." Inwardly he cringed to use the name, with Mariana so determined he should not, but it sprang easily from his tongue. His story seemed to satisfy the cautious Mr. Roher, who dropped the key back onto his desk.

"What kind of artifacts?"

Relieved, Lyman held an arm out to Mariana, which she was quick to take. "Egyptian mummies," he explained, slipping into his jovial persona.

"Well, Mr. Chandler." Roher's smile didn't reach his eyes, but his expression became friendlier than it had been. "Let's say we take a look at these mummies. Then perhaps we can take a look at your room."

Lyman had grown accustomed to the artifacts opening doors for him, but he would never have expected to find enthusiasm among the likes of a small-time innkeeper in the middle of Amish country. The man had more questions than even the learned among Philadelphia's elite, and when Lyman patiently answered them all as his imagination supplied, Roher suggested displaying the mummies and scrolls in the hotel.

While the location was not ideal for lending credibility to the exhibit, Lyman realized that may be the very reason he could consider using it. Once Quinn discovered they'd left Baltimore, he would likely waste little time in pursuing Walker's clever misdirection. But if he lingered, he'd be less likely to trace them here than to a major museum.

Lyman shook Mr. Roher's hand and took the room key. Mariana would not be well enough to travel for at least several days. He didn't object to making a little profit in the meantime.

*****

"I don't need a doctor, especially not one from some God-forsaken backward village in Pennsylvania."

The argument had been raging for three days. "Mariana." Lyman rubbed his tired eyes. "There are many ways you might describe Lancaster, but God-forsaken it's not. In fact, there's a little too much of God here for my liking."

Despite Mr. Roher's insistence there would be plenty of interest in Lyman's exhibit, there had been little. A steady stream of travelers filtered through the hotel but few remained for long, most road-weary and sullen. The Amish influence in the area dictated a squeamishness about embalming practices and a focus on a spiritual eternity separate from the earthly body. Mummies did not hold great appeal in such a place.

"And now we're back to the damned mummies. If you're as unhappy as I am, why are we still here?"

"Because you're sick. You need rest. And you need a doctor."

Mariana stood and tugged at the tight-fitting sleeves she wore to keep herself from clawing at her arms. Anger etched a crease in the skin above her nose. She pushed at his chest, taking him by surprise, and he stumbled backward, nearly hitting the wall before regaining his balance.

"I'm well enough to knock you off your feet." She raised a clenched fist, the sight so unexpected and childish, he laughed.

She lowered her hand and laughed, too. When her giggles subsided, she said, "I'm feeling a little better. I don't need a doctor to tell me that."

"Okay," he relented. "But we won't go far, just to Harrisburg. There'll be more traffic there, especially with the canal about to open."

"And maybe there won't be so many religious fools and I can dust off my orb."

"And if you are not as fully well as you think you are," Lyman added, taking advantage of the positive turn in her mood, "Harrisburg is sure to have a doctor."

Once again she raised her fist in the air and shook it at him, but her eyes were smiling. "You're an impossible man, Lyman Moreau."

"But you'll see a doctor, if you get worse again."

She sighed. "If you will take me out of this Amish hell and if my health takes a turn again, I will see a blame doctor."

21

Lyman had a good feeling about Harrisburg. Despite its status as Pennsylvania's state capital, it was a quaint town surrounded by expansive farmland on three sides and the highly navigable Susquehanna on the fourth. Like so many places they'd traveled through, Harrisburg vibrated with the energy of change, and though sophisticated was not the descriptor he might have chosen once he'd seen it, Lyman believed in the city's potential.

Tucked into a great river bend, Harrisburg served as a transportation hub where merchants and tradesmen outfitted travelers beginning the long journey west through the winding Pennsylvania countryside and across the Allegheny Mountains. At the heart of town stood the stately brick capitol building from which a wide set of stairs spilled onto the tidy grid of streets.

Lyman secured lodgings on the edge of the commercial district and left Mariana, still ill and exhausted from travel, to rest as he scoured the town for potential exhibit locations.

His credentials from Titian Peele did little to recommend him here. Not a cultural center, Harrisburg couldn't lay claim to any world-class museums, nor to the scholars who might frequent them. But what it did not lack, Lyman soon discovered, were Freemasons.

Pillars of their community, highly esteemed and undeniably influential, the Freemasons often sought to promote educational opportunities, but after his experience in Philadelphia, Lyman was not anxious to turn to them. Then, too, there existed an underlying mistrust of this secretive organization among the general population, whose money Lyman hoped would soon line his pockets.

The three-story stone Masonic Lodge was spacious, well-maintained, and centrally located, just steps from the capitol. Without a clear alternative, it would serve well enough for the brief time Lyman hoped it would take Mariana to recover her health, and its membership proved just as willing as the Philadelphia Masons to welcome an intriguing exhibit into its space.

The public trickled in and he soon hit his stride, his tales blending mounds of crumbling remains with winding stone passages where a man could become lost, both in body and in spirit. Adapting many of the details from Belzoni's travel writings, Lyman described the dust of the dead that threatens to choke the breath from a man like a great curse, deep pits in which a man could fall to his death, and treacherous locals who would sooner sell the bones of the explorers than to see them profit from Egypt's past.

Each evening, Lyman brought supper to Mariana. While coaxing her to eat, he relayed the highlights of his day and delighted in her questions, imagining that it might be a sign of her returning health.

Then one afternoon, nearly three weeks into the exhibition, Lyman looked up in the middle of an explanation to a gray-haired patron of priestly temple carving and saw Mariana walk into the gallery. Moving with obvious care, she was poised and fresh in appearance with her hair pinned beneath a bonnet that suited her much better than the scarlet dress she loved that now hung from her too-slender frame. To her cheeks she'd added a splash of rouge, which lent her the illusion of healthy color.

At the sight of her, Lyman lost the trail of his speech, so pleased was he to observe her anywhere but her sick bed. With a mumbled apology, he left the visitor to puzzle over the mummies on his own and rushed toward Mariana, his arms outstretched to her.

He clasped her elbow and she leaned into his touch. "Look at you," he whispered. "What a pleasant surprise."

She smiled at him, though he thought her expression might be better described as a grimace and it worried him.

"Why are you here?"

His question caused her lips to fall into a pout. "Do you not want me here?"

The gray-haired man acknowledged Lyman's return with a glance, but when his gaze fell on Mariana, he stepped further away, tugging on his close-trimmed whiskers. He appeared to focus on the flattened scrolls, but Lyman got the impression the man's attention was divided.

Lyman lowered his voice. "Of course I want you here. But are you well enough?"

Mariana released a halting sigh. "We can't stay here, Lyman."

He pushed his finger to her lips, leaning into her. "What are you talking about, my dear?"

A blush rose in her cheeks, her eyes downcast in apology, but she did not relent in her attempt at warning. "*Michael*, we've been here too long already."

The gray-haired gentleman returned to examine the scrolls and Lyman grew uncomfortable at his nearness to them. Two new patrons had come in and approached the exhibit. Lyman needed to collect their entrance fees and see to their questions, but Mariana had begun to tremble. He could sense the instability in her posture and then the quaking stopped, the weight against him increasing.

"Mariana," he spoke too loudly, his outburst commanding the attention of everyone in the room.

Mariana's muscles had gone slack and her eyes had closed. He quickly wrapped both arms around her before she could slide off the stool and together with the assistance of another set of agile hands, he lowered her onto the gallery floor.

The extra hands belonged to the gray-haired gentleman who spoke before Lyman could thank him. "I'm a doctor." The elder man adjusted his wire glasses and looked Lyman over. "Is this young lady your wife?"

Lyman nodded, grateful. "She's been ill for some time, growing worse as we've traveled."

The doctor placed his fingers on Mariana's wrist and then, removing her bonnet, pressed a hand to her forehead. "She's only fainted. Let's move her to a more comfortable location and I'll examine her more fully."

Lyman scooped Mariana in his arms and carried her to a divan set in the temple entryway just beyond the door to the exhibition hall. He left her there with the physician long enough to speak with the remaining patrons who left disappointed as Lyman closed the exhibit.

When he returned to Mariana, she was regaining consciousness.

"Madam," the doctor began. "I'm Dr. Warrick. Your husband has asked if I would take a look at you."

She turned glassy, unfocused eyes on him and then buried her face in a cushion. "Go away."

"Mariana, please," Lyman whispered. He knelt beside her, aware that their location set inside the temple entrance was hardly private. "You collapsed. Just allow the man to examine you."

"I won't be killed by a doctor." Even muffled by a cushion, her forceful words carried.

"Madam," the physician balked, "I assure you I mean you no harm. Your husband is concerned."

"He's not concerned about me. He's not even my husband."

Warrick glanced sideways at Lyman, his head tilted with a silent question.

"She's been confused," Lyman offered, thankful the doctor seemed to accept this explanation. He nodded solemnly and stepped toward Mariana, taking her head in his hands and examining the blotchy skin of her neck. She yielded to his touch, her eyes closed, sweat beading on her brow. The doctor stepped back again, as if he didn't wish to be too close to her.

He straightened, slid a hand into his coat pocket, and spoke to Lyman like they were the only two in the room. "I recommend cold compresses to bring the fever down, and bloodletting wouldn't be out of the question. She's clearly out of balance."

"No bleeding," Mariana moaned.

Dr. Warrick's eyes rolled as he offered a sympathetic smile that made Lyman's stomach clench. Over his shoulder, the doctor said, "Young lady, I should very much like to see your medical degree."

Mariana hissed at him, evidently the only reply she could muster. Lyman might have thought her possessed if he believed such a thing possible. He touched the doctor on the arm and guided him back into the gallery.

"Your wife is delirious with fever," the man said once they'd stepped beyond the door frame. "We need to bleed her before it's too late, and I would recommend mercuric chloride as well."

Mariana screamed and Lyman shut the door behind them, shaking his head. "She's unwell, but she is not, I think, delirious." Lyman would have been inclined to take the doctor's advice, but even weakened, he trusted Mariana's insight. If she did not wish to be treated by this man, he would not force it upon her. She was not, after all, his wife.

"Are you feeling ill as well?" the doctor asked him.

Lyman didn't bother to answer. "Thank you for seeing her, Dr. Warrick, but I will not force treatment on her if she doesn't want it."

"You're making a grave mistake, Mr. Chandler. You were right to let me examine her. Your wife might not be long for this world."

"That may be, sir, but if I have learned anything about her it's that she will only do what she wants."

He saw the doctor out of the building and returned to Mariana, who had managed to pull herself to almost sitting, supported by the arms of the divan. She was calmer, but still her complexion remained pink with heat.

"Are you feeling better?" he asked, not hopeful that she was.

"Much better. Thank you for caring enough to ask a doctor to examine me. And thank you for throwing him out when he proved he was a fool."

"Don't thank me for sending him away. I don't know if I did the right thing."

"But you trusted that I knew. And that's what matters."

"You collapsed. You might do it again. You're too weak to be out of bed."

She reached her hand toward him, which he accepted with one of his own. "I feel as well as I need to, Lyman. And he's still coming."

"The doctor?" Lyman asked, confused. "Between your lack of cooperation and my curt dismissal, I doubt we'll be seeing him again."

She squeezed his hand. "Not the doctor. Martin Quinn. He's coming, I can feel it. He's closing in on us."

"You really are delirious. Maybe I should fetch back Dr. Warrick."

Mariana shook her head. "When I look into the orb, he's there. When I close my eyes he's there. And sometimes I catch a vision of him from the corner of my eye."

Lyman pressed his free hand to her fiery cheek. "Mariana, Quinn is halfway to Detroit by now. Walker sent him chasing McKinstry weeks ago. We're well shut of him."

He'd surprised himself with the confession that he'd known Quinn was in Baltimore. His words made him cringe in anticipation of her anger, but Mariana barely reacted to the news. She only smiled, her expression filled with a sorrowful pity. "That won't matter. He'll retrace his steps and when he does, we won't be far enough ahead of him. With you showing the mummies in every blame town in Pennsylvania, he'll find us."

He looked at her eyes, clouded with sickness, and his strength to oppose her, to force her to see reason, faded. It was clear that she would not recover with the threat of Martin Quinn looming in her mind, and as long as they remained on the move, displaying the stolen mummies, his shadow would continue to haunt her.

Lyman put his arm around her and gently laid her back onto the pillows. She didn't resist him as he kissed the top of her head.

"If it's that important to you, my dear, we will leave in the morning. We'll find a place for you to rest where you'll be safe. Perhaps we'll seek out another doctor, a better one."

"No doctor," she replied and rolled to her side, her long curls falling over her face as she buried herself in the cushions. "All those quacks want to do is drain your blood and feed you poison. I won't die that way."

He brushed the hair away from her face, sliding the long locks through his fingers. "You won't die at all. Not for a long time."

He hoped what he said was true as he felt the import of the words press on his heart. Even if this woman were not yet his to love, he still wanted to protect her.

22

Once the steamship began to paddle upriver, leaving Harrisburg more than a mile behind it, Lyman finally relaxed. Mariana rested against him, her eyes beginning to close at the sound of the lapping water. The remaining six mummies were secured in the cargo hold, their identities safely obscured from the captain and crew by the thick wood of crates.

There were few other passengers on the steamer, which was headed north up through Pennsylvania and into New York State. It wasn't the route Lyman wanted to take—back toward all he'd been running from—but for now, he didn't have a choice. With Quinn looking for them and Mariana growing increasingly weak, they would be wise to take the mummies off exhibit and rest for a while. Lyman knew of only one good option, and the mighty Susquehanna would deliver them there.

"Lyman," Mariana said. The sound of her voice surprised him. He looked down at her head on his chest and felt her warmth seep into him.

"I didn't realize you were awake."

"Only just." She yawned. "I don't think I've felt this safe in a long time."

He pulled her closer, wrapping his free arm around her as she bent into him. Lyman was skilled at making people feel safe around him, putting them at ease with his careful manners and bold confidence. But it had been a long time since he'd deserved such trust, and he didn't take for granted this gift Mariana had given him.

He noticed the glistening trail of a tear on her cheek and swept it away with a gentle finger. "Are you all right?"

"Yes." She pulled free of his arms and dabbed at her eyes. "I was thinking about Horace."

Lyman closed one hand in a fist at his side, squeezing his fingers tight in frustration with himself for feeling jealous of a dead man. "You must miss him very much."

Mariana's eyes narrowed, her expression becoming difficult for Lyman to read. It was as if her sorrow had been clouded by something he couldn't place.

"I do," she began, and then hesitated, dropping her eyes to her lap. "He could be a difficult man." She raised her glistening eyes and met his. Oil lanterns provided low light in the passenger compartment, but he could see her expression. She bit her lower lip and her gaze dropped once again to her lap.

"Was it bad?" He hated the hopeful tone of his own voice. "With Horace, I mean."

"I know what you mean. And the answer is both yes and no. I loved him and he loved me. But since he got sick, he was different. Mean and confused and confusing. He got so he wouldn't trust me. He was jealous of any man I spoke to."

"Did he hurt you?" Lyman tried to conjure the image of his mentor beating a woman, but couldn't, even with the memory of the beating he had taken, and had well deserved from the old man.

"Nothing like that. He was old and weak. I don't think he could've hurt me if he wanted to. Just sometimes it felt like he went out of his way to make sure I was unhappy, is all. I shouldn't complain, not of the dead, but like I said, the man he was when I married him, the one who was so smart I thought he knew everything, and who could deal on the black market and no one would dare take advantage of him because they knew he'd outsmart them, that man died a long time ago.

"Doctors killed my husband."

"I thought Martin Quinn killed Horace."

"Yes, but you saw him, Lyman. The man you knew, and the one I married, was dead a long time before that night. It's the doctors that did it. And the blame mercury."

Lyman reflected on his last interactions with Horace and realized that what she said was true, that he'd had the same thoughts himself. The shrunken old man, so quick to anger, who reeked of whiskey and defeat, was not easily reconciled to the gentleman he'd once known.

"It was like he was a shell," Mariana continued. "His brain addled so he didn't understand fully what was happening most of the time, or he'd mistake it for evil."

"Like you and Quinn?"

"Oh." She dropped her face into her hands and groaned. "Quinn was the biggest mistake of my life. I allowed him to seduce me. Horace was right not to trust him. And me."

The confession hit Lyman in his gut. He slid away from her, putting as much distance between them as he could across the bench seat, which was no more than two feet, only enough to garner startled looks from other passengers. Lyman opened his mouth to speak, but found his throat had gone dry.

"Please don't despise me." Mariana wiped her nose with the back of her glove. "I couldn't stand it if you did."

Lyman didn't know what to say. He should hardly have been surprised, but during his many weeks with her, he'd manage to convince himself of her devotion to Horace, a man brutally taken from both of them too soon. For her now to confirm his earlier assumptions—that she'd been an unfaithful wife—and to confess that in some ways she believed her husband worthy of death, and even counted him as dead already horrified Lyman. The revelation filled him with rage and sadness that doused any inkling he might be coming to care for her himself.

"Have you been telling me the truth?" he asked.

"What?" Her eyes darted to the other passengers. They'd returned to their own business their own conversations, and the noise of the engine offered at least some sense of privacy. Still, Mariana lowered her voice with her next words.

"Of course. I never told you I wasn't with Quinn."

Lyman took her cue and spoke quietly, but with no less venom. "You told me you were afraid of him, that he'd killed your husband for daring to defend your honor, and that Quinn was coming for you next because you'd sent him to jail."

"All true, I swear." She didn't attempt to scoot closer to him, but there was pleading in her eyes and in her choked words.

"If you were having amorous congress with Quinn, why would he want to hurt you? Why wouldn't the two of you have run off together once Horace was dead?"

Mariana cleared her throat and slid toward him on the bench seat until their legs were touching, her face barely an inch from the tip of his nose. "You remind me of my Horace. He was the kindest man who ever lived, and I treated him so badly." She sat back and blew out a long breath.

"He rescued me from the most awful life a woman can live— one of sin and danger. He always saw the best in me, even though I wasn't educated like he was."

Lyman regretted how much the speech moved him. His own experience with Horace had been similar in some ways. He'd been the young son of a woman who lived a life of sin and danger. With a pang, he wondered if, had met Horace sooner, he'd have redeemed his mother the way he redeemed Mariana and become Lyman's father and protector rather than his criminal mentor.

"He was charming and no man had ever treated me with the respect he did, but he was so old. I woke every day afraid he'd be dead and I'd be right back to where I was before. When Quinn came along and looked at me the way men do, I saw a younger man, clawing his way into success. He was easy to flatter. Men always are."

She patted Lyman's knee and his heart gave an unwelcome flutter.

"Then Horace started going mad. It was the mercury, I know it, but he insisted he needed it. And then he started drinking more, too. I think it was how he tried to hide the fact that he had a hard time getting around. He figured if he was always drunk then he had an excuse to be stumbling about."

"So you just abandoned your sick husband?"

"No," she insisted. "Not at first anyway. I tried to be the best nurse I knew how to be. I tried to get hold of healers, but Horace would have none of it. His over-educated brain didn't want anyone but a trained physician. I didn't know what to do, or who to turn to. The people I knew was worse off than I was and wouldn't be able to help even if they'd been willing to. The people Horace knew was bad people. And one of those bad people was Quinn, a man who'd been kind to me.

"So I went to him, and begged for his help, and he became a big part of our life. He brought in a new doctor, and Horace did seem to get better for a while, but his price for helping was steep."

"He took advantage of you."

"I wish it was fair of me to say that, but I let him do what he wanted, because I knew Horace was going to die, and sooner rather than later. Quinn was the man who would rescue me the next time."

"Except he wasn't."

She shook her head. Her shoulders slumped. The flush of fever rose again in her cheeks. Lyman became aware of his own growing discomfort, caused by the inescapable and familiar shame of pushing a frail woman to her breaking point. He could not sit in judgment of a member of the fairer sex, more vulnerable to the harshness of the world than the most unfortunate man.

"Can you forgive me?" she asked, the sight of her misty eyes and long, dark lashes causing his heart to swell.

"Yes," he whispered. His anger still burned, but on the scale of despicable actions, hers were far outweighed by his own. "I doubt you deserve it, but I can."

"Because you're a good man, Lyman Moreau, despite what you'd like me to think."

Lyman sank against the back of the bench, rubbing his eyes with his hands. "Well," he said. "You don't know me that well."

"I think I'm starting to." She placed a hand on his knee, which caused him to sit upright again. "Tell me, Lyman, what happened to your wife? Did you love her?"

He tensed at the question, and Mariana's grip tightened. He tried to move away from her, but part of him craved her closeness, and in the limited space of the steamer, it was hardly worth the effort. Her dark eyes bored into him, probing him, reading him as if he were her glass ball, and he felt all of his secrets pleading for release.

"I did not." The information tumbled out of him as never before, and he found it was cathartic to utter the words. Mariana's face remained expressionless. She only continued to search his face, unsatisfied with this one small answer. She shifted in the seat and turned her attention full to him so that the steamship all but disappeared. There was only Mariana, her sad eyes pleading with him to share his darkness with her, as she had shared hers with him.

"Katherine was a widow, wealthy. She had land up in New York. And she was sick."

He tried to stop after each new piece of information, but the press continued to tighten. He didn't know what power Mariana possessed, if any real power at all, but he was bound to her in this moment, trapped and captivated.

"I was traveling through with a medicine show and she took a fancy to me. She'd seen doctors and they'd failed her. She bought my patent medicine and claimed she felt better than she had in years. I don't know, maybe she did. Really, I think she was just lonely for a man." Lyman smiled. "And I am quite charming."

Mariana did not laugh. Perhaps she didn't find him so charming. Instead, she prompted him to continue, asking, "And you were pleased enough to poison her?" Suddenly, Mariana's delicate hand on his thigh might have been made of lead. He squirmed, but she held tight.

"The medicine didn't have anything in it that would have harmed her. It was made for me by an associate, a gifted healer I once knew, but it wouldn't help her either. I thought if I gathered some of the herbs I'd seen my associate use, heard him talk of, maybe I could help ease her suffering."

Mariana released her grip on him and sat straight-backed in the seat. "So we are no different, you and I. Who did you blame for Katherine's murder?"

"Katherine wasn't murdered. She died peacefully in her sleep after a long illness, her devoted husband by her side."

Mariana chewed her lip and seemed to think about his words for a long time before she asked her next question.

"Lyman, have you ever been in love, truly?"

He slumped in the seat, the energy fed by concern for Mariana that had aided in their quick departure from Harrisburg had left him and his fatigue became suddenly overwhelming.

"Once." he admitted.

"What happened?"

"She was wise enough to choose a better man."

23

The steamship stopped for the night at the tiny town of Duncannon, Pennsylvania at a busy ferry crossing. Lyman arranged to have the crates unloaded and taken to the only nearby inn, explaining to the captain that, due to Mariana's illness, they would likely not continue travel the next morning.

His concern for her health did inform his decision. He couldn't deny that. But he'd also grown increasingly worried about the indiscretion they'd both displayed in discussing their private business in close proximity to other travelers. Abandoning them to their own journeys was a relief.

Clarks Ferry Tavern was a charming place—a whitewashed, two-story house with a big brick chimney and a wide front porch. It served as watering hole and rest stop for both stagecoach and steamship travelers. Lyman settled Mariana into their room and descended to the first floor to have a drink and find some supper for the two of them.

"Whiskey if you please, sir," he said to the bearded fellow behind the bar, who complied by handing him a short glass filled to the brim.

"That can't be Lyman Moreau?"

He started at the sound of his name, turning to find a scraggly man in a rumpled suit, smiling at him with a mouth full of rotten teeth. "Barkeep," the man said. "Keep the whiskey flowing."

"Ben." Lyman opened his arms and caught his old friend in a hug. Ben Seymour was one of the few criminals Lyman knew with integrity, the kind of man you could count on to have your back, which made him unique among Lyman's acquaintances and also singularly unsuccessful in his life of crime. Well connected by virtue of his willingness to spread favors and complete dirty jobs for contemptible men, Ben was likeable, even if he didn't smell very good.

"It's good to see you. What are you doing in Middle of Nowhere, Pennsylvania?"

Ben helped himself to a seat next to Lyman and laughed. "This ain't the middle of nowhere. We're on the Mighty Susquehanna. I'm headed south, making a delivery for a friend. What about you?"

"Headed north. By the way, I'm not Moreau."

"And I ain't Seymour, but I bet that's no surprise. You left a hell of a mess back up in New York. You sure you want to go back?"

"What do you mean I left a mess?"

"You brought your medicine show through a little town Sherburne, right? Made a lot of people sick. They ain't too happy with you. Like to string you up if they get hold of you."

Lyman mulled over the accusation, which rang false. He'd not been in the medicine show business for several years, but that didn't mean his name couldn't have gotten dragged into a mess anyway. That was the risk one took when engaged in life as a criminal.

"I never was in Sherburne as far as I can recall. I sold my medicine wagon and got married."

"Really?" Ben's unsightly grin widened. "Congratulations! Where's the missus?"

"Dead, I'm afraid."

"Best kind of wife there is, you ask me. Are you traveling alone then?"

"No. I'm with the widow of a friend. Her husband and I pulled a job in New York and it didn't end well for him."

"Now that I'm sorry for. Friends are harder to come by than wives. What kind of job?"

"We confiscated some antiquities. I've been traveling with them from Philadelphia to Baltimore, but there's some unwanted interest in them now. We're looking for someplace to lay low for a while."

"With the woman?"

"I feel like I owe it to her late husband to try to keep her safe. And she's sick."

"So blame noble." Ben's words dripped in sarcasm that could be heard even through his clipped words and poor grammar.

"What can I say? I'm a romantic at heart, I suppose."

"Ha! So where is this grieving widow? She pretty?"

"Too pretty for the likes of you. And sick, remember? I need to get her to a doctor, but she won't see one, doesn't trust them."

"You know who that sounds like?"

Lyman nodded. He knew exactly who that sounded like—another former associate, the one he swore he'd never see again, the one who'd stolen his love.

"I came across John not too long ago." Ben threw back his whiskey and signaled to the bartender for another. "He was on the run, too. You boys need to take it easy."

"Men like us don't stay still for long." Lyman paused, unsure whether he wanted to ask the next question, but decided if he didn't it would haunt him. "Was Harriet with him?"

Ben took a drink from his whiskey and looked down at the table, allowing his greasy, black hair to fall into his eyes. "She was there, and a little girl."

Lyman nearly choked on his drink. "They have a child?"

"Well you'd think so, but no. Said she's a niece. Brave little thing. Harriet torments her."

Lyman mulled over the information. "Do you know where they were headed?"

"I got a good idea. They was looking for a place to stay where John could find work and the little girl would have a home for a while. I sent 'em on to Hartwick. But Lyman, you sure you want to follow them? They won't be happy to see you."

"I think if there's a chance John can help Mariana, I've got to try. Besides, I may have a card to play."

"Good luck to you. She must be some cherry."

Lyman smiled in spite of himself, his thoughts wandering to Mariana's eyes as she gazed into him. Helpless as she made him feel, it had been a relief to unburden his secrets to another person, one as flawed as he was.

"She is a lovely woman. Thank you." It occurred to Lyman that Ben might be able to help him out with his other problem, too. "Hey, would you be interested in a job, one you could do at the same time as your other one?"

Ben licked the whiskey from his lips. "What can I do for you?"

"Can you place some advertisements for a mummy exhibit in a few local papers along your route?

"You want to give the impression you're moving south."

"That might buy us enough space for us to get to John and let Mariana recover. Maybe I can even unload the mummies and be done with this business."

"I could do that. What do you want it to say?"

Lyman reached into his coat pocket and handed Ben a few clippings from papers in Baltimore and Harrisburg. Ben stuffed them into his own coat pocket without even looking at them.

"Where exactly am I headed?" Lyman asked, sliding money down the bar toward him.

"Not sure I can exactly say, but I can promise you your phantom mummies will mark a good trail all the way down to New Orleans."

"I'll drink to that." Lyman raised his glass and finished the whiskey in a single gulp.

*****

When he made his way upstairs to the room with supper, he found Mariana sitting next to the window, gazing into the dark sky, the oil lamp beside her burning low.

Lyman set the bowl of soup next to the lamp and raised the wick. "You should eat something."

Without turning to look at him, she spoke. "Why bother? I'm dying."

"What are you talking about? You can't know that."

"But I do know it. Horace died and now I'm going to die." She held something in her balled hand, but there was not enough light for Lyman to see. He could hear in her voice that she'd been crying, but she now appeared composed, as if it were possible to become truly placid about death.

"No, darling. You're not going to die." He knelt, brushing aside her wild curls, and stroked her cheek with one hand while gently pushing open her tight grip with the other. Inside her hand was a soft, dark bundle. "What is this?"

"It's falling out." Her stoic façade crumbled and she brought her hands up to cover her face, letting the tangled lock fall to the floor. "I don't know what to do. I know a doctor won't help, but without one, what chance do I have?"

He clasped her shoulders and whispered, "I know a man, a healer. Not a doctor. If anyone can help you it would be him."

"Really?"

He cringed at the hope in her voice, the grasping at a promise on which he could only hope to deliver. "Where is he?"

"A small town up north, back in New York."

"Why are you doing this for me? You don't have to."

"I think you know why."

A fleeting smile lit her face and she wrapped his neck in her arms. "You are a good man, Lyman Moreau."

When she let go, he lifted a spoonful of soup to her lips and said, "I'm not."

24

By stagecoach, the journey could have taken as little as four days, but given the limitations of Mariana's health, Lyman considered two weeks a more reasonable estimate. What he hadn't taken into consideration was the determination of his traveling companion with the promise of a healer at the end of the road.

They arrived in a week.

The stagecoach took them as far as Cooperstown, New York, just to the northeast of the village of Hartwick. There, Lyman negotiated the purchase of a horse and a long, curtained wagon with room enough to comfortably convey the two of them, as well as their deceased cargo. At Mariana's insistence, they started out again right away and arrived only a few hours later in Hartwick.

Otsego Creek divided the village, consisting of only a handful of streets, into east and west. Lyman guided the horse across a bridge barely wide enough for the carriage. At the end of Main Street, Mariana pointed out a large house that identified itself as a hotel.

A buxom, ruddy-cheeked woman greeted them at the door and introduced her husband, a Mr. Field, summoned from the supper table.

"What is it you need?" Mr. Field couldn't have been more different than the hotel proprietors of the cities. He'd clearly cleaned up for his evening meal, the skin of his face rubbed red with the effort, but he wore a dingy shirt and suspenders with the patched trousers of a man who worked hard for his livelihood.

"My wife and I would like a room, if you've one available."

A snort of laughter drifted into the room from the hallway through which Mrs. Field had exited. Mr. Field glanced over his shoulder toward the sound, but made no comment. He sniffed and looked them over, his discerning eye catching on Mariana's flushed face and the tilt of her body pushing into Lyman.

"We have room for a married couple, Mr.—"

"Durand, sir." Lyman extended his right hand. The innkeeper shook it before turning to open a drawer of the roll top desk beside him to retrieve a key.

"Horse and carriage, too?"

"Yes, sir," Lyman responded.

Field sniffed again as he handed Lyman the key. "If you need supper, my missus will fix you plates." Again he looked at Mariana, his eyebrows raised. "What was it you said you was doing in Hartwick?"

"I don't believe I mentioned," Lyman answered, "but we're looking for an old friend who may have settled here recently. Maybe you know him? His name is John. He's got a wife and a little girl."

To Lyman's relief, light sparked behind the man's otherwise dull eyes, his features draining of tension. "I imagine you're talking about the Powells, Mr. Durand. Strange folk, but he's a good sort of fellow. He witches wells. So does his girl, from what I hear."

"Yes, John Powell. That's just the man. He's a healer. Do you know where he is?"

Mariana perked up beside him.

The innkeeper smiled at Mariana, his eyes full of pity. "They're boarding at the Clark residence on North Street. I can point you in the right direction in the morning. For now, you'll need something to eat. Maybe the missus can find you some broth. Looks like it's been a rough journey."

*****

A walkway led to a whitewashed house, modest in front, with an extension in the back that protruded into a large vegetable garden bursting with the last crops of the season.

Lyman helped Mariana from the carriage.

A night of rest, along with the ministrations of Mrs. Fields and her hearty broth, had done much to rejuvenate her. Motivated as she was by the promise that John would be able to help her, she refused Lyman's arm once she'd climbed safely to the ground.

Lyman frowned at her. "Appearing strong will not benefit you here. I don't know if John will agree to help you. He and I didn't part on good terms."

Mariana held her head high despite his words of caution, but it mattered little. The blood-red dress she so fancied now hung off her frame, and the matching turban into which she'd swept her thinning hair washed any hint of healthful color from her face.

"Did you try to steal his wife?" Mariana joked, but her laughter trailed off when Lyman failed to respond. "You didn't, did you?"

"Not exactly, no. But I told you I loved a woman who chose a better man." Lyman paused, offering his assistance once again. "John was the better man."

Mariana frowned as she accepted his help.

Once on the porch, Lyman cleared his throat, smoothed his coat, and rapped on the door. "Let me do the talking," he whispered to Mariana, who made no attempt to counter his advice.

When the door opened, his breath caught and for a moment, he could conjure no words. The woman who stood before him was older than he remembered, the effects of a rough life of toil obvious in the lines of her face. In other ways, however, she remained exactly as he saw her in his dreams.

Not a classic beauty, she was tall and angular, all sharp corners. But her hair, pulled back in a tight bun, was the color of sunshine, and her freckled skin reminiscent of childhood and warmth. Her crystalline eyes bored into him, momentarily sapping any semblance of strength he'd summoned for this moment.

"Harriet," he said at last.

Her eyes narrowed. She raised her gaze to Mariana who stood behind him, propping herself against the porch rail and then back to him before she spoke. "What are you doing here?" She spoke with a strength that suggested he stood on unstable ground.

"I need to see John."

Harriet drew a sharp breath and shook her head, backing away from the door. He followed her inside, Mariana inching behind him.

"Please, Harriet. I need his advice."

"You have no right to ask for anything from him." Her volume escalated. "Or from me, Lyman." She raised a hand and pointed a long, dagger-like finger straight at his chest where a stab of heat began to spread through him.

He held up his hands, palms toward the angry woman. "Just listen." With one hand still stretched in front of him, he reached behind, grabbed Mariana's arm, drawing her forward. He could feel her tremble beneath his touch and regretted his roughness, but she didn't complain. In an uncharacteristic moment, Mariana followed his advice, allowing him the space to explain their presence to the unforgiving Harriet who so clearly despised him.

"My companion is sick. John can help her."

"You would dare to come ask my husband to perform sorcery for a whore?" Harriet's words dripped with disgust, spurring Lyman to an even more deferential tone. She had many reasons to be angry with him, but Harriet was only the gatekeeper. John was a reasonable man. He would not deny help to a dying woman, and he would not resist a beneficial arrangement, no matter what Harriet had to say about it.

"You're not being fair, Harriet. Mrs. Laurent is the recent widow of a friend. She has done nothing to incur your wrath."

"She associates with the likes of you. That's enough. Get out of this house, Lyman. Spread your poison elsewhere."

She'd always been a stubborn woman. He didn't know how to calm her, how to make her listen, but as he considered his next move, another woman pushed through the door behind him.

"Goodness, Harriet, what's going on here? We heard you all the way down the street." The newcomer wore a plain day dress and stood a full head shorter than Harriet, who did regain some composure at the subtle reprimand.

"What's going on is that this beast is not welcome here."

"Now, Harriet," Lyman responded, infusing his speech with a smooth, reassuring calm. Though he couldn't blame Harriet for her anger, his heart still ached to hear it. "Where are your manners?

"Madam," he addressed his new potential ally, "I assume you are the proprietor of this fine boarding house. Allow me to introduce myself."

The woman stared at him, her lips pursed with mistrust, but she nodded for him to continue.

"My name is Dr. Lyman Durand and this is my dear friend and traveling companion Mrs. Mariana Laurent." He bowed as he spoke, sweeping off the top hat he'd failed to remove when entering the house. He indicated Mariana, who stiffened at the attention and coughed lightly into her handkerchief.

"Forgive us for our intrusion into your peaceful home. I am an old associate of your tenants. Upon hearing they were so nearby where I was traveling through, I stopped to pay my respects."

The landlady eyed him. "Sir, it seems odd to me that you should claim you wish to share your respects with this dear lady and yet you obviously cause her such grief."

"It is true, I admit, that Harriet and I did not part on the best of terms when last we met, and for that I can only apologize and appeal to her Christian mercy."

Lyman had always excelled at flattery. Harriet would not be swayed, he knew, but the landlady, a kind soul if ever he'd seen one, would not be immune to his charms. He was confident his excessive manners had begun to win her over.

It was she who informed him that John was working on a nearby farm. Likewise, it was she who invited Lyman to supper that evening that he may have the opportunity to talk with his old friend, a man he had little hope would refer to him so but who would certainly be more agreeable than his wife.

Once again on the porch, Lyman caught his breath. A young girl stood, staring at him with the same crystal gaze he had once loved. She was the very image of Harriet, or she would be one day—gangly and stern, but she possessed something else as well, a curiosity that bordered on hypnotic. Lyman removed his hat once again and tipped his head to the little girl.

25

"That is the woman you love?" Mariana was weak after the interview with Harriet, but not so weak she couldn't express her disbelief; and, perhaps, disgust.

They'd returned to the hotel. Mariana had removed her scarlet dress as Lyman turned his back to her, and now she sat on the bed, poised to fall back against the lumpy mattress.

He sighed. "She was my first love. We were young."

"Your only love, to hear you tell it."

Her words rang true, though he was shocked to hear her say it. Lyman had been romantically involved with many women, most far more beautiful than Harriet, but never had he felt as he did with her. She was his childhood, his safety when his world crumbled around him, when his mother vanished, most likely dead at the hands of a licentious man, and there was nowhere for him to turn.

The strange neighbor girl with straw-colored hair and crystal eyes, the daughter of a mystic and a musician, rescued him. Influenced by the teachings of the mission society that attempted to improve the lives of immigrant guttersnipes, she welcomed him as her personal project.

When her family took him into their home, Harriet pulled him through his grief and tried to help him find his way. She'd been full of a sweet grace then, and possessed of a heart that longed for goodness. He admired her for that and he wished he'd known how to provide it.

Lyman did eventually find his way, but he never forgot the girl who had saved his life. In his heart, he loved her, even after she had grown into a bitter woman, hardened by too much religion.

"She's the first woman I ever met who was worthy of love."

Mariana groaned. "That's lofty talk for a first-rate criminal. She's a hag. And you're well to be rid of her." She dropped back onto the mattress and closed her eyes.

Lyman resisted the urge to offer a retort. In truth Mariana was right, but he couldn't help the way his heart fluttered and his blood pumped, shooting heat through his veins when Harriet was near. She was more adversary than love interest now, of course, but he could not imagine his life without at least the idea of her in it.

He hadn't expected her to be pleased to see him, but her hostility still stung. Perhaps the evening would go better. John was a balm for Harriet's angry soul. Lyman had known it as soon as he introduced them, and he'd comforted himself with the thought as he watched them wed.

Mariana still slept as Lyman dressed for supper, unwilling to wake her. His conversation with John was likely to be a difficult one, and she needed the rest.

*****

The neat little house was well lit and welcoming. The girl opened the door when he knocked, and invited him inside with a broad, gap-toothed smile.

"And who might you be, my dear? We weren't properly introduced."

"I'm Ada." She attempted an awkward curtsy that looked out of place with her simple homespun dress and showed him into the parlor. In an apologetic tone, she added, "Harriet is my aunt."

Lyman nodded and sat on the sofa, inviting her to settle alongside him. Even her mannerisms reminded him of the little girl Harriet he once knew.

"You are a charming young lady, Miss Ada. Are you sure you're related to Harriet?"

The girl blushed and Lyman knew he had her affections, even if he could not sway her guardians. "I think so. Harriet is my father's sister," she explained.

"Ah, you're Albert's girl." Lyman remembered him well— Harriet's younger weasel of a brother. The girl beamed at him, and he chose not to further reveal his thoughts, deciding instead to let her chatter on like little girls do. As she did so, he slipped into thoughts about what he would say to John to convince him to help

Mariana. He didn't have to wait long before the man himself stood in the doorway.

Despite his small stature, John Powell was a well-muscled and formidable man with thick red hair and a full beard. His face was scrubbed and he wore a clean shirt, but he smelled like a man who'd toiled all day—like sweat and grime and wild things.

"John, old friend." Lyman extended his hand, pleased that John took it after a moment's hesitation.

"Why are you here?" The gruff questions served as the only greeting Lyman would get from a man like John Powell. He was not the sort to play the role of a gentleman.

"I heard a rumor about a man," Lyman grinned at Ada still seated on the sofa. "And a little girl that could sniff water from rocks."

John's eyes crinkled at the corners, and he looked at his niece with unmistakable pride. The girl was the way to move him. Lyman wasted no time in bringing her and their situation into the conversation.

He listened as John explained their presence in Hartwick, the result of a late-night escape from a money-making scheme gone poorly.

"Good man." Lyman clapped him on the shoulder, inspiring a subtle flinch. "Always one step ahead of the game, but mind you, only a step. A dangerous way to live." Lyman leaned back against the sofa, his gaze causing his former friend to wither just enough. "You're a family man now, John. You've got your princess here to think of."

Ada sat taller and clasped her uncle's hand. Lyman had captured her attention, and she would do much to further his agenda. He might have set a deal before John right then had they not been interrupted by the entrance of Harriet looking worn, but no less furious at his presence.

"And here at last is the lovely Harriet! Haven't left this old scoundrel yet, then?"

The glare she gave him carried heat, as deadly as any weapon. He shifted his weight.

"Where's your companion, Lyman?" she asked.

He laughed with relief. The notion that, of all the anger she might fling at him, what mattered to her most was the whereabouts of Mariana. His heart leapt to his throat at the thought Harriet might be jealous.

He rolled his eyes at Ada, inviting her to conspire with him. "Too intimidated in the company of such brilliant beauties as you, I should think."

"'A whore is a deep ditch, and a strange woman is a narrow pit.'" Any glimmer of fantasy he might have held that she cared for him vanished with the cold words of Scripture. She loved not him, but to stand in judgment of him.

"Phew! Is that from the Bible, Harriet?" His heart hardened, resisting the crush of her antagonism. "I'll have to remember that one the next time a strange woman comes my way."

Harriet's mouth formed a silent o and she motioned for Ada to come to her side, as if to shield her from his indecency. A moment's regret flashed through his mind. "Mariana is the widow of a dear friend. We were traveling the same direction. I couldn't leave her to traipse across the country alone. What's a gentleman to do?"

"Are you what passes for a gentleman, then?" she scoffed, turning on her heel and exiting the room, pulling her reluctant niece behind her.

Lyman looked to John, who stood at Harriet's exit. "Do you think your wife and I will ever get along?"

"Harriet does not forgive easily. Nor do I."

"I don't think that's true, John. I may not deserve it, but I think you have forgiven me. I can see it in the ease of your mannerisms."

"I only want to know what you're doing here, Ly. I don't want to play games."

"No games, my friend. I'm here because I need your help. More precisely, my companion needs your expertise. I brought her to you because you're good at what you do. And because you need a fresh start. I think we might be able to help each other."

John tugged his beard. "I think we'd better sit down to supper."

26

A charming hostess, the landlady Mrs. Clark laid out a hearty meal of roast pork, boiled onions, and corn bread. She made every effort to keep the conversation moving in a civil fashion—not an easy task in the presence of the sullen Harriet.

Through much of the meal, Harriet kept her head bowed and at least one hand rubbing her temples, looking up only to interject a jab at Lyman.

Mrs. Clark persevered, asking him about his line of work. At this question, Lyman launched into a lengthy speech about patent medicines, the business he had previously shared with John, infusing his explanation with as much respectability as he could muster.

He made no mention of the mummies currently stashed in nondescript crates in the barn of the only hotel in town. Harriet and John knew nothing of his new venture, and he thought it best not to mention it. Though John would likely find them fascinating, Lyman feared Harriet would see them, and him, as a curse. He couldn't risk giving her more reason to turn him away when Mariana so desperately needed John's help.

"You're a snake oil salesman?" the landlady asked, her skepticism displayed by one arched eyebrow.

Perhaps he had underestimated Mrs. Clark. He dabbed the corner of his mouth with his napkin and placed it alongside his cleaned plate. "Oh, now, when you say it like that, it sounds like I'm some sort of fast-talking criminal."

"Are you?"

In the corner of his vision Lyman could see Harriet lean forward, fully engaged, her crystal eyes daring him to somehow win the landlady's trust. If Harriet expected him to fail, he would have to disappoint her. He had a way about him, an inherent impression of trustworthiness. Had Lyman been anything like the man he pretended to be, his relationship with her would have been very different. But he could not bear to dwell on such thoughts.

"Nothing of the sort." He launched into an earnest response about seeking remedies and partnering with talented herbalists to provide healing. Every word true, Lyman failed to discuss the darker side of his business, which had made him and his former partner an angel of death for hire. Harriet, he trusted, would not risk her current home by mentioning it either.

The speech had worked well. When he met her eyes, he could see that while Mrs. Clark still harbored doubts about him, there was a flush in her cheeks and crinkles at the corners of her eyes, the hint of approval, despite the downturn of her mouth.

"But my own talents pale in comparison to John's." Lyman clapped his old partner on the back.

"What do you mean, Dr. Durand?" Mrs. Clark's attention flew to her quiet tenant.

"John here is a gifted herbal healer."

"It's true." It was the little girl Ada, who spoke up and the grimace on her face indicated that her boldness had earned her a kick from her aunt.

"Time for bed, Ada," Harriet scolded. The little girl frowned at her aunt, who marched her from the room, the softening of her hard expression unnoticeable to those who did not know her well. Lyman saw it, the worry he'd introduced into her home, into her family. He could see that Harriet treasured her little family, loved them fiercely, and that she viewed him only as a sickness that must be contained and eliminated before its evil spread.

He regretted causing her grief, but with Harriet's exit from the room, Lyman had won his uninterrupted audience. The little girl, clearly more smitten with him than she was fearful of her aunt, had been and probably would be a useful ally. He would have to keep a close watch on her.

"Well, you are a man of many talents, Mr. Powell." Mrs. Clark stood, and John and Lyman stood with her. "Why don't you gentlemen discuss your business in the parlor? I'll clean up and leave you to it."

Lyman nodded to the landlady he was beginning to like very much. John said a few words to her and followed Lyman into the parlor.

John sat on the sofa, his arms spread wide, the very picture of a comfortable man with a full belly and a willing ear. "That was quite a performance. You nearly had me believing you were some great miracle man."

He lifted his right foot and rested his ankle across his opposite knee. "Why are you really here, Lyman?"

That was the John he remembered—straightforward. It's what made him a good business partner, and also a dangerous one. Lyman would never intentionally leave a partner out to dry, of course, but when someone had to pay for a crime, he'd always rather it be someone else.

Skilled as he was at manipulating a situation, surrounding himself with the nefariously talented, Lyman rarely found himself entirely blamed for illegal activities. When the mobs came out, it was for the mystic they roared rather than his cunning gentleman handler.

Fortunately John had proven slippery as well, and had it not been for the introduction of a pious Harriet into his life, the lucrative partnership might have continued for a long time.

Lyman crossed to the opposite corner of the room to sit in an upholstered armchair, far less comfortable than it looked. "I need your help, John. You're the only man I can come to. I'm in the middle of something—

"When are you ever not in the middle of something?"

"True enough, but this is somewhat delicate."

"Harriet tells me you're traveling with a woman. Will you let a mob try to hang her, too?"

Lyman sucked air through his front teeth. "Look, John, I knew you'd come out of that mess. You always manage to land upright. You've got a better sense about these things than I do."

John slouched in the corner of the sofa, a man weighted by responsibility. "I'm a wanted man because of you."

"Sounds like you've managed to get yourself in trouble, too, without any help from me. Ben Seymour said you got run out of

Norwich a while back. I'm not sure you're far enough away, my friend."

"I know. That'll catch up to us if we stay here too long, but I'm a family man now. I need stability. Farm work's not exactly greatness, but it's honest."

"Then I think you'll be interested in what I have to say. My companion, Mariana, is very ill. That's why she isn't here tonight."

"Who is she?"

Lyman explained to John who Mariana was, who she really was, for he saw no reason to lie to this man who may hold her life in his hands. Lyman tried to make John understand how important she was, a thing he didn't quite understand himself. Harriet was no longer the savior of his childhood. As an adult she had become something different, something colder, but Horace had also helped him out, helped him become the man he was. And though he was now decidedly colder, too, this young widow was alive and in need of protection.

John didn't interrupt him as he spoke, but listened, giving Lyman the impression it was more than the words he heard, but the meaning behind them. John was an interpreter of spirits and often displayed a good understanding of the spirit of living man.

As he spoke, Lyman heard a soft melody, familiar, though he couldn't place it, coming from the kitchen as Mrs. Clark finished cleaning up the supper dishes. Then a bump and a gentle scraping sound reached his ears from around the door frame to the dining room.

"So let me get to my point. I need your help. And you want a stable life for your girl. I was married, briefly, a while back, and came into some land. It's not a lot, but I have a small farm in a little town called New Barker, far south in New York, tucked along the Susquehanna. It would be a wholesome place to raise a little girl."

"You're not going to convince my wife any place is wholesome if you're in it."

"That's one thing she's right about." Lyman laughed. "But as I explained to Harriet, the road calls to me. Once Mariana is well enough, we have some business we need to see to. Then, perhaps with your help, I'm thinking of getting back into the snake oil business. New Barker is too sleepy for me anyway. You could have a good setup there, John."

"And what do you get out of that deal?"

"A caretaker I trust. And a business partner who would be permanently located in a town in which I will not conduct our business. Nothing can go badly for you this time unless you bring it on yourself.

"Come on, John. I need you. I got more charm than I know what to do with, but only you can bottle miracles. You're the goddamned mystic, remember?"

John laughed. "If I could bottle miracles, I wouldn't be a farmhand. I'd be a great prophet off somewhere starting my own religion."

"Well, now, that's an interesting thought. But you're a family man. You've got Ada. How old is she?"

He could see the pride swell in the man's demeanor as he sat up straighter. "Ten or so, I'd say."

"Good age. Old enough for deceit, but still young enough to feign innocence."

"She is innocent. And she's got a real gift. Only reason I'd consider your offer is to give her some sort of stable life."

Lyman stood and crossed to the doorframe, his steps silent on the plush rug. "I know that, John. She deserves a good life and she'll have it. I can see it in her. Potential, she's got. And plenty of curiosity, too." He smirked. "Probably likes to eavesdrop, the little sneak."

He bent and peered around the doorframe to where the little girl sat, her knees pulled up under a shabby nightdress. Her eyes widened at the sight of him, and she looked for a moment as if she might run, but when he reached his hand to her, she took it with resolve.

"Come now princess. Your uncle and I have no secrets from you." He led her to the sofa and directed her to sit next to John, who glared at him as he shifted his weight so Ada could curve into him.

"That's a fine picture. A father and daughter, like it was meant to be." Lyman smiled, and the little girl blushed. He gathered she rarely received such lavish attention.

John's expression remained cold. "I'm not so easy to manipulate."

"Oh don't get all upset with me, John. I'm just saying if I suddenly found myself with a little girl, I'd want to take care of her. Give her some stability."

John hugged his niece into him and kissed her on top of the head, a most fatherly gesture that looked odd coming from a man of such rough appearance. "Time for bed, girlie," he said, and this, too, sounded strange.

Ada pulled away from him and leaned onto the opposite arm of the sofa. Yawning, she responded, "But I want to stay with you, Papa."

He brushed a straw-colored strand of hair from her forehead and whispered more fatherly words, giving her a gentle push that sent her stumbling sleepily from the room.

"Papa, is it?" Lyman asked. John answered with a shrug and a sheepish grin as though he had been caught in a sinful act. "We'll discuss this in the morning." He stood to follow his surrogate daughter out of the room. Looking back over his shoulder, he added, "Thank you, Ly."

The expression of gratitude surprised him and Lyman couldn't help but grin, too, as he watched the unlikely father and daughter pair disappear into the darkness of the rear of the house.

He let himself out the front door, confident the battle had been won.

27

The pounding on the door came early the next morning and Lyman leapt from the chair, startled and embarrassed that though he traveled with a beautiful companion most believed to be his wife, he did not share her bed.

Mariana's sleeping figure didn't move at the sound. Lyman's heart thudded as he fought to recall where they were and wished he was the sort of man who kept a pistol handy. The knocking grew more insistent, spurring Lyman, wearing only his trousers, to throw open the door. John wasted no time in pushing past him into the room.

"I got work to do. Where is she?" he grumbled before kneeling by the bed. Mariana woke and turned tired eyes to the wild newcomer. "This her?"

"Yes," Lyman answered. "Good Lord, who else would it be?"

"I don't concern myself with which women wind up in your bed. I just want to know if this is the sick one."

Mariana raised herself to a sitting position, rubbing sleep from her eyes. Her curls had woven themselves into a gnarled mass, a crazed frame for her narrow face. "Are you the healer? The one who can cure me?"

"I wouldn't suggest that yet, but yes, I'm a healer." He placed his rough hand on her forehead. "I need more light."

Lyman threw open the curtain to let in the growing light of dawn. John looked over Mariana, his face inches from hers, the same way Lyman had observed learned men study the mummies. The similarity made him shiver.

The herbalist touched the skin of Mariana's cheeks and neck. He asked her about the skin on the rest of her body, about lesions, abscesses, and ulcers. She denied the presence of them, which seemed to please him.

He also interrogated her about pain, weakness, blurred vision, and loss of balance. Mariana answered all of his questions thoroughly and with precision. As far as Lyman could tell, John approached her much like the doctor had done, but instead of pushing away from him, Mariana cooperated, even volunteering information he did not demand.

At last John stood and, thanking Mariana for her candor, motioned for Lyman to follow him out of the room.

"Well?" Lyman asked, with enthusiasm that fell flat when he saw John's serious expression.

"I need to ask you a question, Ly. And I need for you to be honest with me."

"Of course. I'm nothing if not honest." His joke was lost on John, which made Lyman appreciate the gravity of the situation.

"What is the nature of your relationship with this woman?"

"Well, if it's honesty you want, I hate to disappoint you, but it's exactly as I described to you. Mariana is the widow of an old business partner, and as such, she's become something of a partner in his stead. She's a woman in need of help."

"And that's all?"

"My goodness, John, are you asking me if I am having amorous congress with a woman in mourning? What would Harriet think?"

"Harriet doesn't think about you or your women at all. Are you having amorous congress with that woman?"

"Not that it's any of your blame business, but no."

"Not even a brush?"

"Not once."

John exhaled then, and Lyman realized just what he had been insinuating.

"Oh, God, it's the French pox." Lyman leaned against the wall, steadying himself. "Will she die?"

"Eventually, yes. I can't cure her, but I won't poison her like the doctors would do with their damned mercury."

Lyman's thoughts flashed back to the small glass bottle of Horace's nightstand. "That's what she was afraid of. Her husband was mad with sickness."

"Mad because of the mercury, most like," John said. "There's no cure I know of, but I may be able to help. It'll take some time, but I can't have you with us for long. Harriet won't stand for it."

"How long do you need?"

"Two or three months maybe. I can have her well enough to travel by then."

"I can't leave her." He was surprised to hear himself say it, but the moment the words escaped his lips, he knew they were true. He never expected to be forgiven for the death of his wife at his own hands, even if he could have justified it as merciful. Abandoning Mariana would not have been merciful, not after he'd decided to care for her, perhaps even love her.

"I won't. Tell Harriet I'll be gone as soon as Mariana is better, and the house and farm are yours. I'll even sign it all over to you if I have to."

John sighed. "Come back to the house with me. Harriet won't listen to me. She won't listen to you either, but whatever it may look like, she loves her little niece. Ada's welfare is important to her, and I know she'd like to see us better settled than we are. You've always been a charming bastard. Maybe you can work some magic."

*****

Lyman followed John into the house to find a new face, a vaguely familiar man with thick muttonchops and a friendly face that turned to an angry mask when he locked eyes with Lyman.

"You." The man pointed a stubby finger at Lyman and fixed him in a fiery glare.

"This is our other boarder," a happy Mrs. Clark chimed, walking into the parlor. "John Powell, this is my husband Jerome Clark, just arrived back home this morning."

The landlady turned to her husband, whose attention stayed fixed. Mrs. Clark paused. "And this is Dr. Lyman Durand, an old friend of the Powells, come to pay them a visit."

Jerome Clark did not greet either of them, meeting them with stony silence.

"Have we met, sir?" Lyman asked, a cold sweat breaking out across his forehead. He didn't know the man, but he didn't doubt they'd run into one another before. He recognized the implication of threat in Mr. Clark's cold eyes and briefly wondered which of his villainous acts might have earned it.

"We haven't met, but I know who you are. You're Michael Chandler, that bastard with the mummies. A good man is dead because of you and your curses."

"I'm afraid you have mistaken me, sir. I don't know a man by that name, and I have certainly never cursed anyone."

"How dare you come into my home and spread your despicable lies! I ought to have you thrown in jail!"

"Now, my good sir," said Lyman, "be reasonable. No matter what you may think of me, I'm only in town to visit my dear friend here. A fine upstanding man. A family man. I had no intention of causing you grief. I will, of course, take my leave."

"This man," Mr. Clark roared in the direction of his wife now, "is a filthy burner and a whoremonger who brings the Devil with him wherever he goes. I will not have him or his so-called friends here a moment longer."

"Surely you're mistaken," his wife responded, but there was no calming her husband, who Lyman now recognized from the Masonic Hall in Philadelphia. He'd been one of the gentlemen at the exhibit when that preacher collapsed, dead amidst the mummies he'd come to preach against. As much as Lyman had benefitted from the tragedy, he'd had nothing to do with it. The doctor who came for the body had determined the death to be apoplexy, not in any way supernatural or somehow caused by either the mummies or the man who displayed them.

"I think there's been a misunderstanding," Lyman began, the injustice of the accusation burning in his chest.

Mr. Clark would not allow him another word. "If you will not leave the premises, I will send for the police." Then he pointed an angry finger at John. "And that goes for you, too."

Lyman bowed to the stunned Mrs. Clark and backed through the front door. His business in Hartwick was completed and this could work to his advantage. With the Powells evicted, Harriet would have little choice but to agree to come to New Barker and Mariana would be treated. Then he would see about selling the mummies.

But when he turned to descend the front steps toward his waiting carriage, he saw that his getaway from Hartwick might not leave him unscathed because there in the street stood a man, tall and lean, with a tarnished metal star pinned to his vest.

"I heard a disturbance. Is everything all right, Mrs. Clark?"

The woman stepped through the doorway, but before she could answer, her husband pushed past her and jogged toward the waiting lawman. "Sheriff," he said, reaching for the man's hand, which he shook with vigor. "How fortuitous that you should be here. This man is an accessory to murder."

The sheriff turned cold eyes toward Lyman, his chiseled features glowing red in the morning light and, for a moment, Lyman considered running. The notion, of course, was ridiculous. He didn't know this sheriff, but he did know that of all the illegal things he had done, killing that preacher had not been one of them. Mr. Clark's word alone would not be enough to keep him imprisoned. John would get Mariana to New Barker. Lyman would catch up with them.

He raised his hands in a sign of surrender. The move seemed to surprise both Clark and the Sheriff, but the latter motioned him forward.

"Mr. Clark says you were involved in a murder. Is this true?"

"If it is, sir, I swear to you I know nothing of it. I have not been detained nor have I been questioned by the police."

"And why then would Mr. Clark suspect you?"

Lyman sighed. "I suspect this is related to the unfortunate passing of a quarrelsome man who attended an exhibit of mine. The timing was sad, but there were plenty of witnesses that could assure you I had nothing to do with the poor man's demise."

"I think you'd better come with me."

Lyman bowed. "Of course, officer. I've nothing to hide."

Clark smirked, but Lyman ignored him, instead glancing back to John who stood on the porch, Harriet's face visible behind him, red with anger. John's expression did not change, but he offered a slight nod to Lyman, an indication, he hoped, that his friend and once again partner would hold up his end of the bargain.

The sheriff shared a quiet word with the Clarks and indicated that Lyman should enter the carriage. He did so with a lighter heart than he'd enjoyed in weeks, knowing Mariana was in good hands.

"Where are you taking me?" he asked the sheriff once they'd begun to move.

"Cooperstown. I'll need to ask you a few questions."

"Why not ask them here?"

"Because the only thing I know about you right now is that you are a showman, probably skilled at manipulating crowds. I'd rather not give you one."

Lyman fell silent in the rhythm of the horse hooves. He considered trying to run, but the sheriff was right about him. He was a skilled manipulator. Flattery and seeming compliance would always get him farther than either strength or stealth.

Two horses pulled the light carriage, covering the distance to Cooperstown quickly. The sheriff directed the horses to a small brick building that looked from the outside like it couldn't have held more than two people.

The inside wasn't any more spacious than expected. A desk sat on one end of the room. Across from that, an empty cell took up half the space. It contained a single thin mattress on the floor behind metal bars. Lyman's head throbbed at the thought of spending time there.

Fortunately it didn't seem to be the sheriff's intention to place him in the cell. Instead, the man threw his hat onto the cluttered desk and indicated a chair.

"Thank you," Lyman said as he sat.

"Now," began the sheriff, "what should I call you? Mr. Clark seems to think your name is Chandler, while Mrs. Clark believes it to be Durand. Mind telling me why that is?"

Lyman smiled. "I would like to know your name, Sheriff, if I may."

The man frowned. "I'm not the one on trial here."

"Nor am I, to the best of my knowledge, but I will gladly answer your questions. My name is Lyman Durand. I am a traveling showman and when Mr. Clark encountered me, I was exhibiting a collection of mummies and Egyptian artifacts using a false name."

"And why would you do that?"

"Names are powerful. Isn't that why you won't tell me yours?"

"It's Morgan. It's always been Morgan. Because I don't have anything to hide, Mr. Durand."

"Well, Sheriff Morgan, I don't either. The collection belongs to a man named Michael Chandler. They were bequeathed to him by his uncle, a respected Egyptologist. The real Mr. Chandler is not a showman, and so he recruited me to exhibit the collection in his stead. It was his idea for me to use his credentials as the nephew and heir, feeling it would be simpler to do so. For me then, Chandler is only a show name."

"And where could I find the real Michael Chandler?"

"If you wished to, I expect you could find him in New York City, but of course, he has nothing to do with this current situation."

"So tell me about the murder."

"There was no murder. A fiery preacher got himself excited over nothing and died, in front of witnesses, without assistance. If you are expecting me to try to convince you, a reasonable man, that there is more to it than that, I can't. I am not superstitious myself."

"Mr. Clark seems to think you had something to do with it. I've known him for a long time. He's a respected citizen of this county. I can't ignore that."

"Mr. Clark may well be all you said, but I only know him to be a superstitious man who thinks that, because I travel with the dead, I somehow hold power over life and death. I have no such power. Surely you must see that. I've come willingly with you. I've answered your questions. I have made no attempt to supernaturally murder you."

A snicker escaped Sheriff Morgan's lips before he managed to subdue it. "All right, then. Let's say I believe you. Where are the mummies?"

"I left them in Hartwick, stored at Mr. Field's Hotel."

"And so if I let you go, Mr. Durand, you will return to Hartwick?"

"Only long enough to gather my exhibit and move on, I assure you. I'm not one to remain where I am unwelcome."

"Okay. Get out of my jail, then. And get out of my county."

"You have my word. It has been a pleasure meeting you, Sheriff Morgan. I sincerely hope we never meet again."

"You and me both, Mr. Durand."

28

The day had grown late during the interrogations and Lyman found himself some supper and a room for the night before hiring a carriage to take him back to Hartwick the next morning. There he discovered Mariana had gone, leaving the mummy crates stacked in Mr. Field's stable, and the anxious innkeeper himself who was relieved to see Lyman's return.

He paid the man for the extra night's lodging and, wasting no time, bought passage toward New Barker.

A tiny village tucked along the Susquehanna River in southern New York, New Barker consisted of less than two dozen homes at its center. Farm houses lay dispersed along the river and to the settlement's west. A central church building served both the spiritual and educational needs of the community and next to that stood a single general store.

Lyman didn't stop to declare himself returned to this community which, despite all odds, had welcomed him largely on the word of a devoted woman whose love he never deserved.

The farmhouse was much as he had left it. Just a couple miles from the village center, its long drive was littered with fall leaves. Lyman had not been back to it since Katherine's death nearly a year before. He'd been planning to sell it, had even entertained an offer, but when it came time to let go, he found it more difficult than he'd imagined and had instead left it all behind him to return to the city.

Now he was glad he had the house to come back to, to offer to Mariana as a resting place and to John and Harriet to whom he would be indebted. What few guessed about Lyman and what he himself was often surprised to realize was that he wanted to be the person others believed he was, before they found out he could not be trusted. Before they discovered how truly self-serving he was, Lyman was generally well received, trusted, even beloved. He'd had to leave New Barker because it was the only place he'd ever been where he had managed to maintain that persona. As long as he didn't live there, he felt New Barker was a place he could call home.

He ascended the wide porch steps and let himself through the front door, secured, he was pleased to find. The rooms were untouched, dusty and close, but tidy. He finished his examination and walked out the back door of the house when he saw a horse and rider coming up the drive, kicking dust and leaf bits into the air.

"Is that Lyman?" The voice was that of Fred Dyer, the man who lived on the neighboring farm with a wife and two pretty young daughters. He dismounted and shook Lyman's hand. "Come back to sell me the farm?"

"No, sir," Lyman responded. "But I have a tenant moving in soon. He'll be taking care of the place—a good man, an old friend."

"Well, it'll be nice to have a neighbor again. Need help opening the place back up? I can send Gracie and Emily if you'd like."

"I'd appreciate the help." Lyman in fact was overwhelmed by the offer and a short time later, the man's two daughters arrived. Emily, the younger of the two, came ready to work and, blushing, passed by Lyman with barely a nod before she hurried to the kitchen to begin scrubbing.

Grace, the elder sister, took her time getting started, flashing a smile at Lyman, who noticed her dimpled cheeks and the alluring way she swished her hips as she entered the house.

"Welcome back, Mr. Big City. How was New York?" Her easy manners startled him. He'd not known the girl well when he'd lived near her as a married man, nor had he noticed her creamy skin and mischievous smile. When he left, she had been just another farmer's daughter, but the salacious gleam in her wide set eyes indicated that the year had been transformative.

"New York was fine," he stammered. Her wide smile encouraged him to continue. "I've been all over, actually. Philadelphia, Baltimore, Harrisburg."

"Oh, how I would love to travel like that!" She unfastened her long gray coat, draping it over the back of the sofa and revealing a crisp white blouse, the top several buttons undone. "You must tell me all about it."

The clink of pots and pans carried from the kitchen and Lyman turned toward the sound. "Perhaps Emily would like to hear, too."

Grace stepped toward him and grabbed his hand in hers. "I'm sure she would. We've all been worried about you since poor Katherine passed on."

Lyman wondered if that were true, if the people of New Barker had really been concerned about him, if he'd sold his invented grief so convincingly. He tried to summon a tear now, but failed.

He cleared his throat. "I miss her every day."

"Of course you do." Grace moved closer still, and her free hand reached out for his so that they might have been dancing. She smelled of soap and a hint of something else his brain refused to recognize until she tipped back her head, her eyelids fluttering closed. The tantalizing scent of lavender drifted from her, calling to his mind the sharp image of Mariana's curls tumbling from her coiffure, sliding through his fingers.

He took a step back. "Do you want to see what I did in New York?"

Grace's eyes flew open, the corners of her mouth dipping down as she dropped his hands. To her credit, she recovered her warm smile quickly. "I would love to."

Lyman led her outside to a ramshackle shed in back of the house. He'd placed the crates just inside the door, and with Grace looking on, her curiosity clearly tickled, he pried open the first to reveal the ancient, gaping mouth of the mummy Horos.

The young woman screamed and backed away. Tripping on her skirt, she would have fallen had Lyman not reached out to catch her.

"What is that thing?" she asked, wrenching her wrist from his grasp.

"It's a mummy. My uncle was an Egyptologist. He passed on recently and left me some of his findings."

"It's a dead person," she mumbled, her voice weak and trembling. "A real dead person." She sat on the grass, dropping her face into her hands.

Lyman sat beside her. "Yes, long dead. Three thousand years, even. And I promise he means no harm to you."

Grace looked up, wary, but smiling. "No, I suppose he doesn't."

"Would you like another look?" Lyman asked. "That one is the most ghastly. There are five others. All quite harmless, I promise."

"Are you sure about that?"

"Well, they've been my traveling companions for months now and no tragedy has yet befallen me." Lyman stood, brushed the dust from his trousers, and offered a hand to Grace. But as she accepted it, he wondered if his statement were true. While no harm had struck his person since he'd taken possession of the mummies, fortune had not exactly smiled on him either. Mariana had nearly died, one man actually did, and Lyman had been pursued from city to city through three states.

Grace cocked her head to one side. "I'm glad you're back, Mr. Moreau. But I think I'll leave the mummies to you. There's work to be done, and I imagine Emily will be wondering where I went."

She turned on her heel and walked back to the house, her hips noticeably less swishy than before. Lyman sighed and replaced the lid of the crate. If he'd been cursed, he thought, it wasn't the mummies that had done it.

*****

With the sisters' help, the house was aired and scrubbed by nightfall. Emily agreed to come cook a welcome meal for Lyman and his new tenants should he wish. Grace tossed him a lingering look as she left.

It was another day before the road-weary crew arrived from Hartwick, tattered and exhausted. Grace had returned, dressed to seduce, with a new attitude about the mummies and Tarot cards in hand. Lyman was grateful to hear the rattle of the wagon near.

"How do you like my country estate?" Lyman gushed at them as Harriet and her niece tumbled out of the carriage. He pushed past them and extended a hand to Mariana who smiled at him, flushed and weepy, but in most ways unchanged from when he last saw her. He showed her to the porch steps where she asked to sit for a bit before continuing into the house.

Lyman kissed her cheek, blessedly cool on his lips, and returned to John, who busied himself with the horses while Harriet and the little girl continued into the house.

When Lyman entered the house it was to find that Harriet and Ada had discovered Grace, dolled up, her hair inexplicably tussled. Ada spoke to her with wide, innocent eyes. Grace beamed at the girl and snarled at the aunt, whose wide mouth had nearly disappeared in a stern line.

"Gracie," he said. "I think it's time for you to go lest your fortunes take a turn. Out the back door would be best."

Her eyes filled with pain and she turned to stalk out the door. He'd hurt her, he knew, but he'd not led her on and he was grateful for her discretion. Lyman felt a twinge of regret at his refusal of something so graciously offered. He'd go to her house soon with the excuse of asking Emily to come cook for all of them and would take the opportunity to tell her of Mariana and smooth the girl's ruffled feathers.

"We're leaving." Harriet's glare burned a hole in his heart.

"Did I offend you somehow?" he asked, mocking her with his deference.

John walked through the doorway behind her, carrying a small trunk. "Be reasonable, Harriet. You know how Lyman is."

"Yes," Lyman piped. "You know how I am. Just go pray for me or something."

"And what about your Mariana?" Harriet's anger on behalf of Mariana startled him, but the vitriol she expressed hit him like a dagger, and he found his own temper flaring.

"What about her? She's a friend. I owe her nothing but kindness and, thanks to John, I've been able to give her that." He shrugged. "She knows better than some what kind of man I am."

Harriet opened her mouth to speak, but the bang of the front door stalled her. Mariana stepped into the room, a fragile china doll. Lyman rushed to her, offering his support, which she accepted with a weak smile.

"My dear, I told you I'd come back for you. I'm sorry I made you wait." He flicked his eyes in Harriet's direction. "I was being scolded for my sins. Both real and imagined."

At John's suggestion, Harriet took her niece up the back staircase to find a quiet bedroom. Lyman waited several minutes and escorted Mariana back through the sitting room and up the main stairs to a hallway of bedrooms. He led her through the first door, to the room he'd shared with his deceased wife, and the featherbed he'd not slept in since his return to New Barker.

"Your home is beautiful, Lyman," she gasped, gazing at the rich furniture he'd not chosen. A tall, intricately carved wardrobe stood against the wall between two wide windows, beyond which the sky grew darker with ominous gray clouds. "Why'd you leave?"

"Ghosts."

Her eyes grew wide at the suggestion and she sat on the edge of the high bed. "Please don't joke about such things."

He sat beside her and clasped her hand. "Only being melodramatic, my dear. It's memories I meant—the shadow of a man I thought I might be and, in the end, never could become."

"You came back anyway. Because I needed a place to rest."

He patted her knee and stood. "I did. I suppose you think that makes me a good man?"

"No, Lyman Moreau." She shook her head. "That's only a symptom of your goodness."

He couldn't speak for a moment, so touched was he by her words. She held his gaze with her dark eyes that had become like large, endless pools in her thinning face. There was much he wished to say. Thanking her for her kindness seemed insufficient for the moment, but to tell her he loved her, a thought that had been haunting him at the edges of his mind for longer than he fully knew, seemed even more impossible.

He turned away from her. "How are you, Mariana? Has John been good to you?"

She sighed before answering, as if sensing his unspoken words drifting through the air. "He made me swallow all manner of terrible things and smothered me with foul smelling poultices. But, yes. He's been kind. That's more than I can say for that horrible woman. I can't imagine why you ever loved her. Out of spite, I told her we were getting married. I hope you don't mind." Mariana's tone suggested that whether or not he minded made no difference to her, but what disturbed him was that he didn't.

What had he seen in Harriet? He might ask himself the same question, except that she hadn't been the same person. Or perhaps she was in part, but her desire for goodness outweighed her bitterness then. In many ways, she was much like Mariana— determined, manipulative, and cold when motivated by fear, but warm and lovely when she felt safe. He assumed Harriet had not felt safe in a long time, and for that he was truly sorry.

*****

"How's your lady friend?" John sat in the kitchen, a cup of coffee and his flat cap on the table in front of him when Lyman returned from settling Mariana.

Lyman crossed to the wooden hutch beside the stove and collected a plate of small tea cakes Grace brought earlier. He set them on the table and sat in the straight back chair across from his friend. "Resting. But I should be asking you."

John shrugged, waving off Lyman's offer of a cake. "She survived the journey, and in the presence of my wife who was not at her most gracious."

"So I heard." Lyman bit into the oily cake. It was covered in a thick icing so sweet he nearly gagged before setting it back down on the table, thankful that it was Grace's sister Emily who would be returning to prepare their supper.

"She can't continue to travel. Not until she's had time to heal. A month or two at least."

"Can Harriet tolerate our presence for so long?"

"She's coming around to the idea of this place, and I think seeing it, she'll have strong motivation for handling our current situation. Having a place to call home for a while will be good for her, for all of us. Just stay out of her way as much as you can. And stay away from Ada."

The command hit Lyman like a slap. He knew he didn't yet deserve John's trust, but the implication that he might consider Lyman a threat to a child was more than he could tolerate. Quietly, he asked, "Is that a warning from Harriet, or from you?"

John looked at the floor and rubbed the back of his neck. "Consider it an edict from both of us."

"Very well then, my friend." Lyman brought his hands together in a clap. "I shall remain as scarce and unobtrusive as I can manage until you tell me Mariana is well enough to travel."

John's eyes shifted over Lyman's left shoulder. He followed the gaze and found Ada standing in the doorway, as thin and wispy as a wraith, like she might be the sick one in the house. His heart swelled at the sight of her, an embodiment of innocence that had long ago departed from his life. With a glance at John, he decided no one could be angry with him for sharing a supervised conversation with the young one.

"My goodness, don't you feed her?" Lyman rose from the table and offered the plate of cakes to the girl, who eagerly took one. "I expect Harriet's in charge of that, is she? Probably living on crusts of stale bread, by the looks of her, the poor skinny child."

Lyman smiled his approval at her as she stuffed the cake into her mouth, tickled by a momentary pang of guilt over criticizing Harriet's care.

"A change of scenery is in order I believe, John. It'll never do to have a perfect lady skulking around a kitchen table. We'll have a proper conversation in a proper sort of room."

He led them to the parlor where Ada grabbed another cake the moment he set down the plate. The pastries, as revolting as they were, brought a light to her eyes. There was something about her, a haunting presence in her sunken, underfed features. Perhaps, Lyman thought, he recognized something of himself in her, the child no one quite knew how to love, who would have to find her own way beyond the suffocating possession of her aunt, seemingly determined to strike the ethereal from her.

"Does your aunt rage at you, darling? She excels at that." The question and comment slipped from his lips before he could pull them back, and he looked anxiously at John who only shook his head. "Well, no matter. I'm sure Uncle John here will protect you from her madness." The child's shoulders slumped at his words, the sight of her slender bones stabbing him with regret.

"You'll all find a wonderful home here in New Barker," he continued. "And maybe there's a project you could help me with. I hear you have a supernatural gift just like your uncle."

"That's enough," John grumbled.

"Of course. I don't want to interfere with young Ada's rearing."

The girl looked at her uncle and then at her toes, a tangle of pale hair falling over her face. For the time being, Lyman could do nothing for her. That was the price he would pay to save Mariana. For the woman he loved he would, for now, sacrifice this child, this younger, less wounded Harriet.

29

The next two months Lyman spent in introducing John to the community of New Barker. He was a quick study of people and soon forged relationships with many of those who might help him get going on the farm in the spring. John would be suited for this life in a way Lyman never could be.

John surveyed the fields which had lain fallow the past planting season and drew up plans for them. Lyman watched with great interest as John designed the framework, very carefully, for a side business as a water dowser, with no mention of treasure. He also did not speak of his talents for healing but still often gathered various plants he deemed useful.

Lyman helped him to set up a workspace for handling and storing them in the shed behind the house, where the mummies lay undisturbed in their crates, probably relieved to have been left alone for a time. John insisted on careful labels, which Lyman applied with a steady hand, though his friend knew every plant intimately by sight at least as well as he knew himself.

"For Ada," John explained. "She's bright and likes to learn, but some of these are very poisonous if used incorrectly."

Lyman had heard the warning before, and had even picked up on useful knowledge from the talented herbalist. When John told Lyman one clear January day that Mariana was at last strong enough to travel, he reached into the box labeled "Henbane" and slipped a small amount of the dried, poisonous leaves into his pocket.

That night, he asked Emily to prepare a nice meal and he paid her well knowing she would not be asked to come and serve the family once he and Mariana were gone, especially since he asked her to place the crushed henbane into Harriet's wineglass.

He watched with nervous anticipation as Harriet's speech slurred and her thoughts wandered until she slumped in her chair, her eyes closed, a thin line of spittle dangling from the corner of her wide mouth.

"What did you give her?" John asked, more weary than angry, which greatly amused Lyman.

"There may have been a touch of henbane in her wine."

"You could kill her with henbane!" John's face became a bright shade of purple and he bent toward his wife, checking for signs of life.

"Could we?" Mariana asked with a healthy giggle that filled Lyman's heart with joy, though even he cringed at the unseemly comment. John looked at Mariana, his complexion darkening to a furious red and for a moment, he looked as if he might strike her. Before Lyman could decide to intervene, Ada cracked a smile, letting loose a quiet giggle that caused her uncle to turn his attention to her instead, his fury replaced by deep lines of sorrow.

"Obviously we can't." Lyman put on his most responsible voice to break the spell. "It was only a small taste. To create an opportunity."

"How much did you give her?" John asked as he lifted the lids of Harriet's eyes, one at a time.

Lyman waved his hand in front of his face. "No more than five drops of a tincture I made with some of your stores. Nothing could kill that woman. She'll be fine."

John looked up at him, the corners of his mouth turned downward, and shook his head, dangerously calm. "She'll have terrible dreams. She won't wake very happy."

"Does she ever?" came the small voice, directed at the floor. Lyman smiled toward the top of the little girl's head and felt sure he'd done the right thing. There would be a price to pay for the evening's adventure, but the benefit to Ada was an ample reward.

*****

Twenty minutes later, John, with Lyman's help, had tucked Harriet safely into bed.

"So," Mariana began. "What's the great mystery? What did you plan for us tonight?"

"I thought we'd celebrate your returning health by showing John and Ada your special skill. I've an acquaintance, Mrs. Woodruff, an old friend of my late wife. She'd very much like to see your gift. And," he turned to John, "she'd like to meet you as well. You and Ada."

"Ada will not be coming." John's stern proclamation insisted there was no room for negotiation, but Lyman didn't hesitate.

"Harriet will suffocate her with her stern form of motherhood. You've admitted it yourself. Let her have some fresh air, John. Let her come and see what possibilities and wonders the world holds."

John had already begun to shake his head, emphatic, but to Lyman's delight, the little girl spoke up. "I want to come with you, Papa.

With a grin, Lyman jumped on her use of the endearing moniker. "Yes, Papa, let her come."

*****

Mariana hadn't scried in months, largely at Lyman's insistence. The images she saw always frightened her so, that for her health alone he would have been glad to have her stop. Harriet, too, would not likely have taken kindly to sharing space with any hint of the occult. Her religious ferocity, he feared, would have torn her from New Barker, and with her Mariana's best chance for recovery.

But Mariana was strong now, like when Lyman had first met her, many months ago in the home she shared with her husband. This, he decided, was his way to launch her back among the living, and perhaps to bring another with her as well.

Mrs. Woodruff waited on her substantial front porch, ready to welcome them. She was plump and jolly, a bejeweled and privileged middle-aged wife with too much time on her hands and more charm than she had reason to use in her small world.

She lavished greetings on them and particularly fawned over Mariana, the beautiful young woman at the receiving end of Lyman's affections. Her sitting room had been prepared for the evening—the plush sofa set against the walls, a round table with three chairs in the center of the room.

Mariana placed her orb, cold and dark from underuse, on its stand in the middle of the table and sat. Mrs. Woodruff took the seat beside her.

"I wasn't expecting so many of you," the kindly woman explained apologetically. "We will bring over more chairs."

"No need," Lyman said. "Ada can take this one. John and I are unnecessary. We'll sit against the wall."

The girl moved forward to claim the chair, but her uncle gripped her hand and she stepped back again. Lyman shrugged and took the seat for himself as the other two shrunk back to one of the displaced sofas.

Mariana lit a candle and prepared to interpret whatever the glass had to tell her. As she did so, Mrs. Woodruff prattled on about the whirlwind courtship and short-lived marriage between her friend Katherine and a handsome young snake oil salesman. Where others might have found scandal, Leah Woodruff saw only romance, and it was her outspoken faith in Lyman that allowed him to slither into the good graces of New Barker's citizenry even after Katherine's death and his inheritance of her estate.

Mariana reacted to none of this, if she heard it at all, intent as she was on the shapes materializing and fading within the glass. The room was dim, the only light coming from low-burning gas sconces and the single flame dancing above the candle. The shadows it cast flitted across Mariana's face, bathing her delicate features in a grotesque mist.

Though he understood this was the old Mariana, the one full of life and energy, Lyman disliked seeing her draw into herself again in this way, to somehow grow smaller as whatever phantoms whispered to her grew larger. He took in the sight of her, his breath slowing, mimicking hers, until she blinked rapidly and sat back in her chair. Whatever mystical effect he'd witnessed was all at once gone.

"What can I do for you this evening, Mrs. Woodruff?" Mariana's calm unnerved him, but he didn't doubt that she had taken command of the conversation.

Mrs. Woodruff laughed and flung her hands toward the orb. "Tell me about my future."

Mariana pursed her lips and, spreading her arms out wide, leaned forward with her face close enough to the orb her nose might have been touching the glass. Then in a low, hollow tone the likes of which Lyman had never heard, she began explaining to Mrs. Woodruff the very details of her life that Lyman had recited earlier.

Mrs. Woodruff's face fell in disappointment and the woman glanced at Lyman, her eyebrow arching in disbelief. Mariana must have caught the skeptical expression because she changed tactics, sitting upright again in her chair.

"If you'll give me a direction you wish to pursue, that's how my gift usually works best."

"Oh, well," Mrs. Woodruff stuttered. "It's fine. You mentioned my son George—"

"He got married recently." It wasn't Mariana who spoke. Instead, Ada had risen from the seat beside her uncle and now approached the woman. "The marriage is a happy one, but not entirely maybe."

Mariana exhaled audibly, but Lyman's eyes were locked on the strange little girl now seeming to float across the room with unfocused eyes. If such a thing could be possible, he would have believed her possessed of a spirit, one who knew how to play at something a child so young should have known nothing about.

"I'll thank you not to interrupt," snapped Mariana.

Ada shrunk at the reprimand and returned to her seat beside John, but seconds later she was on her feet again, approaching the table as if she no longer had control of her own actions.

Before Mariana could admonish the girl, Lyman spoke. "Why don't we let young Ada have a go? Sometimes the spirits are more willing to speak to the innocent, yes?"

Mariana crossed her arms and glared at the girl, who seemed not to notice.

Ada asked, "Are you hiding something, Mrs. Woodruff?"

To Lyman's surprise, Mrs. Woodruff laughed. She withdrew from the pocket in her skirt a ring set with a large gem that sparkled in the flickering light. The ring, she explained, had belonged to her grandmother, and when her son had asked to give it to his bride, a woman Mrs. Woodruff did not like, she'd given him a fake. The guilt she felt had been a festering wound, poisoning her relationship with her son and his bride. Her relief at having been discovered was palpable.

"You are a wonder, Ada." Mrs. Woodruff patted the girl's shoulder as her uncle looked on, the trace of a smile across his face. Ada had once again become withdrawn and spoke little as the foursome said goodnight and lit a pair of lanterns to light their way through the cold night.

Sullen, Mariana accepted the arm Lyman offered in silence. He let her wallow in her thoughts as they plodded to the edge of town. John, too, had little to say. He'd doused his lamp and now carried his niece, who drifted to sleep in his arms.

Lyman looked over his shoulder to the sweet scene and whispered to Mariana, "She's something, isn't she?"

"I suppose," came her curt response. Then she added, "I did see things in the orb, you know."

Lyman gave her arm a gentle squeeze. "I know you did."

"I just didn't see anything about that woman. I only saw Quinn. Always Quinn."

"He can't hurt you here, Mariana."

They approached the farmhouse, a gas porch light still aglow, and she stopped, letting John walk ahead of them. "But we aren't staying here, are we?"

"No," he admitted, setting the lantern on the ground and grasping both her hands in his. "We'll leave in the morning. And if Martin Quinn is still out there, we'll deal with him."

She stared ahead into the night toward the house where John and Ada had already disappeared. "I envy that little girl, to be loved as she is."

Lyman gathered Mariana in his arms and held her close. Despite her thick wrap, she shivered. He felt her warmth escape with each puff of her breath. He placed a finger beneath her chin and, even in the dark, imagined he could see her soulful eyes as he lifted her lips to his and whispered, "You are loved."

30

They left the next morning, a mild late February day in which the snow dripped off low hanging branches and birdsong welcomed a false spring. Mariana sheltered in the carriage with the mummies and might have been one of them as silent as she remained for the journey.

Their destination they had determined to be Utica, New York, to the northeast on what locals referred to as the long level on the Erie Canal. The canal itself would soon be open for the season, once the thaw could be trusted. They intended to board a packet ship headed west, sure that their mummies would create a sensation among the ruffians and travelers of the canal.

Utica was a delight to Lyman from the moment he arrived. A thriving, booming community, it reminded him of a nest of snakes wriggling around one another, not sure where the center should be or which way any of them might be trying to go. It was a small city in which a man could get lost or could make a big impact, whichever he had the inclination to do. All manner of business had risen up to welcome the tide of canal travelers, and one got the sense that anything might be possible in such a place.

"Someday I will come back here," Lyman said as Mariana linked her arm through his. Together they strolled through the shop-lined streets.

"There." He stopped short, pointing to a corner building with stairs leading below the street level to a nondescript glass door. "That's the perfect place for a little shop, don't you think?"

"Lyman Moreau, a shopkeeper?" Mariana giggled beside him and gave his arm a gentle squeeze.

Perhaps, he thought, she really was well. Her cheeks glowed with the rosy complexion of health in the chilly air, so different than the veil of death she'd worn when she first arrived in New Barker.

Lyman said a silent word of thanks to the air, hoping John would somehow feel it.

"And why not?" he replied. "I could see myself settling down in a place like this, a place where everyone seems to be going somewhere. Let my customers come to me for once."

"We could do it now, you know." Mariana stopped walking and turned to him, all seriousness. "We could open a permanent Egyptian display, right here."

Lyman almost said yes. He could envision it, a future here in this place with this woman by his side, but then he remembered John's warning. He could not build a life with Mariana, not the kind she was asking for or would be contented with. He shook his head. "It would be unwise to stop moving."

"Maybe." She frowned. "You're right, of course. But it would be nice, wouldn't it?"

"It would. I could see a shop filled with wonderful, mysterious things, like your glass orb and talismans and elixirs that would attract a certain type of crowd, the kind that might also travel the canal and wish to fade into the swirl of a busy port town."

"And would you sell your mummies?" Mariana asked, a playful smirk on her lips.

Lyman teased her by enumerating the most distasteful practices to which the mummified ancients had been subjected in recent years. "I would. I'd sell their wrapping to the paper mills, chop off their fingers and toes as charms for good luck, and grind up the rest of them into powdered mummy for the customer who will only be happy with the promise of everlasting life."

"You should hope our companions don't hear your plans," she replied lightly. "I think they're attached to their toes."

Lyman chuckled. "And they told you this?"

She grew thoughtful for a moment, her eyes gaining a faraway stare. "They tell me a lot of things. On the road, we've spent quite a lot of time together."

Lyman didn't know what to say. In a way he wanted to believe her that the mummies spoke to her, but of course he knew they could not. The only speaking they could do was through the symbols on their scrolls, and no one could interpret those, no one living. But then, he wondered sometimes how Mariana saw details in her orb. He wondered if perhaps she did commune with the dead, with Horace her deceased husband, and with Horos, the ancient, screaming figure who haunted his dreams.

*****

They had been to the docks every day since their arrival. The state of New York would declare the opening of the canal any day. Lyman and his mummies, nearly as whole in death as they had been in life, would find an audience among the travelers. Perhaps he would find a buyer for the mummies themselves, someone who would respect them as the remains of great men. Lyman would wash his hands of them. Then he could think about the future and what it might hold for him, and for Mariana.

Finally, in mid April, water was allowed to rush into the canal. Once known as Clinton's Ditch, after former New York governor Dewitt Clinton, the Erie Canal had become the life force that drove an unbelievable growth in trade throughout the state and established New York City as the major port city of the Eastern United States.

Three hundred sixty-three miles of waterway, much of it manmade, crossed the state from Albany to Buffalo, connecting the Hudson River to Lake Erie. Packet ships changed elevation by five hundred and seventy feet from one end to the other through a series of locks, transporting goods and people and mummies.

Lyman helped Mariana descend into the belly of the long packet ship that would haul them to the west. What they would do when they reached the end of the journey they could only imagine, but among the hardened and superstitious canawlers, Lyman felt at home. When the boat captain asked him to identify his cargo, Lyman did not hesitate to reply.

"Three-thousand year-old dead men, sir."

The captain was a man named Ainsworth whose tobacco-stained beard and leathered skin struck Lyman as belonging to the captain of a large ocean vessel rather than that of a canal packet ship. That was perhaps why Lyman liked him so immediately. As a man who frequently dressed as he wished to be perceived rather than as a descriptor of who he actually was, he felt a kinship with this man.

Captain Ainsworth spit a stream of dark juice and wiped his mouth with the back of a dirty hand. "Lots of dead men have made their ways down these waters. Some of 'em start that way and plenty of 'em come by it on the journey. I don't expect age of the body matters so much."

Lyman watched as the crew loaded his crates into the midsection of the boat with the rest of the cargo and then watched as a flood of travelers filed into the main passenger room where the men bunked and where all gathered around crowded tables for greasy meals, too much drink, and a healthy dose of gambling.

Surveying the waterfront, Lyman felt as if the entire city of Utica had been waiting for the arrival of spring and the opening of the canal. Boat captains and crews rushed through preparations, harnessed mules and horses, and urged an impossible number of passengers into the flattop cabins.

Though most of the boats had been named for the companies that ran them, Captain Ainsworth called his *The Mermaid*, and he seemed to take great pleasure in yelling to the passengers, especially the handful of women, "Everyone pile into *The Mermaid*!"

Lyman fell into line to enter the cramped cabin, counting twenty-two passengers in a space that may have comfortably accommodated ten. A crewman followed him in and pulled the gangway from the bank, storing it on top of the cabin, leaving just enough room for a man to walk beside it on the boat roof.

Another member of the crew, barely more than a boy, then slid off the roof and leapt onto the tow path, next to the two large horses that would pull the boat. Neither beast flinched as the boy landed beside them with a soft thud. He grabbed hold of the mane of one and pulled himself up to its back.

As a whistle blew, the boy gave the horses swift kicks in the side. With a flurry of excitement and a great deal of calling and angry exchanges with boats that had rather gone first, *The Mermaid* shoved off to begin her voyage.

The passengers, most of whom had stood at the small windows and lurched backward with the first pull on the tow rope, now milled about, many finding places to sit at the tables. A few of the men bellied up to the bar and were served, even though morning was still fresh.

All manner of characters were aboard—a handful of ladies, four besides Mariana, one old and fat and traveling with her equally fat and uglier daughter; two young married women with three small children between them and, Lyman assumed though he could not determine who they were, husbands lurking nearby, probably at the bar already into their glasses of liquor swirled with foul canal water.

There was no question the packet ship was not a comfortable way to travel, and more than once Lyman wished he had simply attempted to move by carriage, but the snows of the New York winter had been relentless and large mounds still edged the roads, releasing a slow but steady trickle of water that made for muddy conditions difficult to maneuver over long distances.

However, there were advantages to canal travel, and Lyman was pleased to see that Mariana in particular seemed to soak up the life around her, growing stronger in the close company of the other women, cloistered as they were by night in a small cabin in the bow of the boat. They were fast friends by necessity, as there was barely room for a hat box, let alone five grown women and three youngsters.

At night the men attempted to sleep on boards that folded down from the sides of the main boat cabin, supported by chains and covered with mattresses too thin for their task. It wasn't the discomfort that got to Lyman so much as the snoring and wriggling. The odors and sounds of too many bodies in too little space reminded Lyman of his childhood in the slums.

Fortunate enough to be on a lower platform bunk, Lyman rolled from his bed as quietly as he could, slipping into his boots and coat and pushing past his snoring roommates to the doorway where he grabbed hold of the ladder leading to the roof to enjoy great breaths of sweeter air.

Under the stars and a bright moon, Lyman surveyed the gentle waters of the canal. As he did so, a low mumble of voices came from the rear of the boat—that of a man and a woman—and he moved toward them.

He began to make out words as he drew closer, recognizing a voice he knew well. "You couldn't sleep, either?" he asked Mariana when he got to the back edge of the boat. She stood next to Captain Ainsworth who worked the tiller. Mariana gazed at the surface of the water, a smooth reflection of moonlight interrupted only by the few ripples as the slow moving boat cut through it.

She looked back over her shoulder when he spoke. To his surprise, she didn't appear especially glad to see him. Her chin quivered in the cold of the night and though she wrapped herself in a shawl, Lyman had the urge to scold her for taking her health so lightly after all he had done to care for her.

Mariana turned back toward the water and it was the captain who answered. "Mrs. Chandler was keepin me comp'ny, reading the water for me. You didn't tell me you had such a talented wife, Mr. Chandler."

The captain's utter lack of consideration at how the situation may appear sent a shockwave through Lyman, and he fought the urge to punch the man in his bearded chin. "She will catch a chill if she's not careful."

"Nah," answered the captain. "She's a sturdy one. I can tell. And canal air is good for the soul. Even cold canal air. I been working these waters for ten years and never been healthier."

"That may be, but sir, my wife has been ill."

"And I'm well now." Mariana joined the conversation after all, displaying her utter lack of concern for all he had sacrificed to give her. Anger prickled at him, anger with her for taking so lightly her renewed health and a chance at life, but he could not have this argument with her in front of the captain. They had too many secrets between them and in public arguments, truths had the tendency to sneak out. For now, he would let her live in her fantasy where she was cured and on a pleasure cruise through the wilds of New York.

He sighed, defeated. "What does the water have to tell you, then, my dear?"

She turned her face to look at him, moonlight shining off her cheek.

The Captain spoke before her. "She told me she sees extra profits in this run for me and my crew. I'll take a fortune like that."

"I see danger, too." She nodded toward Lyman, who lowered his body, settling to sit on the edge of the cabin roof, his feet dangling. "Danger for us."

"Well, I don't think you need to worry about that, Mrs. Chandler. The canal ain't a dangerous place. A little rough at some of the locks, for sure, but *The Mermaid* and crew will take good care of you."

Mariana shook her head. "I don't know where it'll come from. Maybe not the canal at all. Maybe at the end of our journey, but death is in our future."

Ainsworth laughed, a jolly guffaw straight from his belly as if he might break into a robust sea chantey. "You keep comp'ny with three-thousand-year-old dead men and you're surprised to see death in the water? Everyone dies Mrs. Chandler. They ain't no getting around that."

"Darling," Lyman spoke, his tone serious and low, his words meant only for Mariana though he was sure the captain felt free to listen. "I think you should go inside and get some rest."

Mariana turned back to the water, ignoring his advice, but after a full minute of silence as the captain's laughter faded, she pulled her shawl tightly around herself and walked back toward the cabin entrance, leaving the two men alone in the silent night.

Lyman lost himself in thought. He didn't know whether Mariana's scrying revealed truth or whether it was entirely for show, but he couldn't shake a growing sense of unease.

"Oh, she'll be fine, Mr. Chandler." The captain's voice was still jolly, which struck Lyman as wrong for the moment. "These canal waters been talkin' to people for years and they're just as likely to lie as are the men that travel 'em. I'd like to think I'm coming into extra money, though. It makes a man think."

"Yes, it does."

"She ain't really your wife?"

Lyman shook his head.

The captain motioned for him to come closer and Lyman slid from the roof, dropping to the floor of the boat to stand next to Ainsworth in the spot Mariana had recently vacated.

"Take this." The captain nodded toward the tiller and released it, leaving Lyman scrambling to get hold. "You worry too much, Chandler. This canal ain't no more'n forty feet wide at the top, and only eighteen at the bottom, only four feet down. There's no tragedy to be had here. If we sink to the bottom, we stand up."

As he spoke, the captain pulled a can of chewing tobacco from the breast pocket of his coat and when he finished, he tucked a wad into his right cheek, offering the can to Lyman who shook his head.

"I'm not worried about sinking, Captain."

"It's the demons, then, eh?"

"I don't know what you mean."

"Something is chasing that woman of yours, and maybe you, too. Don't take supernatural ability to see that. Something's eatin' at you. And I'm bettin' it has something to do with those dead men you brought on my ship. Or is it another dead man that has you worried?"

"Maybe you do have a supernatural gift."

"I just know people, running up and down the canal long as I have. Good people and bad."

"And which am I?"

"Everyone has bad, some more than others. Mrs. Chandler, or whatever her name is, more than most. But you, I think you're a man who wants to find the good in her and in you."

"Not sure I've been very successful at that."

"And that's why you keep your eye on the water. Lots of bad gets swept away in the canal, but the good is there, too, if you keep looking for it. Mrs. Chandler will find it, too, if she keeps looking."

"I hope you're right." Lyman left the man then, pondering the stars and the still canal water to try to catch hold of sleep that would not come.

31

The Mermaid continued to drag through the water in a series of jerks and glides at the maximum pace of four miles per hour, slow enough to effectively eliminate troubling wake on the waterway. The speed limit was not the biggest impediment to the packet ship's progress, however, which became much more dependent on when she reached locks and how much competition she faced to get through them.

Captain Ainsworth had proven his mettle when he set out from Utica before the crowd, but ships left from all along the length of the canal, and the competition for good positioning at each of the locks grew fiercer the longer they spent on the water.

While the locks at Marcy and Rome were conquered in a little over an hour each, Brewerton and Baldwinsville each took half a day, and by the time *The Mermaid* and her passengers reached the locks at Lyons, the ships lined up for half a mile one way, promising a nearly two day wait to pass.

That's where Lyman finally convinced Mariana it would be safe enough to display the mummies.

"No one knows we took to the canal. I didn't even tell John where we were going and in two day's time we'll be moving again. The canal is so awash with stories, by the time anyone heard about a traveling mummy exhibit, we'd be long gone. And, Mariana, we need the money."

Reluctantly, she'd agreed. Lyman set to work and soon found a pub just a block away from the canal where the owner agreed to let him display his collection.

Drunken canawlers turned out to be such a superstitious lot, they'd as soon pay him to take the mummies away than look at them and learn about them, and Lyman didn't care how he parted them from their money.

By the time they reached the jammed locks at Newport, they were ending the exhibit with a spiritual cleansing provided by Mariana. This was a much bigger draw for most of the unsavory bits of humanity seemingly dredged up from the bottom of the canal along with the stones locals used to build houses, churches, and factories.

The exhibit morphed into something new. No longer did Lyman tout his knowledge of the tombs at Thebes or claim relationships with celebrated Egyptologists, some of whose names were real, some imagined, but all impressive. The canawlers didn't care about such things. They wanted curses and lore, they wanted to be frightened and rescued again from the brink of disaster. They wanted supernatural powers of protection, and they wanted to believe that this life was intricately entwined with the next, joined in a long stream of time. That was how they saw the mummies, he realized, and how he had begun to view them himself.

To gaze at a body that had lasted through millennia, still recognizable as a person, who lived and toiled as these men did, was to conceptualize eternity as if each individual really was a part of it. It was inevitable that these hardworking and hardy men, with no significant social standing outside of the canal towns, would feel both cursed and relieved by the knowledge.

They looked at the mummies, they gazed at the scrolls, and then they sought the wisdom of another realm. And it worked well for several towns, until they got the three-day hold-up at Lockport, the last lock before Buffalo.

Lockport itself was still miles away when *The Mermaid* nudged into place among the long line of packet ships. Most passengers disembarked during the day, walking up the tow path to see what they might find at the bustling town. Lyman ventured off the boat as well, leaving Mariana, who he felt shouldn't walk such a distance, without a better idea of what they might discover at the end.

He found his way to a neat freestone building with a pub sign in the front and walked in to find a space crammed with small tables and groups of men who might have belonged to the crews of any packet ship, including *The Mermaid*. Interchangeable men engaging in interchangeable conversations.

A woman stood behind the bar, drawing a cloth across it, and it was obvious from her own neat appearance that she was the reason this establishment, with so many of the same kind of clientele as similar watering holes up and down the canal, was tidy and scrubbed.

"Pardon me, Miss."

"Missus," the woman replied, a tart edge to her voice. She eyed Lyman and his clothes, which were of a high quality that did not match his disheveled state.

"Well, Mrs.—"

"You want a drink?"

"Yes, please. I'll take a whiskey."

The woman poured an ungenerous glass and slid it to him with neither smile nor comment. She turned away, but Lyman caught her arm and she flinched.

"Is there someone I could speak to about a business proposition?"

"What kind of business?" A sneer formed on her thin lips. Now that he really looked at her, he could see she was not as young as he'd first thought. Skin sagged from her jaw line and her sharp eyes were rimmed in the dark circles of one who works too hard to accomplish too little.

"I am a showman—"

"Got no use for a showman in this establishment."

"Isn't there someone I could speak to?"

"You're speaking to someone right now."

"Might I at least know your name?"

The woman sucked air through a gap in her front teeth. "Mrs. Mary Anna Wells."

Lyman sipped his whiskey. There wasn't a lot of it, but it was of good quality and he held it on his tongue a moment before allowing it to slip, burning, down his throat. "It's a pleasure to make your acquaintance, Mrs. Wells. This is a fine whiskey, and you run a clean, respectable place."

"That I do. And it's because I don't let any old hustler that dragged himself here off the canal to take advantage of me or my customers. There's no gambling, no whoring, and no two-bit scams."

"And that's why this is the perfect place for me to set up my exhibit, a respectable place run by respectable folks."

Mrs. Wells held up the bottle and when Lyman nodded, poured more into his glass. The second portion was larger than the first, he was pleased to see. She was listening.

"You see, I exhibit first-class education for the people. My uncle is recently deceased, but he was a world traveler and Egyptologist who sent me some of his collection."

"Egyptologist?" She watched him swirl the amber liquid in his glass before taking another sip. Then she reached below the bar for a cloth and resumed her cleaning. Her interest was waning.

"Yes, Egypt. The land of the pharaohs, of great monuments, and mummies. I have several papyrus scrolls with writings of Ancient Egypt and six genuine mummies. I have been traveling with them on the packet boat *The Mermaid*, stopping to display them whenever the locks delay us. I'm sure your customers would enjoy such an interesting distraction."

He expected that at the word mummies he would have her hooked, like most, either out of fear or curiosity. She would want to know more, but if that's what he expected, then he'd been wrong.

Mrs. Wells released a quick breath through tight lips and turned to another customer, a man with long auburn mutton chops and greasy hair that hung in his face. She got him a drink and said over her shoulder, "My customers would rather be drunk than distracted. And I won't have the dead in my establishment. They never drink much."

The man with the greasy hair laughed, spitting a mouthful of whiskey into his glass. Mrs. Wells flashed him an appreciative smile that faded the moment she caught Lyman's eye. "I think you'd better take your business proposition elsewhere, sir."

Lyman threw back the rest of his whiskey, paid for the drinks, and left.

*****

"There's no place here to exhibit," Lyman explained when he met Mariana back at *The Mermaid* for supper. The boat held fewer people as many had disembarked to explore the offerings of Lockport, several declaring this their final destination. Likely more would board once they neared the locks.

"It may be just as well," Mariana said, squeezing his knee beneath the table. "We don't want to be too conspicuous. We're nearly to Buffalo and then we can slip into Ohio. I'll feel safer once we're out of New York."

Lyman looked at her with sadness. "You know, darling, I don't think we have anything to fear. We've not heard even a whisper of Quinn. By now he must have given up."

"I don't think so, Lyman. I've been gazing, into the water and into the orb. There's something awful sinister following us. I know it."

"What I know is that my funds are running low. These mummies were supposed to make me money, but so far the expense of transporting them and us has eaten up profits. The sooner I can sell them off, the better."

"And you think you can sell half-a-dozen at once?"

"To the right buyer I could, but I'm not going to find that buyer on the Erie Canal."

Two days passed, both dreary and raining, and Lyman was forced to admit to himself that he was pleased not to be displaying the mummies. Many of their fellow travelers had abandoned *The Mermaid*, seeking passage instead on one of the boats further ahead in line, but as they approached the five locks that would lift them a total of fifty feet, the captain took on more passengers until the boat was nearly bursting with their travel-weary bodies.

Mariana examined the new faces. None of them mattered to Lyman: dirty children, tired mothers, hard-working men in crumpled suits. They were all the same to him—more people who didn't want to buy his dusty burdens.

The weight of them had begun to crush him like the pressure of thousands of years of windblown sand piled high and suffocating him. Lyman could feel himself being pulled into a despair he couldn't shake off. Contributing to this was the still brown landscape of the New York countryside and the stretching mucky towpath trampled by an endless line of stinking beasts. He found life on the canal increasingly stifling with the odors of bodies stacked on bodies. Each night, he attempted to sleep to the sounds of lapping water, ringing bells, and the endless bump, bump, bump of crew jumping between land and boat, lighting and extinguishing lanterns, yelling out warnings of bridges, and vying for position, which involved frequent fist fights and shouting matches.

In all of this, Lyman forgot to watch the passengers themselves. He failed to notice when a man with mutton chops and greasy auburn hair boarded *The Mermaid* just prior to her entrance into the first of the five locks.

The man did not approach him. As other passengers lined the windows or climbed to the top of the boat to observe the water rushing in through the gates, the new passenger kept his eyes on the gentleman showman across the cabin and on the pretty woman leaning into him, exhausted by travel but as enchanting as she ever had been. The time for approaching them had not yet arrived. For now, it seemed enough for Martin Quinn to know he'd found them at last.

32

After weeks of travel along the canal, Lyman was anxious to reach Buffalo where he might eat a good meal, take a hot bath, and sleep in a real bed instead of on an unsteady plank in a room full of twenty or more odoriferous, snoring roommates.

As soon as *The Mermaid* made it through the last of the Lockport locks, Lyman sought the company of Captain Ainsworth.

He found him at the helm, shouting directions to the boy driving the horses along the towpath. Both beasts were fresh since their long rest in Lockport and the boy was having difficulty convincing them they were back on the job.

"Good afternoon, Captain," Lyman interjected as the man turned back to the tiller, the horses at last seemingly under control.

"Mr. Chandler, good aft'noon. What can I do for you?" The man had turned jolly, the irritation with the horses and the boy suddenly dropped, and Lyman wondered at the ability to let go of worry to focus on the task at hand, something he found increasingly difficult to do.

Lyman stepped up to the edge of the deck, surveying the long line of packet boats and steam ships waiting to enter the locks from the other side. He could see three distinctly before the line faded into fog.

It was a dismal day, not too cold, but enveloped in low-hanging clouds that dropped an almost imperceptible mist forming a wall from sky to water. The boat cut through it, slowly, making little more than a ripple across the murky surface. In it, Lyman could almost sense the same foreboding that had driven Mariana to distraction, but he did not sense such things, could not, even if he believed it were possible.

"I wondered only if you could tell me when we will reach Buffalo."

"Well," the captain began, tugging on his tobacco-stained beard, "it's twenty-six miles to Buffalo Creek from Lockport. Depending on traffic, which will thicken considerably as we approach Lake Erie, we have a good half-day of steady travel." There was tension in the old man's face, his jovial nature no longer in control. As he gazed out at the mist, a small frown formed beneath his whiskers. "That puts us getting into Buffalo well after dark I'm afraid. It would be unwise to disembark before morning."

Lyman chuckled. "I hadn't figured you to be afraid of the dark, Captain Ainsworth."

The captain adjusted the tiller and turned his face to Lyman, his complexion the color of the sky, bleak and menacing. "It's not the dark I fear. It's not even Buffalo, though I warn you it's a rough place. But approaching Buffalo in the dark, and in weather like this, that's a proposition that might concern even the bravest of men."

Lyman, who might not have considered himself among the bravest of men, asked, "What exactly is your concern, Captain?"

Without hesitation, the captain answered, his low words nearly swallowed by the dense air surrounding them, "Pirates."

Sharp laughter fell from Lyman's mouth. The notion of pirates setting upon the packet boats of the Erie Canal was preposterous to him. He envisioned the ruthless cutthroats of the ocean, a threat growing ever more distant as the world got smaller, now attempting to capture vessels in a channel that spanned no more than 40 feet from edge to edge.

The captain's face held no trace of levity.

"You can't be serious."

Ainsworth squinted into the fog. "I am very serious. This promises to be the kind of night we might see 'em. They ain't much to fear as long as you're willing to drop a little cargo their way once in a while."

Lyman heard a tremble of fear in the man's voice. He swallowed. "And if you're not willing?"

The captain spit a stream of dark tobacco juice into the murky water. "It's a nasty crew, operates out of Buffalo. Rough place. A murder a day in Buffalo, if you believe the stories."

"And you believe the stories."

"You can't believe everything ya hear, o' course, but it wouldn't surprise me if it was true. All the bad swept along in the canal ends up in Buffalo and freezes there under a mountain of snow, just waiting until the thaw so it can bubble up some more. Thaw's comin'. There's a lot of bad ain't bubbled up yet."

Lyman didn't find much pleasure that afternoon in the company of Captain Ainsworth, shrouded as he was in fog and pessimism. Mariana would be more cheerful, he hoped, as he climbed below deck to find her

Her company offered little improvement. He found her sitting at one of the tables with her orb in front of her and a sturdy woman with a thick neck and a sensible dress sitting across from her, giving rapt attention to her words. Lyman approached them without noticing the auburn-haired man in the corner whose eyes, beneath his pulled low cap, also followed the women's conversation. His eyes left the women only to track Lyman's slow walk across the cabin as he weaved past tables and bodies of passengers unwilling to brave the ominous weather outside.

When she saw Lyman, Mariana said a few words to the other woman who got up to leave in a huff.

"What does the captain have to say?" Mariana asked when her customer wandered out of earshot.

"Captain Ainsworth expects to arrive in Buffalo late tonight." He did not mention that this made the captain nervous, but her expression suggested she already suspected, her complexion growing ashen as he spoke.

"Are you seeing things in your glass ball?"

"Call it an orb, please."

"Is it more magical if I do?" he asked. She displayed no sign of appreciating his jest. "I'm sorry. I believe in your gift, you know."

"Do you?"

He nodded.

"Because, Lyman, I'm frightened. I see the shapes that can only be human bodies, but I don't know whose they are."

"The mummies?"

"Maybe, but sometimes there are six of them and other times there's three, or four, or only one." She shivered. "And it's always so dark."

"Perhaps just signaling the end of our journey, arriving in Buffalo after dark, and selling the mummies in various bits to whoever might buy such a thing."

"I'd be glad to be rid of the devils."

"As would I," Lyman agreed. He'd begun to believe that a curse had fallen on him, one that threatened the well-being of anyone around him. He thought of the single body Mariana saw in her orb and hoped the curse wouldn't soon land on him.

After the evening meal, the women retired to the ladies' quarters, shooing scuttling children ahead of them, while the men took down the tables and lowered the hinged boards that served as beds. Lyman escaped to the deck as others prepared to sleep.

The night air enveloped him, cold and dense. He tried to see through the fog, but his eyes couldn't find the banks of the narrow canal nor anything more than indistinct shadows beyond the gas lamps of *The Mermaid*.

Lyman squinted on, unsure what he was trying to see, but the night was ominous. He couldn't shake the warnings of Mariana's vision, if only he knew what it meant. But then, it should have been the seer's job to interpret, to know what they were up against. Anger rose in his throat, the unfairness at finding a forbidden love with this woman—a weight around his neck that had pulled him off his course. He wondered where he might be now if she had not been with him, or if she weren't carrying the pox, or if he'd never loved her. He wondered where he might be if he'd never stolen the cursed mummies to begin with.

He sighed, releasing curling wisps of breath into the fog. Goose pimples rose on the back of his neck. He pulled his coat more tightly about himself and descended into the cabin to find most of the men already settled. Lyman took his place among them, stepping onto a low bunk to reach one of the few remaining empty ones, and apologizing to the man whose bedding he soiled with his boot.

"Pardon me, sir."

"Of course. In these close quarters we are bound to get in one another's way, Lyman."

Shocked to hear his name, Lyman leaned over the side of his bunk to see the speaker, whose face remain obscured by shadow in the soft glow of only the few oil lamps that remained lit.

"Or should I call you Michael?"

He knew the voice. As he looked, the man's features materialized and Lyman recognized those as well—the auburn hair, the mutton chops, the air of self-importance.

Lyman would not let this man enjoy the upper hand for long. "You look well, Quinn."

"Do I? I was thinking myself rather shabby, but then, travel will do that to a gentleman. Especially when he is outrunning a bad reputation he didn't earn."

"I'm sorry to hear about your misfortune."

"I wonder if the lovely Mariana will be displeased to hear of it."

"What do you want from us, Quinn?"

"Is it 'us,' then? I should have suspected. I suppose it always was. Clever of Mariana to introduce you as an old acquaintance of Horace's."

Lyman drew a sharp breath. The mention of Horace on this man's lips was too much to bear, as if a knife had been drawn across a tender part of him.

"Mariana spoke true."

Quinn snorted. "That would have been a first. But perhaps you are telling me the truth. You left me in a very difficult position, Lyman. I suppose I may call you Lyman?"

"You may call me whatever you wish. You are the master of names, after all."

The last of the lights was snuffed and the cabin descended into darkness. With it came a curtain of silence so thick it was felt more than heard. Lyman pulled his head back onto his makeshift bunk and focused on the gentle lapping of the water against the side of the lurching boat as the horses continued to pull.

It was the kind of night that swallowed sound, only to spit it back as fear so loud it admitted nothing else. Only a single whispering voice penetrated the fog that now seemed to fill his head, his body, his limbs.

"Goodnight, then, Lyman Moreau."

Panic swept through him as he huddled against the side of the boat. Quinn knew his real name. It did not matter, he reminded himself. Quinn would be ruined if he were to reveal that he had been dealing in false identities, abusing his role as a customs agent. The men were bound by both lie and burglary, yet Lyman felt that Quinn held power over him with his name.

There was not a living soul he could be traced to any longer that mattered. Except that wasn't true. His mother had died when he was a boy, died in violence, the way whores eventually do, but there was another family, a better family, and despite their fallings out, there were still people he cared about. John and Harriet, with their adopted daughter, lived under the protection of his name. And there was Mariana to consider as well. He could have been anyone to her, but she had in recent months become everything to him. Quinn could not be allowed to know that.

Thoughts of Mariana, of Quinn, of Horace, and of murder swam in his head, mingling with the images of Harriet and her family. Lyman could not sleep upon the stiff board that was a poor excuse for a bed. He wondered if he should awaken Mariana, if the two of them should simply jump ship and make their way on foot the remaining miles to Buffalo.

But the night was so very dark, and the waters of Buffalo dangerous by all accounts. And Quinn would still be a threat, perhaps an even larger one, once they were away from the relative safety of the crowded ship.

He would wait, and when they docked in Buffalo, he and Mariana would slip away into the rough town that had hidden scores of hardened criminals.

33

Lyman awoke with his heart pounding and his clothes drenched in cold sweat. The cabin was the shade of thickest dark before the promise of dawn could be felt. His stiff muscles ached as they always did after even a short sleep on the thin mattress that did nothing to disguise the hard, unsteady board beneath it. One arm at a time, he stretched and wondered what had awakened him.

The sound of slow rhythmic breath, of snores, and the murmurs of dreams, surrounded him and with them came the assault of the odors of sleeping men. Lyman sat up with care so as not to bash his head against the sloping wall of the cabin. Fresh air would do him good. He'd not intended to sleep at all. Even in the relative security of the crowded cabin, he didn't trust his safety with Quinn so close, but exhaustion had at last overwhelmed him. Gently he dropped onto the floor and slipped on his boots, gazing with relief toward the sleeping form of his enemy.

His eyes adjusted to the dark, but still he could sense more than see the outline of the sleeping bodies around him. It occurred to him that he could end the chase right now. The knife he always carried still resided in the pocket of the coat lying rumpled on his bunk, within an easy arm's reach. He'd never used it to kill someone, but he kept it sharp enough to slit a man's soft throat with ease.

Lyman drew a slow, silent breath in the darkness, imagining the satisfaction of opening Quinn's throat. The blame for many deaths could legitimately lie at Lyman's feet. His schemes at times had cost men their lives. But the satisfaction of feeling the warmth of an enemy's blood ooze through his fingers was something Lyman had never experienced. The power of that sensation called to him with frightening temptation, but before he could answer, he heard a thump and a splash from above, followed by the squeal and snort of an angry horse.

For a moment he froze. Then carefully he crept past bunks, easing dangling arms and legs out of his path. One man woke just enough to grab Lyman by the wrist, but then fell back, his grip loosening.

The thumps continued as Lyman ascended the ladder to the deck and voices became decipherable. He heard at least four distinct men, one of whom he could identify as Captain Ainsworth, his voice gruff with sleep and sharpened by anger.

"You're a bunch of cowards is what you are, boarding my boat on a God-forsaken night like this."

"Calling a man a coward when he's got a pistol to your head is stupid, Cap'n. Not brave." A silky calm permeated this wise observation, the speaker of which clearly understood the advantage of his position.

Lyman lifted his head through the door only enough to better hear, pulling back just as another man rounded the corner of the cabin. "We got all we can load. Left the lumber, but there was crates of household goods weighing them down."

"Well, now," the calm man said, the clump of his boots retreating from where Lyman could see the edge of the captain's head, barely illuminated by the yellow glow of a gas lamp, his beard streaked with blood. "See there, Cap'n, we didn't leave you with nothing. You got to keep your lumber haul, and your passengers will surely understand this is just business. We gotta keep ourselves afloat, every one of us."

Lyman heard the soft splash and thud of boots that indicated an out-of-sight boat took on a passenger on the opposite side from where he crouched. The horse snorted and stomped on the footpath.

"Cut that damned horse loose. Time to set this old mermaid adrift." A third voice howled the command from mere feet away. Lyman scrambled onto the deck without thinking and spun toward the sound. When his fist connected with the scraggly jaw of the pirate, Lyman heard the crunch of loosening teeth. Lyman dropped back for a second punch, but before he swung, the crack of a gunshot interrupted his heroism.

A shriek shattered the stillness of the air and then fell with the sickening thud of the horse.

"The next bullet goes in your gut, sir." Again, Lyman was struck by the smooth command of the man who'd pointed his gun at Captain Ainsworth, the weapon now trained on Lyman.

The pirate whose mouth Lyman had bloodied rose behind him and punched him in the back. He lurched forward, the blow exploding through his side, injecting every cranny of his innards with excruciating pain as he tumbled to his knees.

He heard the quick steps of his attacker retreat and then drop into the waiting rowboat.

Lyman pulled himself to his feet, his hands searching in vain for the pockets of the coat that remained crumpled in his bunk with his knife tucked safety inside. In absence of the coat, he smoothed his shirt. Disheveled he may be, but he obstinately refused to yield his confidence in the face of the canal pirates.

The armed man stood before him over six feet tall with dark, bushy hair that fell to his broad, muscled shoulders. A fine mist still swirled through the air coating everything and everyone in a shiny, slick film, but the pirate didn't seem to notice. He had backed toward the edge of the packet boat, his gun trained once again on the captain, his eyes locked on Lyman.

His gaze steady, the large pirate said, "A gentleman passenger come to the rescue. I bet you feel much better now, Cap'n."

Ainsworth said nothing, but shook his head in a subtle warning to Lyman that he understood to mean he should remain quiet. Had Lyman been an easy man to intimidate, that might have been the end, but he wasn't and, after traveling for months across the country in the company of dead men, he wasn't about to lose them now.

He raised his hands, shoulder height with his palms outward and willed the waver from his voice. "There are some crates on this boat. They carry more than you're after, an evil you can't understand."

The large man tipped back his head and released a laugh so loud and so jolly it shattered the night as effectively as the gunshot that had brought an end to the horse.

"I suppose you refer to the crate full of mummies. Don't you worry, *sir*. We'll let 'em be your problem. We left 'em."

201

Lyman exhaled in relief as the man lowered himself backward into the second boat, smaller than *The Mermaid*, but sitting considerably lower in the water now that it carried a good deal of stolen cargo.

"We'll see one another again, I expect, Cap'n." The man chuckled and pulled the trigger, firing one more shot, this one into the right shoulder of the captain who fell to the deck with a shriek.

Even the sound of the gunfire was swallowed by the devilish night, but this being the second shot in less than five minutes, it drew a response. A low, but growing murmur rose from the cabin, along with several men in half-dazed and half-dressed states pouring onto the deck.

Lyman dropped to his knees beside Captain Ainsworth who held his arm protectively and grunted as Lyman leaned over him to get a look.

"I think he just grazed me, the blame devil."

Lyman winced at the vicious ache in his midsection, painful enough to make tending to the captain difficult. "Where's the rest of the crew?" he asked.

Captain Ainsworth sucked air through his front teeth as Lyman applied pressure to the bleeding arm. "I sent a man to guard the ladies. The others is bleedin' at the bottom of the canal or run off." He took a moment to bite back the pain and moaned. "They even shot the boy driving the horses."

"Pirates." Lyman shook his head. "Pirates on the Erie Canal."

"Welcome to Buffalo, Mr. Chandler. I'd ruther be lost in the open sea than coming into Buffalo on a night like tonight."

"But we can go after them, surely. Notify the law that these men have stolen our goods."

"There ain't enough law here to take 'em. They hide out on the islands made by the long side canals and they got a great defense. They only strike when the weather favors 'em. Canal boats, on a night like this, are just sittin' on a barrel of gunpowder. But since they don't strike too often, it's not worth the lives it would take to cut 'em down. So long as they take mostly from the private traveler and not from the shipping companies that'd have enough influence to prosecute 'em."

"So we just have to suffer the loss of our property."

"Sounds like your mummies are safe."

"Maybe, but he said they left one crate of mummies. Unfortunately I was traveling with two."

"I got problems of my own to figure out, Mr. Chandler. I got no horses, almost no crew, and a bad arm. Just what do you think I can do for you?"

Lyman withdrew his hand from the captain's arm, his fingers slick with blood just as he'd envisioned they would be had he sliced Quinn's throat. It was a feat he knew he could never have gotten away with in a cabin filled with witnesses. He would have had to dump the body into the canal, something he could not have accomplished without waking his fellow travelers. The same protection had allowed Lyman to live through the night, but he knew that once they'd reached the end of the canal, there'd be nothing to stop the madman's revenge.

"Once we get into Buffalo, Captain, Mariana and I need to disappear."

Ainsworth had grabbed his own bleeding bicep, his eyes scrunching closed. After a moment he said, "You wouldn't be the first. I know a place you can go. There's a woman, name of Essie, runs a boarding house on Canal Street. Not a nice place to take a lady, but if it's discretion you're looking for, Essie's your gal.

*****

"Three mummies gone, just like that?" Mariana huffed, livid, as they disembarked in Buffalo, the sun just beginning to come up and the world still shrouded in fog. She'd slept poorly after waking to the gunshot. All the woman were exhausted, she complained to Lyman, whose every breath spread the throbbing ache in his gut. He had no response for her.

"I can't imagine pirates on the Erie." She sighed.

"I don't have to imagine them," he spoke through gritted teeth. "I saw them."

"And there's no getting the mummies back?"

Lyman pulled her through the crowded dock, glancing over his shoulder as he went. "Ainsworth says no."

"But if the thieves were superstitious enough to leave the one crate, why would they want to keep the other once they knew what was in it?"

"And would you like to go to their secret hideout to convince them they've made a mistake and their best course of action would be to give the mummies to us?"

"I could. I'm very persuasive."

"And also beautiful. And weak. And they are pirates."

He pulled at her hand and Mariana tripped on her skirt. Unable to fully catch her balance, she stumbled into him. "Is that why we're in such a hurry? Are you afraid a dangerous band of canal pirates will come and take me away?"

He didn't slow his pace even though he could hear in her voice that she was struggling to keep up, growing short of breath. "No. Not pirates."

"But what about the crate we've got? Do we even know which one it is, which mummies and scrolls it contains?"

"No, but I'll deal with them later. We have to get away from this dock before the sun has fully risen." Lyman spotted an empty coach, its driver standing next to his tamping horse, rubbing his hands together in the cold.

Mariana allowed herself to be pulled toward it, but before they came to it she stopped short. "Lyman, will you please tell me what we're running from?"

"Quinn," he hissed. That was all he need say. Her cheeks drained of color and she froze in place. He tugged at her arm, encouraging her to move and she allowed him to pull her along. Within moments he'd delivered her to the safety of the coach.

To the driver, he said, "We need to go as quickly as possible to Miss Essie's boarding house on Canal Street. Do you know it?"

The driver, a young man whose frayed coat was as dirty as the oily hair sticking out from beneath his grimy top hat, licked his thin lips, his eyes sliding over Lyman. "I know it." He flicked his head in the direction of the carriage compartment where Mariana waited. "You sure that's the place you want to take her?"

Lyman handed the driver a five dollar coin, satisfied as the young man's eyes grew wide. It was an extravagant amount, and more than Lyman liked to part with, but the driver's silence would be well worth the investment.

"I am certain that's where we want to go, just as I'm certain no one else needs to know how to find us. Do we have an understanding?"

"Yes sir." The driver placed the coin in his pocket.

As Lyman climbed into the seat beside Mariana and the carriage lurched forward at the slap of the reins, the young man began to whistle a tune familiar to Lyman from his weeks of canal travel. He sat back, closed his eyes, and let the words about a ruthless kicking mule wash through his mind and tug at the corners of his mouth. Lyman's aching body felt as if he'd been kicked by the meanest mule working along the entire length of the Erie Canal, but Mariana was safe and well beside him. And for now, that was enough.

34

At Lyman's request, the driver directed the horses north, out of town and along the lakeshore. The morning air was crisp, the clean scent of snow tickling Lyman's nose as he watched April's half-hearted attempt to paint the ground in swirling white confetti. A strong sun, quickly rising, would bring a swift end to that foolishness, and the day promised to be a bright one.

Lyman draped his arm across Mariana's shoulders, pulling her close. To his surprise, she resisted. She pushed her open palms into his chest and he released her.

"Why didn't you tell me about Quinn?" Her bottom lip protruded, her eyes darkened with a brewing danger.

Lyman crossed his arms. "I only just found out about him myself."

"You're a terrible liar, Lyman Moreau."

Her words stung him. After months of tending to her, of delaying and changing his plans for her, of returning to face the demons of his past in order to help her, he believed he might have deserved her trust.

"It's the truth," he whispered.

"Then you're a terrible truth teller." Her anger swelled to fill the carriage and he feared it would overtake the noise of the road, alerting the driver to a problem he might think demanded his attention.

He reached for her gloved hand, her fingers still clinched. At his touch, her fist loosened.

"Quinn approached me yesterday, near the end of the day. You'd already left for the women's quarters. I knew we'd be safer with the crowd on *The Mermaid* than we would be running."

She slid her hand from his grasp. "We aren't on *The Mermaid* anymore, or hadn't you noticed? We're running anyway, and Martin Quinn will sniff us out. I promise you that."

Lyman shifted his weight so he might face her. Then he cupped her quivering chin in his palm, lifting her mouth toward his own. Their breath mingled, delightfully warm in the chill of the carriage.

"Mariana, your safety is the most important thing to me. I love you. Is that a truth you can believe?" Her pupils dilated as only those of a woman in love will do, and her expression softened. He pulled her into an embrace once again and kissed her. This time, she did not resist him.

*****

They arrived at Miss Essie's establishment after a half-day's drive through the countryside and a turn back into town, down Erie Street, across the canal, and into the area known locally as the Flats, or sometimes as the infected district, and always as a place decent people avoided.

No signage identified the house, with its sagging porch and peeling paint that could have been at home as an old farmhouse in the east. Lyman could believe it was a place where the desperate might seek solace, but then there was also something distinctly ominous about the dilapidated old house. It was as if the drab shutters, open now to let in the sunny warmth of the afternoon, at other times held in secrets so dark the rest of the structure trembled.

Lyman handed Mariana from the carriage, but paused, wondering if Ainsworth had steered them true. Mariana squeezed his hand as she gazed at the house. He'd have liked to know her thoughts in that moment, but was too afraid of her response to ask for them.

The coach driver carried their small bags confidently to the front porch. Shaking off his unease, Lyman followed him to the door and knocked, Mariana a step behind him.

In moments a plump but pretty woman in a flowing kimono whipped open the door.

"Pardon me, Madam." Lyman removed his hat and dipped his head in deference.

The woman at the door scowled. "You needn't put on airs here, sir. My gals ain't the high flown types." Startling green eyes sized him up from beneath long lashes and loose skin. In them he could almost see the beauty she had once been.

"Are you Essie?" he asked.

She crossed her arms and pursed her painted lips, creasing the surrounding skin with tiny lines like cracks in a thin layer of ice. "I'm Mrs. Essie Cole."

Lyman flashed his friendliest smile. "Just the woman I was looking for, then. My wife and I have recently had the pleasure of traveling the canal with Captain Ainsworth aboard *The Mermaid*. He suggested we might find your boarding house both comfortable and discreet."

If it were possible to detect a blush through her layers of rouge, Lyman might have seen the heat rising in Mrs. Essie Cole's face. She stepped aside and waved them into the house, closing the door quickly behind them.

Mrs. Cole slipped past, the smooth silk of her gown brushing against the back of Lyman's hand. She beckoned for them to follow her through the front of the house which consisted of a wide open room, a bar along one side opposite a staircase at the top of which, as far as Lyman could see, was a series of closed doors. The middle of the room featured a smattering of small tables around a grand piano, its black surface polished to a gleam.

Sitting on the piano bench, her arms draped across the keys, was a young woman barely more than a girl. Her long hair fell in tangles across her face, and along with the fabric of her kimono sleeves, cascaded toward the floor.

"Wake up, Charlotte!" Mrs. Cole smacked the girl on the back of her head, which crashed into the piano keys with jarring dissonance. She leapt to her feet, frantically sweeping her unruly mane behind her ears. "We have guests. You could be useful today and make us some coffee."

The girl's eyes darted between her madam and the newcomers before she turned hastily to the bar and disappeared into a back room.

Mrs. Cole's eyes traced the path of the girl. "Follow me," she said to Lyman and Mariana.

They trailed the woman through a door, obscured by a velvet drapery. Beyond it they discovered a lavishly decorated sitting room.

"Well." The sternness melted from their hostess, her features now emanating warmth and welcome as she invited them both to sit on a scarlet divan beneath a vivid oil painting depicting a nude couple entwined in one another's arms.

"If Arthur sent you to me, then you can call me Essie." She settled herself into a chair across from them, leaned slightly forward, and asked, "Is he in Buffalo, then?"

"Yes," Lyman said. He removed his gloves and placed them in his overturned hat which he held on his lap.

A wide smile took over her face, revealing deep, jolly dimples and a complete set of yellowed teeth. "He's a dear man. Always good to me and my gals on his way through town. Keeps his crew in line, too. Better 'n most captains. Pack of rats workin' the canal."

She reached into a pocket on her kimono, pulled out a small carved snuffbox, placed a pinch of powdered tobacco on the back of her hand, and inhaled it with a sharp sniff. "But the question is, why would a married couple want to seek lodgings at my place?"

Lyman opened his mouth to answer, but stopped at the creak of the door. The young woman from the piano walked in carrying a steaming kettle and a tray with three dainty cups precariously stacked.

Essie rose and took the tray, setting the cups with gentle clinks on a side table beside Lyman. The girl poured the dark liquid into each, a distinct odor of charred bitterness rising into the air.

Essie returned to her seat, cup in hand, coffee sloshing over the rim. "You didn't answer me, Mister—"

"Chandler," Lyman interrupted. "My name is Michael Chandler, and this is my wife Mariana." He'd have preferred to use a different name, but thought it wise to maintain the identity Ainsworth knew, given that it was evidently only on his recommendation they would be allowed to stay with Mrs. Essie Cole and her kimono-clad gals.

She sipped her coffee and motioned for him to continue.

"We have been pursued across the state by a dangerous man. He caught up with us just outside Buffalo and now we need a place to hide for a time. Just until he's moved out of the area."

"A dangerous man." Essie frowned. "And Arthur thought I'd risk my gals to help you?"

Lyman wasn't sure how to respond, but he didn't have to, because beside him, Mariana began to cry. He'd seen her tears fall before, but this he'd never witnessed. She leaned forward, dropping her face into her hands, and heaved, emotion pouring out of her in waves.

Mrs. Essie Cole rose, thrusting her coffee cup into the hands of a clearly surprised Charlotte who'd been inching toward the door. The plump madam wedged herself between Lyman and Mariana, pressing him uncomfortably into the arm of the divan.

"Now dear." Essie patted Mariana's back, a gentle, maternal gesture so surprisingly tender, Lyman didn't even bother to wriggle out from his tight spot. He couldn't rip his attention away from them as he heard whispers of comfort pass from the elder woman to the younger.

Mariana looked up after a moment, her face streaked with tears, her entire self emanating confession. "I was married before," the words tumbled forth. "He was an older man, and I loved him. I truly did, but I ruined myself with a man who turned out to be a nightmare, who killed my husband and now he wants me dead, too."

Her words poured out of her, nearly unintelligible, but Essie seemed to manage. She nodded and continued to rub Mariana's back until the younger woman's sobbing subsided. Only then did Essie move from her side, standing and alleviating Lyman's discomfort.

"Very well," Essie said. She pointed to the other girl, still standing, open-mouthed, holding the kettle in one hand and a half-filled coffee cup in the other. "Charlotte will show you where you can stay and, if Mr. Chandler would be kind enough to help, set up the tub. I think Mrs. Chandler could do with a warm bath after her long trip."

"Thank you, Mrs. Cole," Lyman said as he stood.

She cast her peculiar green eyes toward Mariana and sighed. "I told you to call me Essie. And you and Mrs. Chandler are welcome to stay here as long as you need. Let it never be said of Essie Cole that she turned out a gal in need."

35

When Mariana emerged at the top of the stairs, clean and fresh after her bath and a good rest, Lyman felt more relief than he expected. Though she'd been relatively healthy since leaving New Barker, he continued to worry, and he was grateful that Essie had taken an interest in keeping Mariana safe under her wing now as well.

Over the past year she had become more to him than the widow of his mentor. More to him, in many ways, than any other woman had ever been. Respect for Horace had bound Lyman to her, but Mariana herself had won him.

Lyman had swindled his way through much of the Eastern United States, creating and severing a number of partnerships along the way, but never had he felt his own fortunes so delicately entwined with another. She was beautiful and insightful, determined and brutally honest. And he wanted only to spend his life caring for her.

"It's sweet," said a dark-haired young woman beside him, close enough he could smell the powder on her skin. "How much you love her. Can I get you a drink?"

Lyman watched the woman as she stepped away from him and toward the bar. She wore the same style of loose-flowing dress as the others, this one in royal blue, a stark contrast to the pale skin of her neck.

The room had filled as Mariana refreshed herself. Charlotte, her hair now smooth and plaited making her appear younger even than she had before, plunked a cheerful tune on the piano. More than a dozen dolled-up adventuresses with painted smiles now settled on sofas and around tables, greeting gentlemen guests, couples forming and disappearing into the rooms upstairs.

The dark-haired woman in blue brought Lyman a drink just as Mariana joined him, looking well with a happy pink flush in her cheeks.

"Ainsworth brought the crate," he said after sipping at his whiskey.

"He's here?" She grabbed the glass from his hand and swallowed a gulp, her eyes flashing mischief. "Essie's glad of that, I'm sure. Where is he?"

She set the drink in front of Lyman. He slid it back toward her. "It was quite a reunion. He disappeared upstairs, I imagine. Don't think we'll be seeing him for a while. And he said he was setting out at first light tomorrow morning, heading back to Albany to do it all again."

"Those canawlers, I don't know how they do it. I would lose my mind drifting up and down that big ditch. I hope he's having a good night at least." Mariana giggled and threw back the rest of Lyman's whiskey. She wiped the back of her hand across her mouth. "Have you looked at the mummies yet?"

"I was waiting for you, my dear. They're in the kitchen behind the bar."

He rose, pulled out her chair, and offered her his arm, which she took with a light touch. Together they snaked their way across the room, winding through the tables and high-spirited clamor. The dark-haired barkeep had become engaged in conversation with a burly man twice her age. Still, she winked at Lyman as they passed.

Behind the kitchen door waited a hush so complete it was disorienting after the din of the main room. The glow from the fireplace served as the only light in the room, but it was enough. Lyman grabbed the poker and pried open the top of the crate, his heart sinking.

Mariana's face registered disappointment almost as soon as he felt it himself. Together they reached into the crate, beneath the straw, and found four tightly wrapped scrolls tucked beside the forms of three mummies. One was not quite five feet long, its arms by its sides with palms open to the world. The second, slightly longer, its hands brought together as if in prayer, and the third, similar to the first, with its hands tucked neatly along the length of its body. Each shriveled face lay bare, and each mouth was closed.

"We lost Horos." Mariana's voice cracked. Lyman's heart might have burst with the grief of hearing those words from her lips had the door not opened behind him at just that moment, letting in the noise and exuberance of a Buffalo rumhole and brothel in full swing. Essie burst into the room, followed by discordant voices raised in a rowdy rendition of "The Raging Canal."

"What are you doing in here?" she gasped, as the door closed and the chorus was swallowed by silence. Her hand flew to her breast. "Sakes alive, you scared the devil out of me."

"I'm sorry, Essie." With her easy tone, Mariana spoke calm over the woman who beamed at her, the shock of finding them there evidently forgiven. "We were inspecting our traveling companions. Captain Ainsworth was kind enough to deliver them here."

"Of course," Essie said, walking around the perimeter of the kitchen, lighting oil lamps as she approached them. "Now what is this about companions?"

She crossed back toward them, stopping short when she saw the dried bodies laid upon her floor. To her credit, she didn't scream, but no amount of rouge could have given color to her complexion.

"Mummies from Egypt," Lyman answered with a smile, deciding to shake off the loss of the mummy called Horos. The ancient dead man was not interchangeable with Lyman's more recently lost mentor, though with its gaping mouth, the desiccated body had come to represent the idea to Lyman that Horace's presence still guided the journey somehow. In truth, three mummies could still incite sufficient interest to make a sale of the collection, especially along with the scrolls.

Essie cocked her head to one side. She stared at the mummies for a wordless moment, then walked out of the room, leaving Lyman to exchange a nervous glance with Mariana and wonder whether they might soon be thrown into the street.

A few minutes later, the door flew open again and in marched Essie, followed by the dark-haired bartender and the man she'd been flirting with, along with three more of Essie's gals and several more loud, drunk, canal-hardened men.

The questions rolled in faster than Lyman could keep up with them, but he did his best, providing all the details he'd recited hundreds of times across three states. When the crowd grew too large for the kitchen, Essie shooed everyone to the main room where more gathered around the tables scooted together to make a platform for the deceased guests.

Charlotte took up on the piano again, pounding out a jubilant tune that further energized the spirits of the gathered, several of whom grabbed partners and started to dance. To Lyman's surprise and dismay, a stout man in a stained coat and muddy boots even scooped one of the mummies into his arms, skipping and twirling with it across the floor.

Lyman managed to catch the man's attention and retrieve his property as the crowd began to swell again. Several more men entered the house, drawn by the inviting atmosphere of frivolity. As busy as he was answering questions about the mummies, he'd had neither time nor inclination to study the faces that streamed through the door. All manner of varmint scuttled in, and Essie had her hands full ushering the rowdiest back out the door.

Those who behaved themselves like gentlemen were scarce and were welcomed by the few young ladies not yet engaged for the evening. But one such man eschewed their attentions. Keeping his low cap pulled down on his auburn hair, he made his way to one corner of the room to observe the frivolity. When at last he spotted the only real object of his desire, he walked without disruption directly to her and grabbed her by her arm.

Over the clamor of spontaneous celebration, no one noticed Mariana's protestations as Martin Quinn escorted her up the stairs, a Derringer pistol pressed into her back.

It wasn't until the night grew late and much of the ruckus had died down that Lyman thought to look for her. One of Essie's gals, a brunette whose gentleman companion had long since stumbled out the door, approached him to ask about the scrolls.

"What do they say?" she asked, her finger tracing the faded figures. She was younger than Mariana but worn by a world that had cared little for her. He wondered how she had come to live and work among these women, what kind of life she'd left behind that might be worse than this.

"They're funerary texts," he replied.

He could see that beneath a thick layer of cosmetics was a bright inquisitiveness etched into the thin creases on her brow. "What's that?"

"It's a kind of book of spells that usher the dead into the afterlife, and this column here," he explained, pointing to the strange letters along the side of the drawings, "reveals the identity of the dead man."

"You can read it?" She leaned in close to him, her hot breath scented with whiskey, mingled with his own.

He cleared his throat. "No, but I knew a man who could. He translated a bit of them before he died."

"You don't know everything the dead have to say, then?"

When he shook his head, she sat back in her chair with such disappointment in her eyes, he couldn't bear it.

"But Mrs. Chandler is a skilled glass-looker. She's been able to commune with them." He regretted the words as soon as he uttered them, but the woman perked up immediately, and so he looked over his shoulder to speak to Mariana, to ask her to bring out her orb. When he didn't find her, fear stabbed Lyman's heart.

He turned to the brunette. "Did you see where my wife went?"

She smiled and leaned toward him again, placing her hand on his thigh. "Yes. I saw her go upstairs earlier, with a handsome man who looked awful happy to see her."

36

He jumped up from his chair, his fear for Mariana forcing away any anxiety he might have felt for himself. The brunette shrieked as he pushed past her and flew to the stairs, scaling two at a time, his heart thumping as loudly as his footsteps. At the end of the hallway, Lyman threw open the door to the room he and Mariana were to share.

It was dark and quiet and empty.

Through the walls he could hear the muffled sounds of amorous activities. As he considered where to look for Quinn and his captive, one sound reached him through the rest. It was a moan, not quite of pleasure, though neither was it a telltale call of distress. But the tone of the voice, he couldn't have mistaken, locked as it was in his heart.

He rushed into the hallway and moved to rip open the next door, but paused at a phrase that came to him so clearly it might have been spoken by someone standing directly beside him.

"I do love you. You know I do." The words, formed by Mariana's own lips, didn't make sense to him at first, and he thought only that she must be under duress. He pressed his ear to the door.

"You have to believe me. None of this was my plan." Mariana sounded calm, her speech smooth and endearing, seductive even. Lyman's pulse quickened.

"My dear, your intention doesn't matter. My life is in tatters. Everything I worked for, everything *we* worked for together, ruined because you were a fool." The man's voice could only be described as cold, his response carried with it something more than anger, more than hatred. It was loathing. It was dangerous.

"You wanted Horace dead as much as I did," Mariana replied, a sheepish avoidance of assuming any blame. From the opposite side of a closed door, Lyman could nearly see her expression, the coy smile, the seductive downcast glance.

"And he would have been! In mere months. The poison had him in its clutches. *You* had him in *your* clutches."

"I couldn't wait," she pleaded. "And then Lyman showed up and he was the perfect setup. I wanted to be with you. It's what you wanted, too."

"I wanted to be with a wealthy widow I could trust, not with a thieving murderess who would betray me at her first opportunity. Is he worth it, this Lyman of yours?"

Lyman's heart filled with an anguish greater than he'd have thought possible. That Mariana might once have loved Quinn, have schemed with him to murder her husband and frame the closest thing Horace had to a son. She had lied to him far longer than she'd have needed to. Lyman could have loved her, had loved her. He just hadn't understood what she was.

"He's nothing. A convenience only." The words stung, but not as badly as the honesty in Mariana's voice.

"Why then did you stop writing to me?"

And there it was. She had pursued Lyman in Philadelphia in order to corner him and betray him to her lover, to finish what she had begun.

"Martin—"

Quinn didn't let her finish. Lyman heard the thump of a body thrown to the floor. Mariana screamed.

"You know what I think?" Quinn spoke softly, but nearer to the door, so that his every syllable reached straight through the crack, piercing Lyman's soul. "I think you left me to hang and ran off with the first man who would have you."

Silence. Then muted sobbing. When at last she spoke, Lyman realized he hadn't been breathing.

"But you didn't hang." The desperation in her plea called to him, but he couldn't deny his need to hear her confession. "You're here. And I'm here. No one can stop us from being together. Not Horace. Not Lyman."

The smack of flesh against flesh, once, then twice. In his mind, Lyman saw it as if he were the man delivering the blows to the woman who'd betrayed him.

"Don't say that name to me! You left me to hang for your crimes! You left me for him!"

Now the words spilled frantically from her. "Horace willed everything to him! Like he was his goddamned son. I knew you'd call in favors. I knew you'd be released. I followed the mummies because I hoped I could finger him in the crime like I'd wanted to. The only way for us to get our happy ending was to let Lyman swing. My husband would have me left with nothing! There's no black market business for me to step in to. He left me ruined. And you with me."

"No. You said yourself, I'd have been fine. I did call in favors. I did have connections. Now I don't. I'm finished in New York. I'm a pariah. And if it were ever discovered how many documents I forged, I really would hang. Too many people would benefit from my death. They'll not stick out their necks for me."

Mariana pulled in a sharp breath. Her next words were strained, as if she couldn't properly breathe.

"Please, Martin," she gasped.

"I loved you, you know."

"I know. I do know." the panic rose in the rasping breath of her voice.

Lyman heard a long scraping noise, like Quinn was dragging Mariana across the floor. He slipped the knife from his pocket, and unfolded it before placing his hand on the doorknob, an expression of his inclination to aid a woman in distress.

Still, he was keenly aware that a better man wouldn't have paused, would have long since come to the rescue of the woman he loved. Or had thought he loved.

Quinn might kill her. Lyman could let him. He had no fear of the man. And now he knew that Mariana had killed Horace and that Lyman's mentor had thought of him like a son, had willed to him the tools necessary to take up the reins of a thriving black market business in the city they both loved. He could slip away into the rough Buffalo night, leave Mariana and Quinn to destroy one another.

But Lyman could still hear her terror and feared he always would.

He turned the knob.

She was a heap of skirt on the floor, the tall frame of her former lover looming over her, his back to Lyman. He gave the man no time to react. Wrapping an arm around Quinn's neck, Lyman plunged the knife deep into the man's belly and twisted. Quinn shrieked in surprise, as a burgundy stain spread across his shirt. In a single fluid movement, Lyman pulled the knife loose and drew it across the man's throat, the slice deep enough to release a spurting torrent of bright red blood.

Mariana stared up, open-mouthed, her torn dress and battered face both drenched in her lover's blood.

Lyman met her gaze as he dropped Quinn's body beside her. Then he turned and walked out of the room.

*****

A few of Essie's gals had heard the commotion and came running in various states of undress. Lyman pushed past them to continue down the stairs without explanation.

The main room had largely emptied. One man sat wobbling at the bar, chatting with the bartender whose grimace revealed she'd like nothing better than to escape.

Charlotte played a melancholy tune at the piano. She stopped when she saw him, a mask of shock overtaking her delicate features. She rose and hurried away toward the concealed door of the back room.

Lyman dropped his gaze and examined himself, taking in the sight of Quinn's fresh blood on his shirt cuff and on the sleeve of his coat. His hand still held the knife that had taken the man's life. He took out a handkerchief to wipe the blade before folding it and replacing it in his coat pocket. He'd just done so when Essie's office door flew open and the woman herself emerged, aggravated in an unfastened dress. Captain Ainsworth followed her, red-faced and barely put together himself.

"Stay there, Arthur," Essie said over her shoulder. The man complied and ducked back through the partially obscured door.

Essie headed straight for Lyman, her hands open and outstretched, asking a question for which she seemed to have no words. She needn't have said anything anyway. Lyman was prepared for her.

"He found her."

Essie wrapped her arms around Lyman and his body sagged against her, enveloped for a moment in the faint memory of motherly comfort. When she released him, his cheeks were moist with tears that she wiped away with her thumb.

"Tell me what happened." She glanced around the room until her eyes settled on the chatty drunk who'd finally collapsed against the bar. "Abigail," she said to the bartender, busy wiping a glass. "It's time for Charlie to go home. Fetch a bucket of water."

She led Lyman to a chair and insisted he sit. "I'm sorry I let her down. We were so busy tonight I didn't see to everyone who came in. I should have protected my gals better. And Mrs. Chandler as well."

"It's not Chandler, you know. And Mariana isn't my wife."

Essie pursed her lips, her complexion reddening in what might have been anger, but it was soon gone and she relaxed, the corners of her mouth turning upward as she patted his back. "Is any of us really who he says he is?"

She dropped into the chair across from him and leaned toward him, her face inches from his. "Did you kill him?"

Lyman averted his gaze, the only confession he could conjure in the moment.

"You've done a service for the world, then, I should think." Essie sat upright, adding, "And Mariana?"

"She—

The words stuck in his throat. He found he couldn't speak of what had transpired, of what he'd allowed to happen to Mariana or of what a small part of him wished had become her fate. But again, Essie didn't seem to need him to say anything. She stood and patted his back once more.

"Leave her to me."

37

A dark cloud had fallen over the occupants of Mrs. Essie Cole's brothel. Essie took charge of tending to Mariana's wounds, a relief to Lyman who now knew himself capable of being a monster that might have inflicted more.

Had he truly been her husband, he'd have felt himself assaulted. As her lover, he should have been enraged. But he was neither of those things, his stomach turning at the remembrance of all he'd once believed Mariana had meant to him.

He sat at the long table in the kitchen, a cup of coffee growing cold in front of him. With him sat three of Essie's gals, disheveled and unappealing in their brightly colored Mother Hubbards. A fourth stood by the fire preparing a breakfast of corn cake and bacon.

"What a terrible night," said the woman across the table from him. He thought he'd heard Essie call her Fanny, or it could have been Annie. She wore a yellow dress that washed out her complexion without the cosmetics she no doubt slathered on her face each night.

When Lyman didn't respond, she stood and rounded the table to settle on the chair beside his. She threw her right arm around his shoulders, and her left slid down the inside of his thigh. "Look, honey," she said. "That man was savage as a meat-axe. He got what he deserved." She squeezed his leg just above the knee, causing Lyman to push himself away from the table, his chair scraping against the wooden floor.

"Annie, stop that nonsense at once." Essie entered the room, a flurry of satin billowing in her wake. Behind her followed young Charlotte, her head bent, her arms folded around herself.

Lyman offered only a quick nod in their direction, not meeting either of them in the eye. The cook slid a plate in front of him with a slab of buttered corn cake and two thick slices of bacon dripping with grease, the sight of which caused him to gag.

Essie crossed the room, threw open a cabinet filled with liquor bottles, and poured a tall glass of dark rum that she shoved in front of him. "That's what the man needs, not this slop you're trying to serve him. All you gals clean yourselves up and head to the canal. There's business to be done."

Annie gave Lyman's thigh one more good squeeze before she stood and followed the other women out the door, leaving only Essie and Charlotte in the room with him.

He sniffed at the liquid Essie offered him. No sweet spices tickled his senses, only an unpleasant burning in his nose that made him sneeze.

Essie's laugh sent tiny waves through her double chin. She picked up a bucket from the floor beside the cabinet and handed it to him. "The good stuff is for celebrating. This swill is for recovering your wits. Drink!"

There was no arguing with the formidable woman. Lyman threw back his head and gulped, half the drink disappearing before his tongue had a chance to complain. The potent liquor singed his throat and hit his stomach like a handful of rocks, ruthlessly battering his insides. To stop the few contents of his stomach from rising would have been an impossible, unthinkable task, and so for what felt like an eternity, he wretched into the bucket, dropping to his knees on the kitchen floor.

The girl Charlotte scrambled away from him with a shriek, her skirt caught up in wrinkled handfuls. Essie, however, leaned over Lyman and patted his back until he stilled, feeling as though he'd spit out his own guts and remained nothing but a hollow shell.

"Well," she said, oddly cheery for the moment. "Now you got that out of the way, we can move on to our serious problem."

Lyman sat back on his haunches, too weak to gather himself fully, and wiped his mouth on a handkerchief he pulled from his pocket, noting the spots of blood on its edge.

Essie had given him all the recovery time she would allow and launched into the problem at hand. She was a woman in charge, calm and collected. "There's a body upstairs, cold as a wagon tire, and we have to decide what to do with it."

"Can't we just dump it in the canal?" asked Charlotte, the back of her hand held beneath her nose, protecting her from the foul smell emanating from Lyman's bucket.

"Ordinarily yes." Essie shook her head. "But word from the watch is there'll be dredging soon."

Lyman snapped to attention at that, pulling himself to his feet, his shirt untucked and stained. "You think they'll find anything?"

Charlotte, her eyes wide, peeked from behind Essie. "Oh, they always find bodies. Scores of 'em, bleached and bloated things, ready to burst."

Had Lyman not recently expelled everything in his stomach, he'd have done so at her words. As it was, he had to steady himself against the table, overcome by a wave of dizziness.

Essie sighed. "That was unnecessary, Charlotte." She picked up the bucket and handed it to the girl. "Take this outside and clean up the mess."

She did as she was told, but the moment she stepped behind Essie, her expression hardened to a scowl that could have frightened the devil.

"She has the point just right," Essie continued after Charlotte exited. "They'll dredge up bodies that, with the exception of a few, lack any notable features. Our body, on the other hand, arrived in town a few days ago and has most like been seen by all kinds of folks. We can't dump him. And he'll be stinkin' too soon to keep."

There was a faint cough at the doorway, drawing attention to Mariana's entrance. She wore her recent ordeal like a mourning dress. Quinn's blood no longer clung to her, her skin drained of color except for a purple bruise, nearly continuous, stretching between the left side of her neck to just beneath her swollen eye that wouldn't open as far as its twin.

The sight of her made Lyman's stomach lurch again and he wished Charlotte had not run off with his bucket. He brought his hands to his head to massage his temples.

The confidence of the woman that had waltzed down the stairs of her New York townhouse and into Lyman's life had disappeared. Mariana stood before him in a dress borrowed from one of Essie's working gals, as broken as he felt. She could have been one of them offering false love to the canawlers who passed through for the night or just as easily to the sailors on Water Street, nothing more than a smile, spit out and stomped on by the world.

Lyman dropped his hands and his gaze.

"You shouldn't be out of bed," Essie fussed as she reached for a wisp of Mariana's hair and tucked it behind her shoulder.

"I—"

"Don't start, girl." Essie grabbed Mariana by the wrist and tugged her toward the table, guiding her to the chair Annie had vacated. "Sit."

Charlotte stepped back into the room no longer carrying the bucket, and as soon as she entered, Essie pointed toward the fire. Still speaking to Mariana, she said, "Charlotte will get you some breakfast."

Mariana looked at her lap and didn't seem to notice when the woman, rolling her eyes at her madam, set a plate of food on the table.

"Well, then, Mr. Chandler," Essie continued, "what do you plan to do with the fresh corpse you've added to my household?"

Surprising him, Mariana was the one to offer a suggestion in a whisper so low Lyman wasn't sure the other two women could have heard her. "I know what we have to do."

The thought of the two of them doing anything together was enough to make his heart pound. He wanted to rage at her, leave her behind with this rats' nest of working gals, and never think of her again. He reached for the glass in front of him and forced himself to swallow the remaining drink. The liquid fire against his throat caused him to cough, but the horrid spirit settled on his stomach this time and with it, a sense of calm melted through him.

He slammed the glass on the table, catching the attention of everyone in the room. "All right, Mariana," he said. "What is it we have to do?"

Even now she didn't look at him, but she spoke more loudly so that all could hear. "We have to make a mummy."

A gasp pierced the otherwise silent room, and Charlotte asked with a tremble in her voice, "Can you do that?"

Mariana looked up at the young adventuress, whose honey-colored hair hung down her shoulders, making her appear younger than she likely was. "It's the perfect solution." She turned to Lyman and placed a hand on his arm. He resisted his revulsion and let her finish her explanation. "We're already traveling with ancient bodies. No one would think to look twice at an extra."

"But do you know how to do it?" The question came from Essie.

Mariana removed her hand from Lyman's arm and picked up his empty glass, bringing it to her for a sniff. She crinkled her nose and winced. Replacing the glass, she nodded. "I think so."

Lyman almost laughed at the idea she'd planted, the wonderful, horrible idea. Mariana's eyes met his and in them, for an instant, he didn't see the pain of her betrayal, but rather the genius of her cruelty.

He scooted his chair away from the table, cleared his throat, and pointed to the empty glass. "Essie, do you have more of this rotgut?"

"A whole barrel of it," she answered. "A couple of grateful canawlers brought it to us. It's too wretched to serve so I use it for medicinal purposes. It makes a good vomitive when you have need."

"Good. That should do. And we'll need a drying agent." Lyman thought back over his conversation with the taxidermist Titian Peale, trying to recall what he'd used to dry his specimens.

"Arsenic," he said with a nod. "Do you keep it on hand?"

The madam shrugged and offered a crooked smile. "I live on a canal full of all kinds of rats. I have large tins of the stuff."

"Well, then." Lyman stood, avoiding eye contact as the horrible plan began to take shape in his mind. He didn't want to see in their expressions what the women thought of his next words. "Let's make a mummy."

Essie only nodded. "Charlotte," she said to the silent girl now returned to her side, "I think it's time to show Mr. Chandler where we poison the rats."

38

A wave of revulsion swept through Lyman as he slung the lifeless body of Martin Quinn, wrapped in four layers of linen sheets, over his shoulder like a sack of oats. It wasn't the act of carrying a dead man through the halls of a brothel that troubled him, but rather the notion of exploiting the sacred to cover up his crime. Even to himself he'd have had difficulty admitting it, but Lyman believed in the curse.

Eleven mummies had traveled with him from New York. All but three were now gone, and Lyman was aware that he and his traveling companions had left a number of victims in their wake. How many deaths could be traced to the mummies since their removal from the tomb in Thebes he couldn't know, but he recalled clearly the fear and disbelief of the first mate when he identified the Lebolo shipment. Lyman wondered what tragedy had befallen the *Intrepido* during its voyage.

It was also not lost on Lyman that of the four people involved in appropriating the mummies, two were dead and one was dying. Only he remained unscathed. How long, he wondered, would it take for his sins to overtake him?

He repositioned the body on his shoulders and followed Essie down the stairs onto the main level of the brothel. They made a strange parade—the plump madam trailed by a bloodied gentleman lugging a corpse, and a battered and limping beauty. Behind Mariana came Charlotte, dressed in blue so bright it would be more befitting for a party than a funeral procession.

Essie led them all behind the bar and stooped to pull open a trap door, barely wide enough to accommodate her girth. She stepped aside and motioned for Lyman to descend the dark ladder.

At his pause, she explained, "There's a short passageway, at the end of which you'll find a heavy oak door to a gambling room. Charlotte has the key. Should be everything you need. You'll find the arsenic tins behind the bar and the rum barrel you wanted. I'll stay back. The door will lock behind you, but knock when you're done and I'll let you back through."

Lyman swallowed. He didn't like the sound of the room any more than he liked their purpose for being in it, but he didn't see a way to turn back now. He dropped to his knees, throwing Quinn's body off his shoulders and down through the hole. He heard it land with a thud.

Essie lit a candle and handed it to him. "Don't drink any of the liquor in that room, Mr. Chandler. Knock when you're ready."

He descended the ladder, which was not particularly long, and nudged aside the corpse. The tunnel was just tall enough for Lyman to stand and look around at its crude dirt walls, held up by evenly spaced boards, bowed and splintered and giving off a slight odor of mold.

Mariana climbed down behind him and soon Charlotte appeared. She took the candle from Lyman without ceremony and hurried down the passageway. As soon as she passed, he grabbed the body by its feet and, walking backwards, dragged the corpse toward the disappearing candlelight.

The faint tinkle of keys came just before the release of a lock and the clunk of a heavy door opening into a wall. Soon the soft glow of oil sconces spilled into the passageway. Charlotte let the door swing closed with a heavy bang as soon as Quinn's head made it through.

The room they stood in was larger than Lyman expected, about half the size of the main room upstairs, but open enough to accommodate a rowdy crowd. Thick overhead wooden beams held up the earth above them, more likely the road than the house, he realized. The air had grown colder as they'd proceeded down the passage and if he had his bearings, they weren't far from the waters of the canal.

Planks, more substantial here than in the passageway, provided the walls, but the floor still consisted only of hard-packed dirt and filth. The musty odor had grown stronger, taking on an intense gaminess.

"What do you use this room for?" he asked Charlotte. Without the presence of Essie, the girl seemed to grow taller, an illusion created when she raised her chin and looked him in the eye, something she'd not done before.

"Making mummies," she said with a coy smile. She motioned toward the tables in the middle of the room, indicating that they must be moved to the edges. She recruited Mariana's help and the two of them slid the rough made wooden chairs out of the way as Lyman pushed the tables aside. Charlotte, it seemed, was more than Essie's lackey. She was her first mate and had no problem taking charge.

As they worked, she explained, "This is where we hold cockfights, and it's where we drug scoundrels, rob 'em and roll 'em out that chute over there, right into the canal." She pointed to a solid panel at the base of the wall.

"You gals are full of surprises," Lyman said, forcing the last table out of the center of the room with a grunt.

"Mr. Chandler," Charlotte answered, "you're about to make a fresh corpse into a thousands year old mummy. I think I can trust you with some of our secrets."

"Only some?" Lyman swallowed. Essie's warning not to drink from the bottles behind the bar flashed into his mind. He'd heard rumors of such places where unscrupulous men and women like Essie's gals, lured the gullible to their deaths. An unsavory business, in his opinion, but then with Quinn's blood on his hands, and soaked into his shirt, he could hardly be the judge of unsavory.

He stepped over the body and asked Charlotte, "Do you have rope?"

She produced a coil from a corner of the room as he began to unwind the sheets from around the body, the inner layers sticky with dark blood and a rust-like stench. Lyman tied one end of the rope to Quinn's ankles, stepped up on a chair, and tossed the loose end over a beam, then hoisted the body up. The loose end he secured to the nearest of the tables and sat on it, a counterweight to a corpse.

Mariana gasped as the blood began to trickle from the neck wound onto the floor, spreading into a wide puddle of black paste as it mingled with the dirt. She sidled up to Lyman and, leaning into the table, placed a hand on his arm. As her grip tightened, his pulse quickened, and he could feel trickles of sweat forming on his temples, an image his mind juxtaposed with the draining blood, until rivulets of red streamed down his face in a terrifying vision.

He could not move. To do so would risk the body tumbling uncontrolled to the floor. Once again he'd become her captive and, despite his anger, Mariana was the only one who could answer the question burning inside of him.

He fought back his disgust and whispered to her, "Do you think it would be an insult to the others if we were to make Quinn into a fourth?"

"Lyman Moreau," she answered, a familiar teasing lilt in her voice feeding his desperation to push her away. "You're afraid of offending people who have been dead for more than three thousand years?"

When he did not laugh, she looked directly into Lyman's eyes, and he into hers, still beautiful despite the deep bruising around one of them and the absence of the love he'd once thought he found there. "I think it would be a peace offering."

He did nudge her then, and the shift in her weight against the table was enough to send the dangling body into a spin. "Are you saying we should make more?" His voice rose in volume, filling the empty space of the room. "Perhaps replace all the ones we've lost?"

He stood, and as he did, the table rose, tipping Mariana to the floor. The end rose a few feet toward the ceiling and Quinn's body sank toward the ground, the neck bending backward with a snap.

"Why not?" Lyman asked, gesturing toward Charlotte, who stared at him with wide eyes and a gaping mouth. "We could just go ahead and kill seven more people and make seven more mummies. That way we'll all be perfectly safe. Is that what you think?"

"Lyman, please." Mariana scrambled to her feet, her discolored features contorting with pain, and placed a hand to steady herself on his shoulder. He brushed it off and fell silent.

"Death has been pursuing us," she said, her tone soothing, though it did nothing to calm him. "You don't need a glass orb to tell you that. You feel it."

He lifted his hand to his eyes, covering his face as his shoulders slumped, and quietly asked, "And what if we make it angry?"

She placed a hand on his back and this time, he didn't brush her away. "I think we've already done that. All we can do now is try to make amends."

Tears threatened to overtake him and Lyman squeezed his eyes shut against them until he saw flashes behind his lids. He brought his hands to his head and slowly he breathed, blocking out the pounding of his own heart. For all her faults, Mariana was right. He had to see this through.

He opened his eyes and loosened the rope, causing the end of the table to crash to the floor. Quinn's body rested in a heap on the ground. Mariana stood beside the corpse that was once her lover and looked on as Lyman sized up the task before him, his grip tightening on the same knife that had opened the throat of Martin Quinn, and that he would now use to perform a horrific autopsy.

Lyman knelt on the dirt floor next to the dead man. Placing the tip of the blade on the waxy skin, he made slices from the bottom of the rib cage to just below the naval. A small amount of blood oozed from the incision, but the draining had helped limit the flow. He made a perpendicular cut across the belly and pulled back the skin to reveal the stomach and intestines.

Lyman gagged at the odor, but in truth, it wasn't as bad as coming upon carrion that nature had already begun to reclaim. The man hadn't been dead for more than fifteen hours, and in the cool of Essie's secret dirt room on a day in early spring, Lyman found this was perhaps the least offended he'd ever been by the presence of Martin Quinn.

The same could not be said for Charlotte who had taken a seat in one of the shoved aside chairs and stared, determined, down at her folded hands. Mariana, on the other hand, remained intensely focused on the proceedings.

Lyman asked Charlotte, "Where's the liquor barrel?"

Still without looking up, she pointed and he retrieved it from the corner she indicated. Slipping out the cork, he splashed the foul liquid into the body, the smell burning his nose and causing him to retch again.

"Titian said you have to take out the innards," Mariana said with so little emotion Quinn might have been a dead deer in the woods. As she spoke, she backed up in order to avoid the splatters of blood-tinged rum.

Lyman coughed, determined to shake off his threatening sickness. With both hands, he reached into the body cavity and removed lungs, stomach, intestine, and all manner of slimy organs, tearing through connective tissue with jagged cuts and exhausting force. Mariana wrapped them all together in the bloodiest of the sheets, and with Charlotte's reluctant help, slipped out the wooden panel to deposit the piles of flesh into the canal.

After another good washing in spirits, the corpse was ready for the arsenic. Charlotte carried several quarter-pound tins from a cabinet behind the bar, along with a pair of thick leather gloves.

Lyman slipped them on, opened the first tin, and carefully dumped a pile of the white powder into the center of the open cavity. With his gloved hands, he spread the powder until it covered every inch of flesh. Then he sliced open each of the four limbs and covered them with arsenic as well.

When he was done, he leaned back on his haunches and asked, "Who sews, ladies?"

Mariana shook her head and looked to Charlotte, whose scowl communicated repugnance so overwhelming it couldn't be hidden even by a woman in her profession. "Oh God," she said. "I'll fetch Annie. She's the seamstress."

Charlotte pounded on the door until Essie came for her. Soon she returned with the gal Lyman recognized as Annie in tow. The woman handled her task well after first nearly fainting. She worked slowly, almost tenderly, pulling together the edges of cut skin and working her needle and thread in and out. After a while she hit a rhythm and might have been stitching a quilt. When she finished and the body, sunken and discolored, had been washed clean with the spirits, the thing that had once been a man looked remarkably whole.

Essie marveled when she opened the door to retrieve her gals for their long night of work, leaving only Mariana and Lyman to cover the mummy in the long linen strips ripped from sheets that had covered the body.

In silence they worked together to wrap the fabric around each of the limbs. Crossing the arms over the chest, they wound more linen strips around to secure them in place. Then they moved to the head, carefully winding several layers over the sewn up injuries to the neck, and up around and over the face. Before they covered the mouth, Mariana reached out and forced apart the mummy's lips.

The entire process, from draining to wrapping and a layer of shellac, thinned with more of the spirits, had taken most of the day and night.

They stashed the new mummy beneath the bar, hoping no one would come looking for the man he'd once been. On that count, Lyman needn't have worried. Though he would continue to inhabit it longer than any of them, the people of the world, it seemed, had forgotten all about Martin Quinn.

39

A terrible weight settled into Lyman's chest, threatening to suffocate him. Lying restless on the floor in the room he still shared with Mariana, he saw himself drag his knife blade across Quinn's throat, releasing a river of blood that flowed continually. The warmth of the man's draining life Lyman felt in the tingling of his hands.

Sleep was impossible. Mariana had finally dozed under the influence of Essie's ministrations and a great deal of laudanum.

He'd tried to settle down elsewhere, but Essie wouldn't hear of it. "You may be mad as a March hare," she'd said. "And you may have every right to be, but you will not leave her alone in her condition."

Mariana was his burden, but for how long he could bear her, he didn't know. When he closed his eyes images swam through his mind, like the fog and shadows of her glass orb. He saw her mangled and bruised. He saw himself drag her across the floor, beaten and bleeding. And then she became Quinn, wrapped in bandages, a husk that was once a man.

Again and again, like a horrific stage show, the events of the previous two days played out before Lyman's eyes, his imagination often rejecting the truth and wandering instead into ever darker fantasies in which he became the creator of monsters. First Quinn, then Mariana, then Horace, their mutilated bodies danced before him. In his waking nightmares he gutted them like animals and preserved them like kings.

In this manner Lyman Moreau passed the worst night of his life.

*****

"I have to go." They were the first words he'd voluntarily spoken to Mariana in days.

She sat up in bed, a tray across her lap spread with a breakfast she would not eat. The bruises down one side of her face and across her neck had lightened to an angry shade of green. A grimace of pain accompanied her every move.

"You're healing."

"Yes," she whispered, her voice still hoarse from her brush with strangulation. Speaking required effort from her and one of her beautiful dark eyes was still barely visible beneath swollen lids. If ever there was a time Lyman would have the strength to leave her, it was now, while his anger at her betrayal was as fresh and as raw her scars.

"Essie will take care of you. When you're able, you can support yourself with your glass looking, or perhaps with your extensive talent for seduction."

Her jaw clenched in anger, but weak as she was, she did not sustain it. Instead, she cleared her throat and asked, "Where will you go?"

"That no longer concerns you." Lyman enjoyed his cruelty less than he'd expected. "I'll find a buyer for my mummies. Then I expect I'll travel back to the city and see what Horace has left me."

"I can explain." Even with only one good eye, Mariana managed to stare directly into his soul, tempting him to hear her out.

"You did, Mariana. You explained to Quinn exactly who you are. I had just been too much of a fool to realize."

"I—"

Whatever she was going to say, she didn't manage. Instead she coughed, brought her hand to her throat, and bowed her head, an acknowledgement, he supposed, of her treachery.

*****

Lyman booked passage aboard a steamship setting out from Buffalo along the shoreline of Lake Erie, taking with him three ancient Egyptians, two tattered scrolls, one freshly mummified corpse, and more horrific memories than he knew how to store.

For the first time in nearly a year, he traveled without a living companion, a solitude for which he was grateful. He'd have made poor company, as preoccupied as he was with the demons he'd brought along.

The cool spring winds along the lakeshore buffeted the valiant little ship which proved resilient under the skilled hands of an experienced captain. Lyman wished he could harness that resiliency to help him see this godforsaken mummy scheme to its end at last.

For a time he found he couldn't even mention the contents of his cargo to anyone. To the ship's crew he listed them as personal household effects and would answer no further questions when pressed. And so the dead remained locked in their crate, a millstone around his neck.

At Euclid, Ohio he disembarked and bought passage on the stagecoach bound for Akron and the start of the Ohio-Erie Canal. Still he felt lost, but this was a landscape he understood. Not as built up as the Erie, Ohio's canal system still boasted a similar rowdy crowd, and Lyman blended well among them. In the taverns and inns beside the locks, he began once again to display his cargo, offering up the original three to scrutiny, answering questions with his unique blend of truth and invention.

Quinn he held back from the public. The body had withered nicely in its wrappings, shrinking as it dried, becoming, to Lyman's eye, the very thing it approximated. Still he remained uneasy in its presence. The act of taking a despicable man's life he could justify, but to appropriate that same man's final rest for personal gain was not an entirely comfortable notion.

It wasn't until he'd left the canal towns behind the following year and arrived at the Mansion House Tavern in Hudson, Ohio that he allowed Quinn out of the crate.

At the invitation of the tavern's curious manager, Mr. Edgerly, Lyman set up the three mummies, with barely a scrap of linen remaining between them, alongside the scrolls, Belzoni's "Address to the Mummy," and the note of authenticity from Philadelphia's finest.

"Why are they not wrapped?" The question came from a well-dressed, middle aged man who shook Lyman's hand and introduced himself as David Hudson, the son of the town's founder.

"They were," Lyman answered. "When my uncle opened the tomb that contained them, these were among the finest of the specimens, likely important people in their day. But I've been traveling the country with them for some time now, displaying them in the most respectable museums as well as some of the lowliest environments. I'm afraid they are somewhat worse for wear."

"I see." Mr. Hudson crinkled his nose, as though after millennia the mummies still stank of rotting flesh. He began to turn away, saying, "Thank you, Mr. Chandler, for enlightening the good people of Hudson."

"Wait!" Lyman placed a hand on Mr. Hudson's arm to stop him. "I have one more, one that has not been as often displayed, and remains well wrapped in its original linen." A part of him regretted the words immediately, but the showman in him found satisfaction in his distinguished visitor's pause.

"I would like to see this complete mummy if I might." He pointed to the ancients. "These are ghastly."

"I'd be delighted to show it to you," Lyman replied with a bow. He retrieved the mummy, now nearly as light weight as its older companions, admiring his own craftsmanship as he launched into his speech about Antonio Lebolo and the embalming practices of the ancients.

Hudson listened intently, his face drawn, his attention fixed on the mummy that had once been Martin Quinn. As he did, a second man, in a worn brown coat, reached out to touch the linen wrappings, darkened by shellac to give it an aged appearance, an illusion much improved by the absence of linen on the older bodies. His fingers shook as he traced the outline of eyes, nose, and gaping mouth.

The moment Lyman finished a description of the tomb in Thebes, the newcomer turned to him, his eyes wild with a terrifying idea. "Let's unroll it."

The blood drained from Lyman's face, dizziness overwhelming him as his world tilted off-kilter. In the corner of his vision he saw Hudson turn away in disgust, melting back into the enthusiastic crowd that murmured support for the idea. The instigator, not waiting for a response from Lyman, began to tear at the layers covering Quinn's head, the linen strips that had once been the bedsheets of a whore.

Lyman stayed the man's hand with a grip tight enough to cause the visitor to gasp. "This one remains as it is." His jaw clenched, Lyman held the man in a cold stare. There could be no mistaking the implied threat carried by his words. Nevertheless, the fingers of Lyman's other hand wrapped around the deadly knife in his pocket.

The man shrugged, relieving the tension that had caused a hush to fall over the crowd. Lyman loosened his hold and the man pulled back his hand, rubbing his wrist.

"The wrappings are stronger than I expected anyway," the man commented in a nervous trill. "What'd they use to seal them?"

"Resin." Lyman's reply came as a strangled whisper and an inward sigh of relief. He'd nearly watched his guilt unravel before him, faced the full horror of it. He'd almost attacked a man rather than have his treachery fully revealed in front of this room full of gullible strangers.

Other patrons stepped forward to examine all four mummies more closely and as they did, Lyman imagined he could distinguish beneath the linen the structure of Martin Quinn's forehead, the shape of his cheekbones, the precise point of the chin, sheathed in the shriveled skin of the ancients, ashen and stony like the others, like the dried husks of oversized cicadas.

"Will you look at that?" marveled a woman in the crowd. "It's got hair!"

She pointed and Lyman's legs grew weak as he spotted the tuft of auburn hair, unruly as it had been in life, poking through the torn portion of the wrapping

Lyman shuffled forward, determined to refocus the attention of the crowd. He indicated the scrolls set out beside the other bodies. "I had eleven mummies originally," he began. "And these were found among them."

"No jewels?"

Lyman's tension bubbled out of him in laughter. "Nothing like that. Just the writings of the dead."

Most of the tavern patrons turned their attention away from the hairy corpse, their imaginations captured by the scrolls.

"Do you know what they mean?"

Lyman had been asked the question hundreds of times. His response varied depending on his audience, but recently he'd found it difficult to include any part of his memory of Horace.

He cleared his throat and addressed the crowd. "I've never found anyone who could make sense of it. My uncle was the scholar in the family, but I do hope someday to discover a man who can interpret them."

Hudson stepped forward again and grabbed Lyman's shoulder. "Well, I don't know that you'll find him in the middle of Ohio, but I wish you luck, Mr. Chandler. Thank you again for sharing your fine exhibit. It's been an intriguing experience."

"It's been my pleasure."

Mr. Hudson left but many of the others remained, mulling over the dead as well as the scrolls filled with indecipherable hieroglyphs. The man in the shabby coat sidled up beside Lyman with a sly look in his eye.

"Mr. Chandler?"

Lyman reluctantly answered, "What can I do for you, sir? I'll not be unrolling the mummy." He took in the man's appearance with a glance. He wasn't poorly dressed as Lyman had first assumed, but bedraggled as the road weary tended to be. Clearly the man didn't remain in one place for long, but his dark beard was well trimmed and he had a bright complexion and friendly face.

"No, sorry about that. Maybe I can do something for you. I couldn't help but overhear what you said about wanting to find a scholar of languages. I might know just the fella."

Intrigued, Lyman allowed the man to show him to a nearby table. The new acquaintance introduced himself as Ezekiel Warren, a seller of patent medicines.

"I used to be in that line of work myself," Lyman told the man.

"Lot of humbuggery about. Makes it hard for an honest man to make a living, but people need their cures and they'll pay for the goods. For the right product, that is."

Warren's easy manner caused a stab of jealousy in Lyman. He used to be as free and nonchalant about the snake oil he peddled, when his business was good health and not the obsession with death. Perhaps, he thought, he could return to that life when he'd put this mummy business behind him.

"You mentioned you know of a language scholar?" Lyman pulled the salesman back on course.

"I do." He flashed a gap-toothed grin. "Or I know *of* one anyway. I was hoping we might make an arrangement."

"I'm listening," replied Lyman, a sliver of mistrust wedging its way into his brain. Dealers in patent medicines were a slippery breed, a truth he knew intimately.

"There's good money in mummy medicine." Warren leaned back in his chair, his hands folded across his belly. "Grind up the parts into dust and put them into pills or elixirs. Sell it as the secret to long life."

Lyman had heard of the distasteful practice. "I'm unwilling to sell my mummies for parts." He met Warren's eyes. They were wide set and clear, communicating a kind of honesty most would find appealing. Even his shabby clothing contributed to the illusion that this was a hardworking, trustworthy sort of man.

Warren took out a handkerchief and wiped at his nose. "I understand, Mr. Chandler. Come to think of it, I might have been wrong about that scholar." He shoved the handkerchief back in his coat pocket and stood.

"Wait a minute, Mr. Warren." The man sat back down with a grin and Lyman continued. "I don't truly care about finding a scholar who can decipher the scrolls. I'm looking to sell it all, and whole mummies sell better than mutilated ones."

Warren ran his tongue along the front of his teeth and breathed deeply. "I see your point, Mr. Chandler. How about a few toes in exchange for a name? I think you'd likely find a buyer as well as a scholar."

"A few toes won't give you much medicine."

Warren placed a hand on the side of his mouth and leaned his head toward Lyman as if he were about to share a great secret. "If you been in my business, then you know as well as I do people just need to think they're getting what I'm selling. A few mummy toes will be just the thing to show people, to convince them I have the secret to long life." He leaned back, crossing his arms in front of him. "And who knows? I just might."

Lyman briefly mulled over the truth of the words before reaching across the table to shake hands with Ezekiel Warren. "Four toes," he said. "In exchange for information."

The snake oil salesman grinned and rubbed his hands together. "There's a group up to the north, settled in the little town of Kirtland. They practice a funny sort of religion and they even got their own Bible. But here's the part I think you'll find interesting. Their leader, a fella named Joe Smith, translated that Bible of theirs from an ancient language he calls Reformed Egyptian."

"I've heard of him," Lyman offered. "I didn't know he was in Ohio."

"Been here a few years." Warren's grin widened. "And I bet he'd take a look at your scrolls. Might even be convinced to buy them off you."

Lyman wanted more than anything to rid himself of all of it. The scrolls, the mummies, Quinn, and the curse that had pursued him across the country. "Thank you, Mr. Warren."

"Don't mention it, but be warned. They're evangelizers, but they're a tightly formed group. If I was you, I'd go up to Cleveland and advertise my presence, see if I can get them to come to me. Might be that's the best way to approach them."

Lyman ran his hand across his stubbled chin, considering the man's words and thinking that this Mr. Warren might have just given him the secret to good health and long life.

40

Relieved to be back in a more civilized city, Lyman set to work and soon arranged to display the exhibit at the Cleveland House Hotel on the west side of the public square. He spared no expense this time. Staking all his weary hopes on attracting the notice of Smith and his church, he placed advertisements in both the *Cleveland Whig* and the *Painesville Telegraph*, the latter to send a reporter to cover the exhibit. With Kirtland, the home of Smith and his followers, just to the south of the halfway point between the two cities, Lyman hoped to flush him out.

The Cleveland House made a worthy location for the display, not as respectable perhaps as Peele's museum, but certainly a large step up from the taverns in Akron and Hudson or any of the little drinking holes along the canal. Lyman was back in his element, the showman surrounded by finery and among the gullible and wealthy. Now all he had to do was sell his exhibit to a new religious sect led by a man whose prophetic vision reached back to the world and language of the pharaohs.

A month passed before any patrons of the exhibit identified themselves as Saints, the moniker they preferred to the derogatory "Mormons" that had been pinned to them because of their so-called Golden Bible. The two gentlemen listened to Lyman speak for a long time, looking over his exhibit with particular interest in the Egyptian writings. They assured him they would relay an invitation to their prophet.

Another two months passed before he heard directly from the busy prophet himself, but finally, in early July, Lyman checked in to the Riggs Hotel in Kirtland, an invited guest of the notorious Joseph Smith.

Smith himself was a man who made an impression. Tall and broad with a strong chin, thick blond hair, and an easy smile, he lacked the seriousness and pretention Lyman expected from a man who claimed to be a prophet of God.

"Michael Chandler, the mummy man I've heard so much about." Smith clasped Lyman's hand in his own strong grip. He wasn't sure whether the man was more likely to baptize or arm wrestle him, and the thought made Lyman smile.

"Thank you for meeting with me. I know you're a busy man."

Smith sat on a stool beside a desk, his attention focused on the crate Lyman now opened. Though Lyman had been escorted by several Saints, all clearly delighted to see him and help him deliver his crate to Smith, this interview involved only Lyman and the prophet himself. They met in the back wing of a splendid white house, a space set up as an office, though Lyman doubted this peculiar prophet spent much time behind a desk.

"I had a vision that you would be coming, Mr. Chandler. In fact, I believe you are an answer to prayer. I've gone to great lengths to improve the education of Saints, particularly in the area of languages, and I believe you have something wondrous to show us."

Lyman could only be described as spellbound in the prophet's presence. Never had he met a man so gifted in speech, so compelling to hear. "Yes," he recovered, shaking off the impression. "I received an inheritance from my uncle, the renowned Egyptologist Antonio Lebolo, including eleven mummies discovered in the great city of Thebes and several pieces of papyrus covered in Egyptian hieroglyphs. I've met a great many experts in my travels who have all assured me of the authenticity of the writings, but none have been able to interpret them. I was told you have a gift for such things."

Smith crossed his arms and chuckled. "God has given me many gifts, Mr. Chandler. On occasion he has granted me the gift of interpretation. I'd like to see these Egyptian writings of yours."

Lyman retrieved the scrolls and smaller pieces of papyrus from the crate and smoothed them across the desk. Smith, a wild gleam in his eye, pored over them each without a word for several minutes, long enough for Lyman to begin to feel uncomfortable and wonder if he should leave. Just when he'd decided he would do so, Smith looked up. His mouth hung open and Lyman could sense the man's wonder.

"Can you understand them?" Lyman asked.

"It's astonishing," replied Smith, and Lyman believed that it was.

"I don't understand, sir. What is astonishing?"

Smith walked around the desk, stood before Lyman, and clasped his arms. "You have been a vessel, Mr. Chandler, a conduit for the revelations of God. What you have brought me is the writing of our fathers in Egypt, Abraham and Joseph."

Lyman might have laughed except that Smith was unquestionably sincere, and briefly Lyman wondered if Horace had been wrong about the contents of the scrolls. But of course he had not. Horace had been in the tombs of pharaohs. He'd studied and learned from the foremost experts in the field of Egyptology. This man was nothing more than a backwater preacher, though no doubt a talented one.

"Do you think so?" Lyman asked him, feigning belief.

Smith dropped his hold on Lyman and turned back to the writings on the desk. "It's not what I think. God has revealed it to me." He pointed to a figure holding a knife that Horace had identified as an embalmer performing the rites of Osiris over the deceased. "This man here is an idolatrous priest attempting to sacrifice the reclining man to the heathen gods. And the reclining figure represents Abraham, father of Isaac."

"From the Bible?" Smith was either the most gifted actor he'd ever seen or the man believed utterly in the words he spoke.

"Yes, Abraham from the Old Testament. I believe these are his writings and that they will reveal much to God's people. I'll need time to examine them and seek God's guidance in interpreting them. I'd like to purchase them from you."

"I'd be honored to place them in such capable hands," Lyman began, "but I'm afraid they form a crucial part of my entire exhibit. I can't part with them. Unless, perhaps, you'd like to buy the mummies as well."

The prophet sized up Lyman with his piercing gaze. He walked to the crate, and studied the frozen, linen-wrapped face of Martin Quinn. "Very well, Mr. Chandler. I believe you are an honorable man, a messenger of God. I suspect the mummies carry secrets of their own to offer up. This one, with his gaping mouth, looks as if he is preparing to prophesy already. How much are you asking?"

Lyman quickly ran through the numbers in his mind. Despite the trouble they'd brought him, the mummies had been a source of income for him, and he had no doubt they would be so for Joseph Smith as well, but he also didn't know how much the prophet and his Saints would be able to afford.

"I would let them go for $2,400," he said, expecting his offer to be countered.

Smith only nodded. "It's a large sum, Mr. Chandler, but give me a few days. I'll consult with the church and pray about it."

*****

Lyman waited a full week for Joseph Smith to accept his offer and purchase the entire exhibit. When at last the deal was done, and the mummies safely delivered to the Saints at Kirtland, Lyman hired a carriage back to Cleveland.

As the wheels bumped over rutted roads, he wondered what he should do with himself. He felt freer than he'd been in more than two years, when the darkness of the mummies had descended on his life. They'd brought him respect, adventure, and love, given him a taste of what life might be, but eventually all these things had proven as elusive as rest in the afterlife had for the dead that found themselves thousands of miles from home. In the end he'd become as dry and lifeless as the bones he carried with him.

He didn't know what would become of the mummies, scattered from Philadelphia to Kirtland, or what havoc they might visit upon those who claimed them now, who would make of them science experiments, side show attractions, or holy relics, their frozen faces constant reminders of death.

Lyman couldn't help but feel a kinship to them. He, too, was far away from where he needed to be, trapped in a darkness that had only now begun to dissipate. It was time for him to seek light, to revel in life rather than wallow in death. He had an inheritance to claim.

And then it was time for Lyman Moreau to go home.

Acknowledgements

The long journey to get to the end of this book and the even longer struggle to get it to press has been exhausting but definitely not lonely. Many wonderful people have helped bring it to this point. I am grateful to the writers of Coffee & Critique, who spent many hours helping me transform mediocre into beautiful. I'm especially thankful to early readers Doyle Suit, Donna Volkenannt, Pat Wahler, Jane Hamilton, Les Thompson, Marcia Gaye, Jack Zerr, and Alice Muschany, who all went above and beyond for me and for this book. Research is often slower and more tedious than I'd like but would have proved impossible without the efforts of the staff at the St Charles City-County Library and the University of Michigan. I'm thankful also for much support provided by the Saturday Writers chapter of the Missouri Writers Guild. No story can be well told without the input of a brilliant editor, and Megan Harris is certainly brilliant. Any remaining errors are mine. I am grateful to Steven Varble, whose beautiful work makes me hope people judge this book by its cover. Thanks also go to Ben Conley, the kind of friend who still returns my calls even after numerous bizarre questions about dead people. And of course I can't forget to thank my family full of encouragers, especially my husband Paul who is always up for a research side trip down the Erie Canal.

Author's Note

The journey toward this novel began several years ago when my Midwestern family and I moved to Oregon. It was our privilege to live for about two-and-a-half years in a charming neighborhood where a church, affiliated with the Church of Jesus Christ of Latter-day Saints, stood on the corner. Hoping to learn more about the faith of our neighbors, many of whom were members of this church, I began to research. I stumbled on a historical conspiracy theory that calls into question the spiritual origins of *The Book of Mormon*. That research resulted in my first novel, *Smoke Rose to Heaven*, and eventually led me to discover the curious tale of Michael Chandler and his mummies, a story that formed the basis of *Gentleman of Misfortune*.

In April of 1833 an advertisement appeared in several Philadelphia newspapers informing the public that a Michael H. Chandler would display a collection of Egyptian mummies at the Masonic Hall on Chestnut Street. Mr. Chandler claimed he'd recently inherited eleven mummies and various artifacts excavated from the Valley of the Kings in Thebes. According to Chandler's own account, the mummies had been shipped to him from Trieste shortly after the death of his uncle Antonio Lebolo. Presumably Chandler acquired them in March of 1833, though no official records of the shipment exist. Possibly legal concerns over bringing antiquities into the United States could explain this lack of records.

Parts of this account check out. Antonio Lebolo did spend a few years working in Egypt for avid antiquities collector and diplomat Bernardino Drovetti. Lebolo died sometime in 1830, leaving behind a sizable estate and several heirs. However, none of the heirs was identified as an Irish nephew named Michael Chandler. The will makes no specific mention of mummies, but other Lebolo family documents do, including one that references enlisting the help of Franceso Bertoli to act on behalf of the family to recover and liquidate the shipment from Egypt.

It is unclear who exactly Michael Chandler was and how he came to possess the mummies, although many records indicate that he had them and that he stuck to his story about being a nephew and heir of Antonio Lebolo. In the course of this novel I have attempted to be as faithful as possible to the known dates and whereabouts, as well as the sales and losses of the Lebolo mummies as they traveled across the country from New York to Ohio. I have filled in a few gaps in the records, specifically with the journey of the mummies on the Erie Canal. This route is assumed by some historians, but not verifiable at this point.

Although he appears to some extent to have falsely represented himself, there is no conclusive evidence that the Michael Chandler who displayed the mummies used any alternate identities. The presumed real Michael Chandler was an Irish immigrant who lived in Philadelphia and spent many years in a protracted legal battle with merchants. Whether that had anything to do with the Lebolo shipment is unclear. The character of Lyman Moreau is invented.

Mariana and Horace Laurent, too, are fictional as are the characters of Martin Quinn and the three Powells: Harriet, John, and Ada.

I have attempted to capture the spirits of those historical figures that pepper this novel, but they are also largely drawn from my imagination and should be considered fictional representations. Included in this category are the characters of Dr. Samuel Morton, Titian Peale, J. E. Walker, Col. David McKinstry, Edgar Allan Poe, Joseph Smith, and others.

In the summer of 1835 Chandler sought an audience with Joseph Smith, the prophet who claimed to have translated *The Book of Mormon* from ancient writing he identified as "Reformed Egyptian," etched onto golden plates found in the earth near Palmyra, New York. At this point in history Egyptian hieroglyphs still represented an impenetrable code to most American scholars, only about thirteen years after the French linguist Jean Francois Champollion offered the first translations with the aid of the Rosetta Stone. It would seem likely, then, that Joseph Smith might have been the only option available to Chandler if he sought a translation as he claimed.

The prophet immediately identified the writings as the work of the Biblical patriarchs Abraham and Joseph and arranged for the Saints to purchase what remained of Chandler's exhibit. This is, of course, where the novel ends, but there's more to the story of the mummies.

Joseph Smith's translation of the papyri forms the *Book of Abraham*, a sacred text of the Church of Jesus Christ of Latter-day Saints, published as part of *The Pearl of Great Price*. For many years, the mummies and papyri remained in the possession of Joseph Smith or his immediate family. Eventually, at least part of the collection was sold to the St. Louis Museum and later moved to Chicago where it is believed to have been lost to the Great Chicago Fire of 1871. Then in 1976, the New York Metropolitan Museum of Art donated to the LDS Church eleven pieces of papyrus that had come into its possession and were determined to have formed part of the original Lebolo-Chandler-Smith collection.

Already troublesome because of the incompatibility of its story and claims with the known histories of Egypt and Mesopotamia, the *Book of Abraham* became an even greater source of questions when scholars from both outside and within the LDS faith began reporting that the papyri held nothing more mysterious than typical Ancient Egyptian funerary text.

Today, the Church of Jesus Christ of Latter-day Saints still claims the *Book of Abraham* as an important scriptural text, though often views it as significant revelation rather than as a direct translation of the words of Abraham. Some other sects of Joseph Smith's original movement do not claim the work as scripture.

I originally intended for this book to be a companion to *Smoke Rose to Heaven*. That novel was picked up by a small press that unfortunately proved unable to see it through to publication. For now it will have to remain unpublished. I hope to see it brought into the world by early 2020. If you'd like to sign up for occasional updates about *Smoke Rose to Heaven* and other projects, you can subscribe to my newsletter at www.Sarah-Angleton.com.

Further Reading:

Peterson, H. Donl. *The Story of the Book of Abraham: Mummies, Mauscripts, and Mormonism*. CFI, 2008.

Ritner, Robert K. *The Joseph Smith Papyri*. Signature Books, 2013.

Questions for Discussion

1. Hidden identities and agendas play a big role in this novel. Do you feel you got to know these characters? Do you feel they got to know themselves? Are there still unresolved issues of identity for any of them?

2. Lyman is a longtime swindler, thief, and murderer, but he does possess a certain charm. Which of his characteristics or actions elicit sympathy or suggest that, under the right circumstances, he might embrace redemption?

3. Mariana is a bold woman of her time, whose survival depends largely on attaching herself to a man. Does her ultimate betrayal of Horace, Quinn, and Lyman suggest that she is incapable of love? Do you believe there were moments when she genuinely loved any of them?

4. Lyman's experiences with love are complicated. As a young man he was rejected by Harriet. Later he married and murdered Katherine to gain access to her wealth, and then he met the beautiful widow of his mentor. Do you believe Lyman fell in love with Mariana? If so, when and why did he allow himself to do so?

5. The mummies are silent, shadowy companions throughout the novel. To what extent does their presence influence the fortunes of the characters? Do you believe they carry a curse?

6. Historical people, though fictionalized, show up throughout the novel, some perhaps better known than others. What encounters with historical figures surprised you? Did you learn anything new about historical events or attitudes?

7. When Lyman seeks John Powell to help Mariana, it is clear there are some unresolved issues between the two old friends. How would you classify the relationships between Lyman, John,

Harriet, and little Ada? In what ways have those relationships changed by the time Lyman and Mariana leave New Barker?

8. At times Mariana appears to be as much of a trickster as Lyman, but at other times she seems to genuinely see something of value in her crystal ball. What makes you believe Mariana either does or does not possess a true supernatural gift?

9. The novel ends with a road-weary and heartsick Lyman who is ready to go home. Where do you believe Lyman's home might be? Is it Horace's townhouse in New York? New Barker with the Powell family? Will he return to Utica to settle down and open a little shop as he suggests to Mariana? Is there anywhere else you believe he might consider home or is Lyman still searching?

SARAH ANGLETON is the author of the essay collection *Launching Sheep & Other Stories*. She lives near St. Louis, Missouri with her husband, two sons, and one very loyal dog. *Gentleman of Misfortune* is her first novel. Visit her at www.Sarah-Angleton.com.

Thank you for reading!

If you have enjoyed this book, please help others find it by leaving an honest review on Goodreads, Amazon, Bookbub, or anywhere you like to review books.